Miranda Nights

Gail Ward Olmsted

Black Rose Writing | Texas

ISBN: 978-1-68513-227-9
PUBLISHED BY BLACK ROSE WRITING
www.blackrosewriting.com

Printed in the United States of America
Suggested Retail Price (SRP) $21.95

Miranda Nights is printed in Palatino Linotype

Don't miss the first of Miranda's stories!

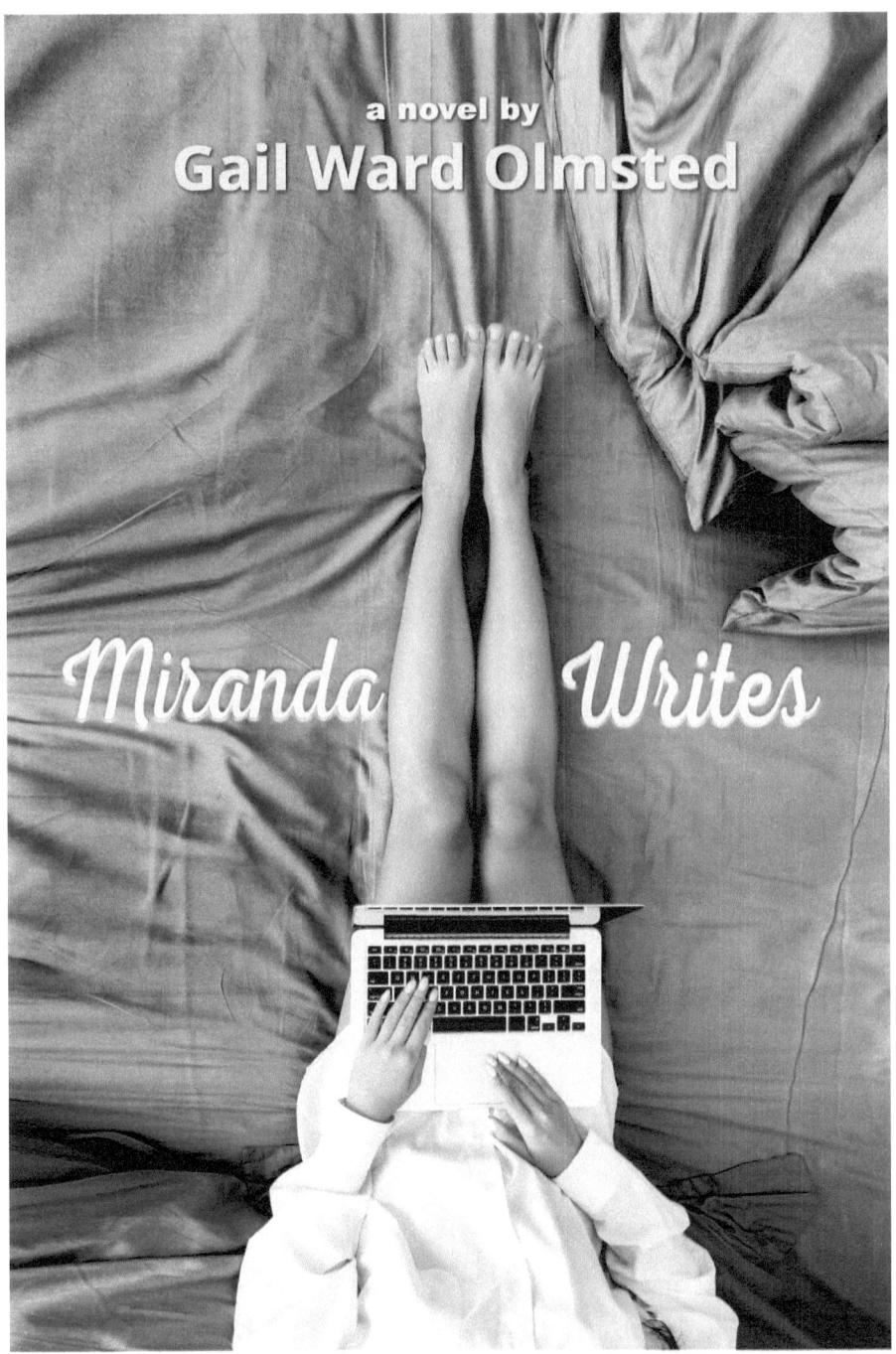

a novel by
Gail Ward Olmsted

Miranda *Writes*

ACKNOWLEDGEMENTS

To my beta readers, **Karen Brees, Phyllis Bultema, BJ Knapp, A.J. McCarthy & Sharon Middleton**: Thank you for your time and talent and your enthusiasm for my work. It is deeply appreciated.

To my editor, **Jenny Toney Quinlan**: Working with you has been a delight. Thank you. Let's do this again soon!

To the team at **BRW**: Thank you for all of your support. BRW staff and authors are the best!

To my dear friends: I can get quite caught up in my characters' lives, but never so much, I hope, that I can't share in yours. Your love and friendship mean the world to me.

To my husband, **Deane**, our daughter, **Hayley,** and our son, **Conor:** You bring more joy and love to my life than I could have ever imagined. I am grateful for you every day.

Miranda Nights

PROLOGUE

I thought I'd heard the last of Miranda Quinn when she blew her chance hosting a TV show two years ago. I was trying to get on with my own life, and not seeing her face splashed across every newspaper or hearing the relentless parade of promos helped. I was living in a rooming house in Bridgeport. I kept to myself, reading the Good Book and working nights at the Grab 'n Go. I had a trusty old beater that got me from point A to point B, and I treated myself to the all-you-can-eat breakfast buffet at Smitty's every Sunday. Life was good, far better than I deserved.

I came across her late-night radio show by accident a few weeks ago. *Miranda Nights*. Seriously? I was driving home after my 3-11 shift, pushing buttons on the dial, and suddenly there she was. Miranda Quinn, know-it-all, big-mouthed celeb wannabe, spouting off and spreading her liberal agenda across the airwaves. I listened to her chatting away with a caller from Albany. Blah, blah, blah. There was a churning in my gut I knew wouldn't go away anytime soon. That voice of hers made me want to lash out, hurt her like she hurt me. What I wouldn't give to wrap my hands around her neck and squeeze until the lights went out. To silence that voice.

But I have to control myself. I get excited thinking that way, but that's not who I am any longer. I've worked hard to redeem myself, and I can't screw it all up because a voice from my past is back. I've learned the error of my previously evil ways.

It is time to teach Miranda the error of her own.

CHAPTER 1

"Thank you for your call tonight. Please stay on the line and my producer will provide you with contact information for your local legal aid office. And to everyone listening, until next time, this is Miranda Quinn signing off. Don't forget to exercise your legal rights, night and day." I took off my headphones and placed them on the desk. Although they fit comfortably, it was always a relief to remove them after a four-hour shift.

I saw my producer, Skip, waving me into his office, but I motioned for him to wait a second and hightailed it to the bathroom. Despite ample opportunities for breaks during the prerecorded commercials that paid my salary, I rarely left the recording studio during an episode. First order of business completed, I headed to the control room, grateful, as always, for the state-of-the-art recording studio my brilliant, sexy architect husband, Eric, had built for me in the basement of our new home. I had originally planned to record my weekly legal advice podcast, *Miranda Writes*, from home, but I had gotten a call five months ago from Infinity Holdings, the second-largest talk show syndicate in the country. When my TV show got shelved before we even shot the pilot, I'd figured I was damaged goods and no reputable media outlet would come near me. But the public protest that occurred when Sterling Broadcasting pulled the plug had piqued Infinity's interest in signing me to offer legal *information* (not to be construed as *advice*) to their nighttime audience. I was much more comfortable on the radio than TV. Things had worked out for the best.

For the last three months, I had been going live with *Miranda Nights* from eight to midnight two nights a week. Infinity wanted me on-air four or five nights a week, but I had no plans to expand. I was finally enjoying a healthy work/life balance and intended to maintain it. Skip and I chatted for a few minutes. He was studying communications at the University of Connecticut, my alma mater. Go Huskies! He reminded me final exams were looming and he would miss our weekly staff meeting via phone on Monday morning. I squeezed his shoulder. "Good luck, Skipper," I said with a smile. He grinned in response.

"Go straight home," he said in a mock-stern tone as I climbed the stairs toward the bedroom I shared with his uncle. Skip had been working with me for nearly five years, and there was no one I trusted more with producing my podcast and radio show. Plus he had earned extra points by introducing me to his uncle three years earlier. I planned to pull every string I could to get him a position at Infinity or one of the networks when he graduated.

By the time I reached the top of the stairs, I had unbuttoned my shirt, and as I tiptoed to bed, I dropped trou and left a trail of discarded clothes in my wake. Entering our bedroom, I nearly tripped over the large gray tiger cat lying in the doorway.

"Seriously?" I muttered as I bent to scoop him up. "Hobes, my man, you are an accident waiting to happen." He purred loudly and swished his tail against my arm.

When we visited the local pound, I had been envisioning a tiny kitten, not a fully grown cat. But one look into those wise green eyes and I had been hooked. I had wanted to name him Catticus Finch or Purry Mason, but Eric felt one lawyer in the family was plenty and suggested Hobie, after the type of boat he'd first learned to sail on.

"He looks like a Hobie," he'd said, and I'd thought, *Well, why not?* The poor thing had been found in an alley in New London. In the year since he had adopted us, he had put on a few much-needed pounds and his fur glistened with good health. He was a real homebody, content to enjoy the great outdoors through a window from the top level of the carpeted cat hotel Eric had built for him.

I pulled a T-shirt over my head and quickly brushed my teeth. I wasn't wearing any makeup—one of the many benefits of working from home—so I left my face unwashed and slid into bed next to Eric.

"That you, Quinn?" he mumbled.

"In the flesh," I assured him, and to prove it, I pressed myself into his back, warm with sleep. He groaned with pleasure.

"You solve the world's problems tonight?" he asked, sounding like he was only seconds from falling back into slumber.

"We knew world peace was gonna be difficult, and I thought term limits were a no-brainer, but . . ." I began but was interrupted.

"Quinn for the Win," Eric said and immediately fell back to sleep.

I rolled onto my back and snuggled beneath the down comforter, concentrating on my breathing and trying to match Eric's slow and steady rhythm. After Hobie jumped up and curled himself into a ball near my head, I drifted off myself.

CHAPTER 2

The next morning, I stumbled into the kitchen. I found the coffeepot ready to go, so I pressed *Start* and waited as the tantalizing aroma of freshly ground beans filled the air. I recalled Eric had an early meeting off-site this morning, so he must have prepped a fresh pot before leaving the house. Not all angels have wings! I was about to grab a mug when my phone rang. I'd shoved my cell into the pocket of my terry-cloth robe, and now I took it out and checked the name of the caller. Tracey!

"Good morning, T. This is early . . . for you." My best friend ran a daycare center and was raising twin boys with her husband, Dale. She wasn't a morning person despite all that. "What's going—"

She cut me off, sounding just short of hysterical. "I need a lawyer. Well, we do. A lawyer." I drew in a sharp breath. What could have happened? A lawsuit brought by one of the daycare parents? I switched into attorney mode and gave her my full attention.

"Are you okay? Where are you right now?" I crossed the room to grab a pad and a pen. We always think we'll remember the important things, but who are we kidding? These days, I write everything down. I heard Tracey sobbing. I needed her to focus. "Talk to me," I pleaded.

"It's Chase. He's in trouble." Chase and Flynn were her sixteen-year-old twins. Good kids, both of them. *What on earth?*

"Was he arrested?"

"No. They want us to bring him in for questioning."

"Who wants him?"

"The Old Lyme police. I thought you could talk to your dad and find out . . ."

"Pop and Sally are on a cruise," I reminded her. My dad was retired from the OLPD and had recently remarried. The newlyweds were celebrating their second wedding anniversary. "I'll try to reach him if—"

"No, no. It's okay. Right now, it's you we need."

"Do you want me with you?" I asked, mentally rearranging my day.

"Yes, please. Would you?"

"Of course. You know I will."

"Can you meet me outside the station in twenty minutes?"

I gulped. It was a fifteen-minute drive from our new home *without* early morning beach traffic.

"Of course. I'm on my way. Don't hang up." I splashed coffee in a travel mug and headed for the bedroom. A shower would have to wait. I grabbed a pair of jeans and a lightweight sweater. Meanwhile, I had one more question for my friend.

"T, what are they investigating Chase for?" No longer crying, my friend's tone was deadly serious.

"Child pornography. They're saying he's a sex offender. Hurry." The abrupt silence told me she had hung up, and I sagged against the bathroom vanity.

Chase? A sex offender?

CHAPTER 3

I pulled into the parking lot of the Old Lyme Police Department, as I had done hundreds of times before when my dad had worked there. I'd used the drive time to call my friend Lisa, a family attorney. She had helped with a child custody case for a witness of mine in a sexual assault case three years ago. I hoped she could bring me up to speed on laws concerning teens and pornography. I told her I imagined pictures had been found on Chase's computer, but I couldn't guess at the content or quantity. The more she told me, the more anxious I felt. The bottom line? Depending on the circumstances and the severity of the charges against their son, Tracey and Dale could be charged as well, and Tracey would lose her license to operate a daycare center. I squeezed into a space made for a car smaller than my minivan, and as I attempted to extricate myself from my car, Tracey came rushing over. I saw Dale and Chase standing on the sidewalk. Chase had reached his dad's height of 6'2" in the month or so since I had seen him last. A good kid, all grown up. So why were we here? Tracey was frantic, but she was trying hard to keep it together.

"Sorry. Seriously. I just want to tell you what I know so we can get in there. It's not much," she said. She recounted the phone call she had received nearly an hour earlier from a Detective Reynaldo. He had identified himself as the lead investigator for a case involving child pornography and the unlawful storing and distribution of sexual images of a minor. "I was so confused. I thought the images were of Chase, that *he* was the victim."

"I can see how you—"

"But no! He said Chase had possession of the images and was the one who sent them."

"*Allegedly* sent them," I reminded her. "If they had solid proof, they would arrest him, not ask him to come in for a chat." It must have been the sound of the word *arrest* because my friend's pretty face crumpled. Gone was the brave facade she had pasted on for the occasion. I pulled her into a hug, turning her away from the watchful eyes of her husband and son. "Get it together, babe. I'm sure Chase is already scared shitless. We have to keep him calm for questioning."

Tracey wiped her sleeve over her nose and upper lip. "Ugh. This is what I tell my little humans *not* to do. We might as well get this show on the road," she said as she hurried toward her family. I rushed along behind her, my long stride quickly making up the distance between us. I greeted Dale, who hugged me and thanked me for coming. I turned to Chase, who wouldn't meet my eyes, flushing bright red when I leaned in to whisper in his ear.

"We're going to sort this out," I promised him. "Follow my lead and don't answer questions without my say-so. Not a word, got it? Zip your lip," I quipped and squeezed his arm, waiting for even the briefest of smiles, but the poor kid was scared shitless. His Adam's apple bobbed up and down as he nodded at me before turning to follow his parents into the police station. I trotted along after them, second-guessing my decision to not interrogate Chase before the police did. I knew doing so could backfire, possibly making him appear as if his testimony was rehearsed, and I wondered exactly what we were walking into.

The dated lobby and stuffy smell of years of law and order brought me back to a familiar and, mostly, happy place crammed full with memories of Officer Desmond "Dez" Quinn and his cronies keeping the streets safe and sound for the citizens of Old Lyme.

"Is that you, Randi?" a familiar voice called out. "What brings you in today?" I turned to see the smiling face of Sergeant Mike Williams, who had worked the desk as far back as I could remember.

"Hey, Mike. Good to see you. We're here to see Detective . . . Um, T, what's the detective's name?"

"Reynaldo," Tracey said. "Detective Dennis Reynaldo. He's expecting us," she added.

Mike nodded in recognition. "I'm heading that way. Follow me." As we walked through the door leading to the office housing the three-person detective team, Mike and I chatted away like old friends. I confirmed Dez was on a cruise with his wife, Sally. Mike's face darkened as he spoke. "I heard how you got canned by the district attorney's office. And you lost the TV show. And after the crap with the DA's office and Kane going free," he said, shaking his head at the injustice of it all. Here we go again, I thought. The State of Connecticut vs. Terence Kane, the biggest case of my career. The charges against him had been dropped when my sole witness, Becky Lewis, had gone missing right before she was to testify. As a result, I had lost my job and a serial rapist had been set free. Three years later, Kane had been arrested again on rape charges and his victim died from her injuries. Becky had resurfaced, I had consulted with the district attorney on the case, and Kane had been convicted. Finally.

"Well, everything worked out and Kane got life, so . . ." I said in my best "aw shucks" voice. I turned to look at Tracey to see if she had heard our conversation. She rolled her eyes at me, and I knew she was thinking, "Good God, man, it was years ago. Get over it, will ya?" There was nothing more satisfying than exchanging eye-rolls with a best friend or a husband. I was still working with Eric on the subtle differences of various facial expressions. So far, he had gotten quite adept at "Let's get out of here NOW" and "Rescue me from this conversation, please." A work in progress, but he was a quick learner.

"Hey, Denny," Mike called out as we approached the detectives' bullpen and the sole occupant spun his seat around and fixed us with a hard glare. A tall, well-built man of about forty, he stood and introduced himself to Dale.

"Detective Dennis Reynaldo," he said.

"I'm Dale Ryan. This is my wife, Tracey, and our son, Chase." Reynaldo nodded and turned toward me before Dale had a chance to introduce us.

"And you are?"

"Miranda Quinn," I said, extending my hand, which he shook briefly, all the while giving me the once-over. Not in a sexual way, more like a fighter sizing up his opponent. "I'm the Ryans'—" I began, but he cut me off.

"I am familiar with your work, Ms. Quinn, and I have to say, what with your track record with sex offenders, I'm surprised to see you here." Hmm, my track record? That could be interpreted in a couple of different ways. Was today some sort of *Groundhog Day* with me playing Bill Murray's role, forced to relive a seminal moment in my former career as an assistant district attorney?

"Yes, but as I was just saying, Terry Kane is doing a life sentence as we speak, so perhaps we can get down to business and address whatever brought us here today." I must have spoken more sharply than I had intended, based upon the way Dale stiffened and both Tracey and Chase suddenly looked even more nervous.

"My cue to skedaddle," said Mike with an awkward wave. "Randi, tell Dez I'm angling to be asked out on the next fishing trip." He laughed aloud. "See what I did there?" I told him I would pass the message on to Pop and turned to face Reynaldo, who was smirking at me.

"It's like old-home week," I said with a grin. "My dad worked—" He waved me off.

"Come and sit," he directed us. "And let's, um, how did you put it? Address what brought us here today."

We took our seats at the scarred wooden table, and I parked myself next to Chase. I was not above kicking him under the table if I thought he was heading down the wrong path. I refrained from squeezing his hand. I hoped to appear cool and professional to the detective, who had taken an instant dislike to me. I leaned forward and took out a legal pad and a pen from my bag. Reynaldo cleared his throat and began.

"Chase, do you know why I asked you to come here today?" Chase nodded almost imperceptibly. "I'll take that as a yes," the detective said. I was about to object that my client's nod could be construed in several ways and that he did not know the specifics of the case or his alleged involvement, but I held off for now. No sense in pissing off the detective before we knew what he had to say.

"Why don't you fill the rest of us in?" I asked.

"Of course, Ms. Quinn. It seems your young friend here is in possession of graphic sexual images of a minor. The victim is fifteen years old and—"

"My client is only sixteen himself," I protested.

"Yes, but Connecticut law clearly states the age of sexual consent is sixteen. That means that it's legal for anyone sixteen or over to sext and send naked photos of themselves to anyone else sixteen or over. What is against the law is for those sixteen or over to possess and circulate naked photos of anyone under sixteen." Reynaldo sat back, a satisfied smile on his face. Crap, this was bad and quickly getting worse.

"I just need to confer with my client," I told him, and, turning to face Chase, I whispered in his ear. "Is the victim someone you know? Don't speak, just nod or—" He nodded vigorously. I tried to recall the name of a girl I had met at the Ryans' house a couple of months back. "Is it, um, Chloe?" Another nod. "Have the two of you been intimate?" Chase averted his eyes and blushed an even deeper shade of crimson. "Chase," I hissed. "We are running out of time. I need to know." He wrinkled his face in concentration.

"Um, well, I guess it depends," he said.

"On?" I prompted.

"What you mean by *intimate*." Oh crap. He was about to be arrested and he was splitting hairs.

"Have you had sex?" I asked, and he shook his head.

"I mean, not like in a bed or anything. We fooled around a bunch."

"Is she your girlfriend?"

"I guess. I dunno. Do you mean officially? I mean, it's not like . . ."

My patience was wearing thin. The meager amount of caffeine I'd consumed was no longer doing its job, and this whole Gen Z affectation of labeling everything was causing me great concern, not only about Chase surviving this line of questioning, but for the future of our country as well.

"You hung out together, you fooled around, but there was no penetration. Is that accurate?" I asked. He nodded, and I felt a sudden rush of pity for him, my best friend's son. I had taken him to the movies and the park and built blanket forts with him and his brother in my living room. The images now free-falling in my brain made me think of something. "What's Flynn's role in this?" I asked. The two were thick as thieves despite being very different in appearance and personality. Chase was tall and lean, athletic and popular. Flynn was stockier, an excellent student with a smaller, select group of friends.

"He's not interested in girls. He's gay," he whispered. "Mom and Dad don't know yet. He's working up the nerve to tell them." I nodded. A couple of years earlier, Tracey had told me she was fairly certain Flynn was gay.

"You mom and dad will be cool," I said, and he smiled briefly.

"Yeah," Chase agreed, and I turned to nod reassuringly at Tracey, who responded with a worried look. Dale was sitting quietly, lost in his thoughts. When Tracey squeezed his hand, he smiled at her, and I reflected for the millionth time how well suited my friends were. I knew they would get through whatever happened together.

CHAPTER 4

Reynaldo's subsequent questioning—"This is *not* an interrogation, Ms. Quinn", he corrected me several times—was about what I would have predicted. The questions raised were meant to be answered with a yes or a no, but Chase turned them into rambling essays with a lot of mumbling and several contradictions in his responses. "Yes, I took the photos, but it's not like I spent any time looking at them. I just knew they were there on my phone, but I forgot about them." I had to give the detective credit for never once coming close to losing his cool or growing visibly impatient with Chase. His patience paid off as he was able to concoct a summary of the events leading up to today, slow and painful as it was. Apparently, Chase and Chloe, who, according to Tracey, *was* his girlfriend, had been "fooling around" in his room after school one afternoon and she'd pulled off her top and started posing, instructing Chase to take pictures of her. He'd grabbed his phone and begun snapping photos.

"Where were you at the time?" Reynaldo asked Tracey, an accusatory note in his tone. She explained she ran an in-home daycare center and her time in the mid-to-late afternoon would have been spent passing around healthy snacks with the help of her assistant and discharging the kids as their parents arrived. "Did you know your son was entertaining underage girls in varying stages of undress?" Again with the tone.

"You don't have to answer that," I told Tracey. "My client—"

This elicited an actual sneer from the detective. "Ms. Quinn, it is my understanding you are acting merely in a consultative role. The Ryans are here of their own free will. There is no need to restrict a response to a simple question."

"I'll answer the question, Detective," Tracey offered. "Chase has friends over after school sometimes, and I trust his judgment. I'm only one floor away, and I know my son. And I was not aware Chloe was undressing for the camera."

"Let's get back to that afternoon in your bedroom, Chase. Do you recall the exact date?"

"Um, maybe a Thursday cuz we don't practice on Thursdays to rest up for the games on Fridays."

"But which exact Thursday?" the detective asked.

"I'm sure the photos are date stamped, Detective. Can we please move along?" I asked with a forced smile.

"Certainly," he conceded. "I have a few more questions. As you continued taking photos, what was Chloe doing?"

"She was into it," Chase admitted, looking both sheepish and proud at the same time. "She unhooked her bra." Tracey gasped audibly, and I squeezed her arm.

"Did you ask her to stop? To get dressed?" Reynaldo asked. The expression on Chase's face communicated clearly: "Why the hell would I do that?" He shook his head.

"No," he admitted. "I didn't."

"Were you in any of the photos?"

"Yeah, I was," he admitted. Oh no.

"Were you also undressed?"

"Well, she wanted me to take off my shirt, so I did, and I took a few selfies of us. She wanted it to look like we were, you know, naked. Like we were having sex. But we weren't. Naked. And not having sex either." Detective Reynaldo was looking quite satisfied with himself.

"A few more questions. How many photos do you suppose you took that day?"

Chase looked perplexed. "Um, I don't know. A couple hundred maybe?" Oh crap, this was far worse than I'd thought. With that many images, we could be looking at felony charges. Tracey moaned and leaned forward, cradling her head in her hands. Dale looked like he wanted me to put a stop to the questioning. Since Chase had not been read his rights, I knew whatever he said today would be deemed inadmissible if the case ever got to court, and I shook my head. "It's okay," I mouthed silently. The detective continued, clearly on a roll.

"What did you plan to do with the photos?"

"Nothing. I didn't plan any of this. It just happened. She wanted me to send them to her Dropbox, so I did. And I said I would delete mine, but she wanted me to hold on to them. And think about her when I look at them." Tracey sat up, her face drawn, looking like she had aged twenty years. No one liked to think of their kid having sex or masturbating to near-naked photos, especially when it was part of a police investigation. I needed to end this now. I was signaling my desire to wrap things up when Reynaldo fired one last shot meant to implode things for everyone.

"How do you suppose the pictures got leaked to the entire student body and the young woman's parents last night?" he asked. I protested and was about to tell Chase he was under no obligation to answer the question, but he responded anyway.

"I have no freaking idea," he said, and then there was silence.

CHAPTER 5

"Time to go," I announced briskly and beckoned the Ryans to join me. I handed a card with my contact info to the detective and was about to follow my friends when Reynaldo asked me to wait. I told Dale I would meet them outside and turned around. "You can contact me if you feel the need to continue this further," I assured the detective. I spoke casually, but deep down I was scared. Behavior like Chase had exhibited was unacceptable. Sexting among teens had gone on for far too long, and I was familiar with cases where the perpetrators had done real time after being convicted. I knew I was over my head and would need to secure competent representation for Chase. Reynaldo fixed me with his steely gaze and shook his head.

"If you care about that boy and his family as much as you appear to, do yourself a favor and get them a criminal defense attorney." I was about to tell him that was my plan when he held up a hand to stop me from speaking. "The era of a slap on the wrist because 'boys will be boys' is over. If he gets convicted on felony charges, he could spend the next five years in prison." At my shocked expression, his tone softened slightly. "Find someone today. These things can snowball pretty quickly." I thanked him and made my way out of the police station, waving to a couple of officers and staff members as I did. Stepping into the bright sunshine, I realized we had been inside for only about an hour, although it felt much longer. Dale, Tracey, and Chase were walking to their car, and I hurried to catch up with them. When Tracey saw me approaching, she circled back to meet me.

"What happened? What did he say? Do you think they'll press charges?" Her tone bordered on hysteria, and my usually unflappable friend looked harried and desperate as she searched my face for answers. "Tell me, Randi, please. I can take it." She squared her shoulders and drew herself up to her full height, which meant she was laser-focused on my chin. I squeezed her shoulders and flashed what I hoped was a confident smile.

"Don't worry. We'll work things out, I promise." I asked Dale to join us, and he did after telling Chase to sit tight. The kid's shoulders slumped as he slid into the backseat of the family's ancient SUV. As soon as he was out of earshot, Dale spoke to Tracey.

"We gotta get him home. There was a message from the school on my cell. He's suspended and prohibited from being on school premises until this is cleared up." A sob escaped from Tracey as she stumbled into her husband's outstretched arms. Dale's bear hugs were legendary, and I was so grateful she had such a supportive spouse. I watched them for a moment before sharing my thoughts.

"So listen. That's a good idea to get him home. Get him to eat something, eggs or a sandwich. He won't want to, but tell him he needs to." If what I thought might happen did, it might be his last home-cooked meal today. I didn't feel the need to share more on that right now, so I continued. "I am going to call around and see who might be available to help us. I'll call you later on and tell you what I find out." Tracey tried to smile gratefully, but it came across as more of a grimace. "It's okay," I tried again. "Get your boy home." She nodded glumly and climbed into the passenger's seat, buckling her seat belt after a quick glance at her son. I turned back to Dale. There was more he needed to know. Keeping my voice low, I spoke quickly.

"Tell Chase to take a shower before he lies down, just in case. And help him locate a suitable change of clothes. Button-down shirt, pressed slacks, and real shoes—not sneakers. Worst-case scenario, and I mean absolutely worst case, he'll be asked to turn himself in, most likely later today." I kept mum on the possibility the police might show up unannounced and escort him to the station. It didn't seem all that likely, and Dale looked like he couldn't handle much more reality at the moment. He nodded grimly before he walked back to his family. Tracey waved, looking so small and sad, and I waved back and tried to smile. Chase was slumped in his seat, and it looked like his eyes were closed. They exited the parking lot and turned onto Main Street; they would be home in about five minutes.

I walked back to my car and began the drive back to the beach-adjacent home I shared with Eric. I thought I might make a detour and stop by the home reno he was working on today. I needed a bear hug of my own right about now.

CHAPTER 6

An hour later, I arrived home. Eric's embrace had worked its magic on my jangled nerves, as had the fortifying swallows of hot coffee from his thermos. He had offered to pick up lunch and said he would be here by noon at the latest. As I trudged up the front walk, I checked my phone. How was it only 10:45? Was it too early to put on a pair of pj's and call it a night? I debated a walk on the beach, but the tiny face watching from the window convinced me to stay home. I dropped my bag and keys on the front hall credenza and sank gratefully onto the sofa. Hobie jumped into my lap and circled around a few times before settling in. I stroked his head, closed my eyes, and tried to relax but gave up after only a few minutes.

"Hey, bud," I said, nudging my sleeping pet gently. "I've got to find someone to help with Chase's case." He opened his eyes, regarding me silently. "Don't judge me," I protested. "Aunt Tracey needs my help." Hobie yawned and stretched out to his full length before stalking away in search of food or another form of comfort. I turned to my phone. Lisa had texted to say she was still trying to locate a lawyer and had calls out to several candidates. She would know without my saying that Schleyer, Houghton, and Fogarty, the largest firm in southeastern Connecticut, was off-limits. Two years ago, I had sued them and won a seven-figure settlement for my client Becky Lewis. No one there would look to do me a favor. I allowed my mind to wander to my ex-boyfriend, former defense attorney Adam Baxter. He had worked there for years and had been well on his way to making partner when he blew the whistle on them for witness tampering and coercion.

Adam and his child-bride, Kimberly — okay, she was twenty-seven — had moved back to her family home in Vermont after he was disbarred. Besides raising two little boys, Anthony and Alexander, they were amateur beekeepers with plans to double their number of hives each year until the boys were in kindergarten and second grade, respectively. Then Kimmie would run the business, with Adam helping on weekends. He had recently been promoted to manager of the flooring department at a local big box home improvement center. If you are wondering how I know all this, it was in the most recent edition of the family's annual Christmas newsletter, *The Baxter Beeswax*. I kid you not.

I smiled as I pictured Becky, my brave friend whose testimony had secured the conviction of a violent sex offender who had murdered his last victim. Becky was one of his early attempted targets, but she had escaped. She and her sister had moved to Florida last year, and she'd enrolled in school to become a paralegal after earning her GED. Jesse, her son with Adam, was doing well in preschool. We chatted and FaceTimed every few weeks, and I realized we were overdue for a catch up. While I waited for Lisa to come up with a name or two, I busied myself by cleaning out the fridge, tossing past-its-prime produce and anything looking in the least bit suspect into the trash. I was wiping the counters when I had a sudden flash of inspiration. I searched my contacts and placed a call.

I heard Eric's Ford F150 turn into the driveway, and by the time he came in with a paper bag bearing Fortuna's logo, I was leaving a message for Justin Mendez, a criminal defense attorney who had been a frequent guest on my legal advice podcast last year. He had always sworn he owed me one, as his straight-talking style and passionate defense of his clients won over many of my listeners and he had since hired three associates to keep up with the demand for his services.

I ran down the basics of Chase's case and asked him to call me back ASAP. I hugged Eric and nodded approvingly at the sandwiches he had purchased: classic Italian for him and chicken, bacon, and ranch dressing on focaccia for me. We carried them to the patio with cans of soda and a bag of chips.

Unwrapping my lunch produced a whiff of heavenly scented deliciousness, and I dug right in. I had already filled my husband in on the basics of Chase's predicament. In between ravenous bites, I admitted I was freaked out at the idea of him going to jail. Even the prospect of a juvenile detention facility had me panicked.

"Until you talk to Justin, there's nothing you can do," Eric advised. "Let it go for now."

"Ah yes, letting go. I've heard of it. I'll add it to the list," I said, taking a sip of soda.

"What list is that?" Eric asked, his mouth full of capicola and provolone.

"The list of things I always assume I can do until I actually start doing them and I realize I can't."

Eric looked confused. "Like what?"

I put down my sandwich and wiped dressing from my cheek. "Like dancing. You know how I'm always bopping around and tapping my feet to the music, but when I get up to dance, it's game over?"

Eric looked more confused than ever. "But you love to dance," he protested. "At our wedding, you were the belle of the ball."

"I was the bride," I reminded him. "I got a pass, but my actual dancing is not even close to what I imagine it will be.

Within thirty seconds of flopping around on the dance floor, I'm thinking, 'What the hell am I doing up here?'"

"What else?" At my quizzical look, he continued. "What other things besides dancing and not being able to let things go are on your list?"

"Frosting a cake, for one." Eric protested, but I cut him off. "My cakes are like Charlie Brown's Christmas tree. You've only seen them after Sally works her wizardry on them." Eric grinned at the mention of my perky stepmother. Her culinary contributions had upped the standards of cuisine at Quinn family functions in the last couple of years.

"Yeah, she is one class act," he agreed. "What else is on your list?"

"Wow, how long do we have?" I asked, only half-jokingly.

"For you, I've got all night," Eric said with a wicked grin.

"Okay, then, you asked for it. Um, bowling, throwing a softball, playing poker, planning a dinner party, arranging a charcuterie board for that party . . . I could go all night here." Eric looked like he wanted to jump in, but I cut him off. "Yeah, yeah, that's what she said. You're a riot."

"So anything involving balls and food?" I shook my head at his foolishness.

"That about sums it up," I agreed.

"So how about things you're good at, my talented, skilled, and accomplished bride? I can think of two right off the top of my head."

"I know what you're thinking about," I told him. I walked over to him and arranged myself on his lap. He immediately wrapped me in his arms. I snuggled in and sighed with contentment. This man was delightful in so many ways. Sensing my interest, he whispered in my ear.

"You know what they say: practice makes perfect. You up for some practice?"

In response, I gathered up the remains of our lunch and headed back inside. Eric followed close behind, carrying empty soda cans and the unopened bag of chips. We left everything on the kitchen counter and hurried down the hall to our bedroom, closing the door a split second before Hobie attempted to join us.

Who says I can't let go? I thought an hour later. Given the right conditions, I could let go with the best of them.

CHAPTER 7

I felt drowsy and relaxed and briefly considered taking a nap after Eric had showered and gone back to work. But images of Tracey and her family dogged my efforts, and after a few minutes I gave up. My efforts to shut off or at least slow my brain were not working. As I swung my legs around to climb out of bed, Hobie hopped up and made it abundantly clear that snuggling with me was the only thing on his agenda at the moment. I agreeably sank back against the pillows and closed my eyes, the motorboat sounds emanating from my fella relaxing me into sleep.

I woke with a start as my phone buzzed next to me. Stealing a look at our rarely used alarm clock, I saw an hour had passed and that my fur baby had deserted me. I squinted at my phone as I grabbed it but couldn't quite make out the caller's name.

"Hello," I more or less croaked. The deep-throated chuckle on the other end of the line was easy to recognize. My agent, Brian.

"Are the burbs that boring you need to nap all day? Isn't there a quilting bee or a barn raising to attend?" he asked.

"Did it occur to you all that activity is why I need a nap?"

"Snappy comeback, Miranda," Brian said. "All these years away from the city haven't slowed you down." I was about to remind him I had never lived in the city and that the Connecticut shoreline had always been my home, but now I had to pee. Time to move this conversation along.

"So what's going on? Or are you offering free wake-up calls as an added value to your services?"

"Hell no," he retorted. "I've got enough on my plate, what with negotiating lucrative contracts for my favorite client." Hmmm . . . favorite client? Since when?

"Spit it out, Brian. What's up?" I heard him clearing his throat, a classic delay tactic of his. Silence. "Brian?"

"The Infinity folks are happy," he finally said. Happy? That sounded good.

"I am glad they are happy . . ." I began.

"They want to be even more happy, really happy, happi*er*, as it were."

"And what would it take for that to occur?" I asked slowly. I knew what it was. Of course I did. We'd had this conversation only last month.

"They are huge fans of *Miranda Nights*, and they want more of them."

"I told you last time two nights is enough for me."

"And I told *you* last time this was going to be up for discussion again soon. And here we are. Your ratings are epic. Better than what they'd projected. They want to hear more from you. And, um, see more of you too." I drew in and let out a deep breath before I spoke.

"See me? I work from home, Brian. It's a radio show. There's no *seeing* in radio. If the Infinity folks want to see me, tell them to send a Zoom invite or consider a standing FaceTime appointment. How on earth are they supposed to *see* more of me?" Brian was unnaturally silent for just a beat too long, and my spirits plummeted even lower. What the hell was going on?

"You knew when they offered you the contract they wanted *Miranda Nights* five nights a week or at least four." Yes, I knew their long-term plan, assuming my show performed well, but I had been hoping to delay the inevitable.

"Mmm, yeah. But that was going to be part of the discussion in the future. It seems awfully premature."

"And you also know the production for all of their shows takes place in their mid-town studio. *Classic Cars, Frugal Gourmet, Sports Talk*—all of those shows are produced in house." I was growing increasingly impatient, and now I really had to pee. But I needed to make one last point first.

"Yes, but I also know my production costs are a fraction of those shows. I have everything I need right here: a state-of-the-art studio, a mini-fridge stocked with seltzers and Diet Coke, and Skip Hansen, sound engineer extraordinaire. Our quality is just as good at a fraction of the cost. Sounds like a win-win to me."

"I know all this, and so do they. It's more of a security thing. Keep your assets close by and safe, where you can protect them and watch them grow." I'd had it. I was done with this conversation.

"As much as I would love to spend the rest of this glorious day arguing about the relative safety of Old Lyme vs. Manhattan, I gotta run. Talk soon. Don't get mugged. Byeee." I ended the call and dashed to the bathroom, fuming over Infinity's interpretation of the contract we signed just three months ago. *They know I'm a lawyer, right?* I had bigger fish to fry this week. Making nice with my agent, as well as my employer, was nowhere near the top of that list.

CHAPTER 8

After I received calls from both Tracey and Justin, confirming they were meeting at the Ryans' house at six, I decided there was no more I could do for now. There had been no further word from Detective Reynaldo, and I seriously doubted the police would look to make an arrest of a nonviolent juvenile at night. That would require overtime, something all but eliminated when Pop had still been in uniform. I might be needed if things progressed, but as it stood, it was just a meet and greet, and I knew Justin was a terrific fit. He would hold Tracey's hand so she felt safe and be clear and direct enough so Dale wouldn't feel as if he was being handled with kid gloves. How Chase would respond, I honestly had no clue. He had always been a sweetheart—outgoing, energetic, and thoughtful. A total contrast to the moody, scared teenager from this morning. I tried to remember what I had been like at sixteen. Yeah, moody, for sure, as well as secretive and boy-crazy. Tracey and I would giggle and whisper on our parents' landlines into the wee hours of the morning, sharing our extremely limited knowledge on boys, fashion, and makeup. We had even developed our own secret language, a blend of high school French and Pig Latin. I would have to cut the kid some slack, at least until we had the complete story, including a statement from Chloe, the alleged victim.

Hobie was sleeping on the top perch of his carpeted palace, bathed in late afternoon sunshine, so I whispered, "Be back soon," as I tiptoed out the door. Everyone said hello and goodbye to their cats, didn't they? I crossed the quiet street and headed for the entrance to the beach. My happy place. I had forgotten to apply sunscreen, so I took off across the sand, heading east to avoid the direct sunlight. I smiled as I recalled how three years ago, with the pilot for my TV talk show about to be filmed, I'd had to be so careful about the sun, my diet, and the state of my polished fingers and toes. But I had sabotaged my chance for a daily talk show when I pursued justice for Becky. The network had not been pleased with the resulting backlash, which included shocking headlines, unflattering photos of yours truly, and rumors I was unprincipled, a home-wrecker, and a talentless hack. Good times! I recall thinking I should have been disappointed, angry even, at their decision to pull my show. But honestly? I had been relieved. I could focus my efforts on my blog and weekly podcast and explore a burgeoning relationship with a handsome architect from New Rochelle. The pressures of being a TV personality would have been enormous. The free clothes and spa treatments had been nice, however. I looked at the chipped peach polish on my toes. Maybe I could convince Tracey to join me in a spa day soon.

As I walked, I let the gentle waves caress my bare feet and soak the bottom of my jeans. I didn't care. This was where I felt most alive, and if sunburned skin and salt-crusted clothing were the price I had to pay, well, so be it. Along with the TV show, there had been a standing offer from Sterling Broadcasting Group to move me into the city, with corporate housing just minutes from the studio. And leave all this? No way. And now I was once again being asked to compromise my lifestyle. Being on air until midnight four-five nights a week would mean I would have to forego dinner with Eric most nights and change my sleep patterns as well. I was a bear unless I got seven hours of sleep, so I would also miss out on breakfast with Eric since he tried to get to a job site by 8:00 a.m. And no more morning sex, I realized. Oh, hell no!

CHAPTER 9

I wiped a relatively spotless countertop and watered a plant that didn't need it, then stole another glance at the clock. It was 7:15, and I was anxiously awaiting a call from Tracey or Justin to tell me how the meeting had gone. My phone buzzed, and a picture of Eric's handsome face appeared on the screen.

"Hey, you. I thought you were Tracey," I began.

"And I thought you were breaking it off with her and trying to make a go of it with me, so I guess we're both . . ."

"I'm sorry, babe. I'm just dying to know how the meeting with Justin went."

"I hear you, and I won't keep you. I'll be heading home in an hour. Need me to pick up anything?"

"I was thinking of finishing our sandwiches tonight. We must have lost our appetites earlier."

"There is nothing wrong with your appetite, Quinn. Or mine for you either. In fact—"

"Wait, Tracey is calling. Got to go. Hey T. What's up? How'd it go with Justin?"

"He was terrific. Seems like he has a handle on things so far. And he was good with Chase, so there's that." Hmmm. She was saying all the right things, but her tone was flat. She should sound more upbeat but probably did not realize her son could have been spending the night in a holding cell.

"Well, that's great. What's the next step?"

"He's gonna ask to see the evidence they have. He told Chase not to use his phone for now. Dale locked it in his glove compartment." She laughed, but it wasn't funny. Not at all.

"T, talk to me. You sound hollow. Not like you."

"How am I supposed to sound, Randi? Huh? Seriously, is there a guide to how to sound when your son is taking nude pictures with his girlfriend? If there's a how-to manual, please tell me. I've no clue what I am supposed to say or do or think. Except be mad and scared and pissed off. I am so pissed off right now, you have no idea."

"That's good. Let it out."

"I'm sorry. I had no cause to go off on you. I am a terrible person," she said. "I am," she added more forcefully after I told her she was anything but. "As a woman, I should feel for Chloe, the victim. She always seemed like a good kid. Levelheaded, sweet. But Chase is a victim too, isn't he? A dumb-ass, clueless victim, but still. I want it to all go away or for me to run away. Just poof—disappear."

"Damn it, I have asked you to run away with me at least a dozen times over the years, but you're all, 'my husband, my kids, my daycare,' and now, when I finally have a husband, this is when you want to run away? Seriously?"

"Yes," Tracey said, and we both laughed. I asked her to keep me posted and to relax a bit, and she said she would try. I took my own advice and, after changing into an ancient swimsuit, headed out to the deck. I flipped open the cover of the hot tub and slipped into the steaming water. The tension I had been carrying around melted away as I closed my eyes and sank in deeper. That's how Eric found me a short while later. I opened my eyes to see him crouched on the steps of the tub, watching me intently.

"Hey, creeper. How long have you been watching me?" I asked.

"You're a mouth breather," he said. "Seriously, your nose does not take part in the process of breathing whatsoever. It's all in your mouth," he added with a note of incredulity. There were so many responses to his last statement. This guy made it too freakin' easy sometimes. I almost let him off with a smirk, but I couldn't stop myself.

"You wish it was all in my mouth," I suggested. *Ewww.* Not nearly as sexy as I had hoped for.

"You are just too much woman for me," he said. "And I think you're just using me for sex," he mock-complained. "I have feelings too, you know." He stood up and stretched. "Crap, it's been a long day. This reno is not going as smoothly as it should. The investors are growing impatient, and I'm the fall guy. It's hard getting materials, and some of the crew are turning out to be less than reliable." He ran his fingers through his hair, which desperately needed a cut. He looked exhausted.

"Do you regret it?" I asked softly. He didn't respond, and I was about to repeat the question when he spoke up.

"Leaving the practice? Moving here with you? No way, babe. I couldn't be happier." But his smile didn't reach all the way to his eyes, and I recalled, not for the first time, what he had given up to live here in Old Lyme with me. A partner position at a top architectural firm in New Rochelle with a roster of Fortune 500 corporations as clients. The reno he was currently working on, a house flip being mismanaged by a couple of recent college grads with zero experience, was a far cry from the job he'd left and required hands-on effort and constant vigilance.

"Why don't you join me? The sun's about to set, and the view from here is to die for."

"All right, but no funny business," he agreed, and, stripping down to a pair of boxers festooned with smiley-faced lobsters, he climbed in and sat next to me. I kneaded his shoulders, and he groaned with relief.

"Oh yeah, you've got the touch, Quinn."

"We could work something out," I whispered. "For you, I mean. Get a place in New York and you could come here on weekends. Your firm would take you back in a minute," I reminded him. "A New York minute," I added. He half turned, and I saw his face, scrunched up in confusion.

"That's what we said we *didn't* want," he said. "Remember those talks about how we didn't meet each other until we were in our forties and we shouldn't waste any more time apart than we had to?"

"You were in your forties," I reminded him. "I was still a young maid in the blush of womanhood." I had been about to turn thirty-nine when we'd met and Eric was only a year and a half older than me, but still.

"Revisionist history," he complained.

"Updating plans based on new information," I responded tartly.

"What new information?"

"You're unhappy with your job. You come home tired and frustrated, and I hate to see you—"

"Babe, it's work. Sometimes the jobs are terrific and other times, not so much. It's a big change from riding elevators in high-rises, but I get to drive my truck every single day, and that's sexy as fuck, so it's all good, okay?" I nodded, but he was still watching me, waiting for something. "What's this all about anyway? Is Infinity trying to pressure you for more shows, and if so, did you tell them I already called first dibs on your nights?"

"Yes, but there's more," I added. "They want to talk about moving the show to New York."

"Well, you knew it would come up again," he said.

"But it's only been a few months, and until they add more stations outside of the Northeast, what's the big rush? Who cares where the show originates? Look at, um, that show. You know the one."

"I need more than that," Eric quipped. "A noun or at least a vowel."

"That show with the guy. Umm, Keillor. Garrison Keillor."

"*Prairie Home Companion*? That's random, even for you."

"But it's an example of a show originating in Podunk nowhere with monster ratings."

"I'm certain the good folks of the fictional Lake Wobegon would find fault with your characterization, but anyway—"

"Damn it, I don't want to work in New York. I want to live in this gorgeous house you built and work out of my beautiful studio. I don't want to give more nights to anyone but you. I don't want you to work in New York either. I want *Eric* nights, as many as I can get for as long as I live." I let out a long sigh. "Phew. That's what I want."

"Okay, then, I think we have a plan, and as long as we're in the same bed every night and you're happy and I get to drive my truck around town, that works for me." He pulled me into his arms and, after kissing me soundly, admitted, "I am about as shriveled and pruney as I can stand. How's about we towel off, put on some dry clothes, and eat those sandwiches? Find something binge-worthy and hang out with Hobie. What do you say?"

I told him it sounded great. So that's what we did.

CHAPTER 10

Tonight's episode of *Miranda Nights* was going smoothly. Skip did his usual flawless job of screening incoming calls, and I ended up talking to a number of interesting callers with a wide variety of legal questions and concerns. Nothing out of the ordinary, except for Maddie, a young woman from Brooklyn, who wanted to know if her landlord had the right to enter her apartment whenever he wanted to. I told her in the state of New York there are three reasons a landlord can enter a tenant's apartment or rental house: to provide necessary repairs, under the terms of the lease, or to show the apartment to prospective purchasers or tenants. The only time a landlord doesn't need to get the tenant's consent or give notice to enter an apartment is in an emergency. She sounded glad to hear it and said since the two had separated, her ex-husband continued to come and go as he pleased.

"Your landlord is your ex-husband?" I asked.

"Yeah, I thought I'd said that up front. Anyway, thank you. Love your show."

The incoming calls were backed up, and when Skip held up three fingers, I knew we were down to the last few calls for the night. The first caller just wanted to thank me for all the information I had provided during the time she had been tuning in and to ask if I was going to add a few more nights to my schedule. I thanked her, frowning through the glass at Skip, who responded with a shrug. He knew I hated fluff calls, preferring to fill my airtime with more substantial matters. The next call was a hang-up, so Skip held up one finger and drew his hands out, which I understood as "no rush" and I should draw this last call out.

The electronic call log showed the caller's name was Peter, and the subject was marked "General." Ugh. I liked to have a sense of the purpose of the call. I cut my eyes at Skip, but I spoke warmly.

"Good evening, Peter. Looks like you are the last caller on tonight's episode of *Miranda Nights*. This is Miranda Quinn. How can I help you?" When I got no response, I tried again. "Peter? Good evening." Skip was shaking his head when I heard someone clearing his throat. A second later, Peter spoke up, his voice rough, like he didn't talk often.

"Quinn for the Win." I felt a chill run through me. The sound of the nickname I had earned during my years as an assistant state's attorney sounded mocking, almost sinister.

"This is Miranda. Peter, how can I help you tonight?"

"New listener, huge fan, and first-time caller. I'm surprised you bounced back so quick after the state fired you and your TV show failed. A new radio show *and* a husband. You must be very proud." Skip ran a finger crosswise along his throat, meaning I should hang up, but I held up a finger of my own.

"Peter, I am certain you spent a fair amount of time on hold this evening. Please don't tell me all you have for me and my listeners is a recap of my career for the last few years. Is there anything I can help you with? We are live and about to conclude tonight's broadcast."

"Just remember, Miranda, conceit is fuel for the devil. You're on top for now, but it won't last. Nothing ever does. Please be careful. Don't forget that pride cometh before the fall." I couldn't tell who disconnected first, Peter or Skip, who looked as angry as I'd ever seen him. I scrambled to sign off.

"Well, that was our last call of the evening." I looked at the screen in front of me, now flashing with a reminder. "And, oh yes, welcome to our newest listeners tonight who tuned in to *Miranda Nights* on WISK, our newest affiliate in Naugatuck, Connecticut. And remember, if you have a pressing legal question or concern, please contact the bar association in your state for a referral to a qualified attorney. Until next time, this is Miranda Quinn. Thank you and good night." I pulled off my headphones. What a crappy way to end a show. Before I got out of my chair, Skip came rushing in.

"Dude, seriously? What was that?" I asked.

"Randi, I have no clue. He sounded normal, just a regular caller. Said his name was Peter and he had a question for you, and sometimes you don't want me to push too hard to find out more. So I put him on hold, and when I came back on the line and told him he was the last caller, he said something like, 'That's great, can't wait.'"

"And what was that platitude about pride?"

"It's from a proverb. I just googled it," Skip admitted.

"Terrific, so now we have a crazed zealot for a fan. Just what every talk show needs."

"I'm sure it was just a one-off. Probably had too much to drink and wanted to vent."

"I hope you're right. But please try to confirm callers actually have a question or an opinion about a legal issue to share from now on, okay?"

"You got it, boss. Really sorry."

"Are you heading back to school or crashing here tonight?" I asked. Unless Skip had an early morning class, he sometimes stayed in our guest room after a show or drove a town over to his parents. He had told me earlier his final exams had gone well, and he was looking forward to his summer break.

"I'm gonna go back," Skip said. "I have a lot to do tomorrow to clear out of the dorm, and I might as well get the drive done tonight."

"Yeah, no traffic at this time of night, that's for sure," I agreed. Skip grabbed his backpack and headed toward the door.

"Thanks, Randi. Tell Uncle Eric I said hey." I assured him I would and watched him leave.

"Safe driving," I called out. He waved in response, and I heard the door close behind him. I followed his path and fastened the dead bolt. I hated to admit how spooked the last call had left me feeling.

After talking to Miranda, I felt something I haven't felt for a long time. Triumphant! I told her she needed to be vigilant and to not allow excessive pride to rule her. Granted, she had rebounded nicely from her disastrous attempt to become the latest know-it-all on daytime TV, but caution should always be exercised. The woman is a sinner, and at some point she needs to atone for those sins. Pridefulness was just the tip of the iceberg. I had learned the hard way any one of us can fail. What kind of person would I be if I didn't protect her from the same sort of pain and public humiliation? But talk is cheap, or so they say. Perhaps I need to deliver the message to her in a less subtle manner.

But how?

CHAPTER 11

I studied my friend as she pushed her angel hair pasta and clams around a plate rimmed with lemon-butter sauce. We were out together, enjoying a casual dinner on a Sunday night. Let me rephrase that. I was enjoying my dinner, but Tracey seemed to have lost her appetite. Or maybe she hadn't had one to begin with; her enthusiasm perusing the menu had been perhaps a tad contrived in hindsight. She had been putting on a brave face ever since the visit to the police station, but I knew she was worried. And from my legal perspective, she had every right to be.

"They can bring you something else." She looked up at me with a blank expression. I gestured toward her barely touched plate. "How about some grilled shrimp? That would be great with your pasta." She stared as if memorizing every strand on her plate, shaking her head slowly. "Then what about dessert? Do you want to split something?" I had eaten a large green salad with the aforementioned shrimp and still craved something more. She shrugged, and I took it as a positive sign. "Tiramisu with two spoons, please," I said cheerfully as our server approached. "And a decaf cappuccino. T, cappuccino?" She shrugged again. "Make it two," I said. I waited in silence for a couple of minutes, nervously slicking on some lip gloss. Tracey's uncharacteristic silence was unnerving. Just as I began to ask her what was going on, she spoke up. Her words came out in a rush, and at first I didn't understand.

"Hedoesn'tlovemeanymore," she said and buried her face in her hands. I was perplexed.

"What? Who? You mean, Chase? Of course he loves you. You're a great mom. He's just scared and embarrassed and, um, hormones?" She looked at me, really looked at me for the first time since I had picked her up at her house an hour and a half earlier. I saw just how much this past week had weighed upon her. Her eyes were ringed in dark shadows, and her skin, usually a healthy glowing tan, was pale under the restaurant's unforgiving lights. She shook her head sadly.

"No, not Chase. It's Dale." She slumped back against the vinyl booth, and I waited while our server deposited our coffees and a huge serving of tiramisu.

"No calories if you split it with your bestie," she said in a voice that grated on me. Before she continued, I told her we were all set and she scurried away. I turned my attention back to Tracey.

"Dale loves you," I told her. "The man worships the ground you—"

"Goddamn it, Randi, we never have sex anymore," Tracey cried out, and the elderly couple seated nearby glanced our way, a look of shocked surprise on their faces.

"Sorry," I mouthed in their general direction before turning my attention back to Tracey. "You two have been going at it like horny rabbits since high school," I reminded her. "And I don't need to tell you how long ago that was." Tracey shrugged, so I pressed harder. "Let's define your terms. Just how long has it been?" Tracey's face scrunched up, trying hard to concentrate.

"Well, let's see. What day is it?" Relief flooded through me. It must not be *that* bad.

"It's Sunday, so a few days?"

"Three months," she said flatly. "Give or take a week." What the hell? Three months? I was shocked into silence. Tracey was now stirring her coffee with the same level of dogged determination she had given her pasta minutes earlier.

"Wow," I managed weakly. "That's a fair amount of time without, um . . ."

"And believe me, I have tried. Many times. He gives me the same old excuses. 'I'm tired', 'The boys are still awake,' 'I just want to finish this show or this book or whatever.' And lately, with this whole mess hanging over our heads and waiting to see if Chase will actually get jail time, it's gotten even worse." She looked miserable but, suddenly realizing there was a luscious dessert in front of her, grabbed the dish and started loading heaping spoonfuls of cake and custard into her mouth. It was like a car crash or a train wreck—horrible to witness, yet I couldn't look away. I waited until she scraped the remnants of the dessert off the bowl, sat back, and wiped her mouth with a large cloth napkin.

"Have you tried talking to him?" I asked casually. She glared in my general direction before affecting a look of utter confusion.

"Gee no, Randi. Talk to him, you say? Such brilliant advice. I never would have thought of that. No wonder they pay you the big bucks," she drawled.

"I'm just trying to help," I said defensively. "No need to get pissy." She looked chastened and, leaning across the tabletop, pulled my hands into hers.

"I'm sorry. I know you are, and I appreciate it. I'm just so frustrated and confused. It's always been so easy for us. Even with the twins and the daycare. Dale's job in construction. No matter what was going on, we always carved out a little time for ourselves. Just going for a walk or a coffee, having sex, there's always been a connection. Do you know what I mean?" She looked at me, begging for my understanding. I nodded enthusiastically. Their marriage of nearly twenty years was an inspiration to me. I had come close once before, but until I'd met Eric, I'd never dreamed I would have anything like that in my own life.

"It's normal to slow down some," I offered. "Sometimes when men hit forty—" I stopped there. I was just making this up as I went along. "They just . . ." I ran out of words and ended with a shrug. She smirked at me.

"Oh yeah, and just how slow is it with sexy Eric these days?" I shifted uncomfortably in my seat. Married sex was different. When we were younger, Tracey and I talked about sex all the time. How often, where, what positions. Since Dale was the only partner she'd ever had, she frequently relied on me to fill in some of the missing pieces from my own relatively scanty pool of knowledge. But Eric was my husband, not some rando guy I met in a bar. Our sex life was sacred—incredibly fantastic, but sacred nonetheless.

"We're not talking about me," I answered primly. "But if there is a problem, you two should talk to someone. A therapist or counselor? I can find someone who—"

"Someone who'll listen to me complaining my husband doesn't want to screw me anymore while the object of my misplaced affection sits there feeling like . . . like some loser?"

"It doesn't have to be like that. Dale is more in touch with his feelings than most men. He might surprise you." Tracey shrugged noncommittally as our server deposited the check on the table between us. She sat by silently while I pulled out a credit card and placed it on top. "Just something to think about," I added. We gathered up our things to leave as the check and my card were returned to me. I scribbled my signature after adding in a hefty tip for our server. We left the restaurant in silence and walked toward my car. We were still about twenty feet away when I saw it. A message had been scrawled in fluorescent paint across my windshield.

Gluttony is the SIN of overindulgence

CHAPTER 12

I drove Tracey home in shocked silence, each of us lost in our own thoughts. First pride, now gluttony? Was this some seven deadly sins sort of game? When I pulled into her driveway, she turned toward me.

"Are you going to tell someone? Eric? The police?" I put my car in park and sat back in my seat. Tell someone? Well, Eric, for sure. He would see my car first thing. I had to tell him. But the police?

"I don't know," I answered. "I'll tell Eric for sure. And I need to call the folks at Infinity. I'll let them decide if this should be reported."

"It's getting out of control, don't you think?" she asked. Yeah, I sure did. Warnings about excessive pride and now gluttony? What sort of religious zealot was this nutjob anyway?

"It's late," I said simply. "We both need to get a good sleep, yeah?" She nodded and leaned in toward me.

"I'm sorry I ruined the evening," she said into my shoulder, and I absentmindedly patted her on the back.

"No worries, my friend," I said in a tone I hoped sounded reassuring. "Talk to you tomorrow." She thanked me for dinner and, after letting herself out of the car, strode up the pathway to her front door. I waited until she was safely inside before I backed out of her driveway and headed home. Who was this guy, and how had he known I was at that restaurant? Was I being followed? I looked in the rearview, but I didn't see any car lights behind me. I felt numb, worried about my friend. If the world's happiest couple's marriage was in trouble, what did that say about the chances for mere mortals like me?

The next morning, I made my way to the beach and headed west to avoid the rising sun's glare. I needed to clear my head, and a walk on the beach had always been my go-to solution. It had only been a few minutes, and I was feeling better already. Eric had insisted on coming out to check on my car last night. I had backed into the garage a few minutes earlier and his reaction was about what I might have predicted. He'd snapped photos of the message, and I'd convinced him to hold off on phoning the police. But he'd called first thing this morning, and a patrol car was expected any moment. Then he'd contacted one of those companies that come to your home or your place of work and replace your windshield. He had even offered to wait for everyone to arrive, which was how I could go for a walk. I had been alone for a good portion of my adulthood and realized, not for the first time, how wonderful it was to share some of life's burdens. Eric had come along at a time in my life when I desperately wanted someone special, not just anyone. Who knew the joyful moments would outnumber the burdens by such a large margin? But if I were being honest—and why wouldn't I be?—the burdens were growing day by day. Chase's legal predicament, Infinity's desire to double my on-air time, Tracey's marital issues, and oh yeah, let's not forget the looming presence of an obsessed fan. I finally turned and headed toward home to check on my windshield and call Infinity. So much for a clear head.

"Twice as cloudy as I'd been the night before. And I went in seeking clarity," I half whispered, recalling the words of my favorite Indigo Girls song. *Clarity, my ass.*

The patrol officers had come and gone and the windshield guy was just finishing up when I arrived home. Eric filled me in on what I needed to know, and after he left the house I poured the dregs of the coffeepot into a mug and nuked it for a minute. Hobie was sleeping soundly, so I went out to the patio and called Sharon at Infinity. I swear the woman must put in eighteen-hour days as she was in early most mornings and frequently called in with a question or comment to Skip on the nights when we were live. She answered on the first ring.

"Miranda, good morning. How can I help you?" she asked. Oh yeah, and she was the most upbeat, cheerful woman ever. Times like these, it was actually kind of annoying.

"Hey, Sharon. So there was an incident last night. A listener of the show must have followed me to a restaurant near where we live. I came out, and there was a message spray-painted across my windshield."

"A message?"

"I'm texting you a picture of it right now."

"I got it," she confirmed. "Whew. What do you suppose it means?"

"Well, here's the thing. I was eating at a restaurant. But all I had was a salad, and my friend ate the dessert I ordered, so that's hardly gluttony."

"You should have seen me attack a quart of ice cream when I got home from work the other night. Now that was gluttony," she added with a laugh.

"Anyway, I think it's the same guy from the other night. The last caller from Thursday's show?" Silence on her end. Well, it's not like she could listen to every one of the network's shows. "He called himself Peter. He warned me against being too prideful. Said pride cometh before a fall, that proverb, you know?"

Now Sharon's tone was serious. "Why didn't you report this first thing?" she asked.

"It didn't seem like a big deal," I said. "Just some rando with an attitude."

"Did you report it to your local police?"

"The phone call? No, but we reported the vandalism. The police just left with pictures."

"Okay. I'll need to listen to the tape and send it on to network ops. Do you remember the approximate time of the call?"

"Yes, it was around 11:55, possibly as late as 11:57. Right after we ended the call, I signed off the air."

Sharon let out a long breath before continuing. "You'll need to fill out an incident report, you and your sound technician. I'll mark the tape and forward it to Alan. Be sure to add the part about your car too. And send the bill for the windshield with your next expense report. You'll get reimbursed."

"Thank you," I said. "I appreciate that."

"You just take care of yourself, Miranda. And please be careful. Most of the callers like this are harmless. But this guy thinks he knows you, has some sort of God complex, and is trying to warn you about your sins. But the worst part?" Oh no, there was something even worse?

"What's that?"

"He must have followed you to the restaurant. He knows where you live."

I truly believe I am getting through to Ms. Quinn. The look of surprise and something like terror that crossed over her face as she saw my little warning was all the evidence I needed. I wish I could say she reacted by putting in a little elbow grease of her own to erase my message, but no, she paid someone else to do it for her.

And that husband of hers! Don't even get me started on him. I've watched him breeze through his day, crisp and clean in his designer shirts, while the common laborers he employs do all the hard work. Typical of men like him. All show and no go. Neither he nor his wife has ever put in what I would call a hard day's work. Apparently, it will be up to me to provide the opportunity for that.

But first, there's something needing my immediate attention.

CHAPTER 13

My show that night went off without a hitch. Twice, I was certain the male caller on the air would go off on me with some warning about my sinful existence, but despite a record number of calls, my stalker stayed silent or must have given up on getting me to repent or whatever. I tried to not dwell on Sharon's comment that he knew where I lived, but I reminded Eric to lock the doors and set the dead bolts as well. Living in a small town, many of our neighbors left their windows open and doors unlocked. For the time being, we would need to be more vigilant.

The next couple of days flew by quickly. Eric's job site was running fairly smoothly, and he predicted he would finish by the projected due date after all. I urged him to consider taking some well-deserved time off before starting any more jobs, and he was going to try. I rarely traveled during the summer months as I preferred to spend my time on the glorious Connecticut shoreline, but an overnight to Newport, Rhode Island, would be an enjoyable break.

Late on Wednesday morning, I drove up north past Hartford to the airport. I found a parking spot in the short-term lot and hustled to the domestic arrivals wing. Pop and Sally's flight was expected to land at 2:45, but when I arrived, I found there had been a delay. A text from Sally confirmed they were running behind and estimated a new arrival time of 4:05. I wandered around, window shopping in the various gift shops and storefronts, finally deciding coffee and a muffin would work well as a substitute for today's lunch. I got in the short line at Dunkin' and placed my order. A couple of minutes later, I took my steaming cup and a chocolate chip muffin and found a vacant table, sat, and scalded my tongue on the first tentative sip. I consoled myself with a couple bites of muffin and waited for my coffee to cool. My thoughts drifted to my show, and I wondered if I could stall the expected expansion of the show. I felt two nights a week was perfect and would avoid future burnout for both me and the listeners. The number of affiliate radio stations increased every week, and many reported ratings they had never experienced previously. Why mess with success? I was at a point in my life where work was much more than a paycheck. I wanted to do something that mattered, and I liked to think listeners of *Miranda Nights* were not only entertained, but better informed about legal issues affecting their lives. I loved being on the air, working with Skip, and talking with callers. I could do the show in my pj's if I chose, as long as I kept things moving and calls coming in. Radio was challenging but enjoyable.

I heard my name being called and, looking up, I saw a happy, tanned couple of lovebirds rushing toward me. I stood up just in time to get enveloped in a massive hug by my petite stepmom. Pop stood by smiling proudly, waiting his turn.

"Hey, you guys," I said once I was standing on my own two feet again. "You both look so relaxed. You must have had a great time." It was a safe bet, as Sally had posted daily on a variety of social media platforms. I was quite familiar with what they had eaten (an ungodly amount of shrimp and king crab legs at the buffets), the shows they had seen (their favorite being a Beatles tribute band), and the weather (hot, humid, and a daily morning rain shower). As we shuffled over to wait for their bags, Sally chattered away, filling me in with even more details. After a couple of minutes, she excused herself to visit the restroom, and Pop and I watched her scoot away.

I'd needed a bit of an adjustment period when I first met her, but Sally was a wonderful woman who truly loved my dad—and me as well. She had made a terrific addition to our family. I turned to Pop, who was still watching her with a smile on his face.

"You done good, Pop," I told him, squeezing his hand. He beamed at me and nodded happily.

"She has more get-up-and-go than anyone I've ever known. First thing in the morning and well into the evening, she's got a plan. Things to do, places to go." He shook his head, amazed. "I need to get a look at her driver's license. There's no way she's only a few years younger than me."

I studied him closely. "You're doing pretty well yourself, old man. I haven't seen you this happy since . . ." I trailed off. "Since Mom died" were the words that lay unspoken between us. Pop nodded gravely.

"Am I kidding myself to think Nora would want me to be happy again?" he asked wistfully. I was about to assure him she definitely would when Sally approached, dragging two large suitcases behind her.

"Do I have to do everything around here?" she asked in a mock-serious tone, gesturing to the bags, and Pop and I each grabbed one from her.

"Sorry, hon, we just got to chatting," Pop told her, and she smiled at him before turning and heading toward the exit.

"C'mon, slowpokes," she called over her shoulder. "We're gonna get stuck in traffic and be late for Eric's dinner." I assured her Eric was aware of their flight's delayed arrival and was planning to serve at seven instead of six. We took the escalator to the short-term parking lot, and after loading up my car, paying, and exiting the lot, we were finally on our way home. Traffic was lighter than I'd imagined, and Sally's lively commentary, interspersed with Pop's occasional sounds of booming agreement, made the drive fly by.

I dropped them off at their condo at six, and they promised to head over once they had stowed their bags and freshened up. I made it home in plenty of time to toss a salad and warm up a loaf of French bread while Eric worked his magic on the steaks he had been marinating. I hastily prepared a plate of cheese and crackers and uncorked a bottle of red wine. Sally would join me in a glass while the men each had a beer. Eric had already set the table on the patio, and I joined him outside. I set down my tray and hugged my husband from behind.

"I love you," I told him. He put down the long grilling fork he had been holding and turned to face me.

"I've been thinking of getting a 'Kiss the cook' apron," he said. "Thoughts?"

"Hmmm . . . that's kind of basic. I think we can do better. How about 'My wife's chilling while I'm grilling'?" He appeared to consider my suggestion right before he snapped his fingers.

"Or maybe the all-time classic, 'My meat can't be beat'?" I laughed at his silliness. He lowered the flame on the grill and kissed me thoroughly. The kind of kiss that made me want to skip dinner and drag him off to bed, but we were interrupted by the sounds of our company arriving.

"To be continued," I promised and headed into the house to greet our guests. Hobie had center stage as he strutted across the marble-topped kitchen island, slowing down just long enough to allow the newcomers to pet him. I greeted my folks before addressing my fresh feline. "Hobie, you bad boy. What are you doing up there? You know you're not allowed." He looked at me disdainfully but jumped onto a barstool and allowed Sally to pick him up. While she found his treats, Pop and I went outside.

"Dez, good to see you," Eric called out, and the two exchanged one of those one-armed bro hugs only men seem to pull off. "Can I get you a beer?"

Pop assured him he could help himself and offered to bring one out for Eric as well. I poured wine for Sally, and soon we were sitting around the table talking and catching up on the cruise, Eric's projects, and my show. I had already warned Eric not to bring up my stalkerish caller or the vandalism to my car, so other than announcing a newly revised affiliate station count, I was happy to change the subject.

My meager cheese tray sat largely ignored, and we started on our salads before Eric passed around platters of perfectly cooked steaks and ears of grilled corn. Sally moaned happily as she bit into her corn.

"I always used to boil my corn. That's the way my ex liked it. But Dez made dinner for me and threw the corn right on the grill, husks and all." She beamed at him. "Genius." Pop finished chewing his steak and washed it down with a sip of beer.

"I can't take all the credit. Dale showed me that trick," he said.

"Ooh, how's Tracey these days? And the boys? What are they up to?" Sally asked. I shifted uncomfortably in my seat, not sure how much I wanted to share.

"Oh yeah, they're good, you know. Good, really, really good," I added awkwardly.

"They're all great," Eric said. "We should plan something soon. Get Jake and Meg, Julie and Brad all together, the Ryans, my brother and Tricia. How about a lobster bake on the beach? Is there anyone with some pull at the police station to get us a permit?" I shot Eric a look of thanks for helping to avoid an uncomfortable conversation, but I saw Pop watching me in full-on cop mode. I would bet anything he would ask me to spill my secrets before the night was over.

We lingered over our food, but everyone declined my offer of coffee. It was getting dark out, and when the solar-powered lights came on, Pop announced it had been a long day and they would have to eat and run. Sally, in particular, looked positively exhausted.

As we hugged goodbye, he whispered to me. "Coffee at the diner tomorrow." It was a statement, not a question. I was about to agree when he added, "Nine a.m. We need to catch up."

"You betcha," I told him, and Eric and I watched as the two of them walked hand in hand to their car. "Cute couple," I said. Eric looked at me, a knowing smile on his face.

"You're busted. He knows you're holding something back," he said, and I nodded.

"That man can see right through me," I complained. "And he's crazy about the twins. I hate to be the one to burst that bubble."

"Your dad is a smart guy, and he's seen a lot worse in all his years on the force. I don't think there's much you could say to shock him." I agreed, and we went inside, wrapped up the leftovers, and stored them in the fridge, except for a chunk of steak I chopped up for an appreciative Hobie.

"Let's leave the dishes," I said. "I'll have plenty of time to take care of them before I go to meet the grand inquisitor." Eric agreed, and we locked the door, turned off the lights, and went to bed.

CHAPTER 14

"What's going on with you, Randi?" Pop's voice was tinged with worry, and his weathered face showed concern. I had been all set to offer a neat and tidy explanation of the issues facing Tracey and her family, but I had not prepared my own defense. Stalling for time, I took an ill-advised sip of scalding black coffee. Then I needed to gulp some cold water to soothe my throat. Ugh. The only thing worse than the coffee at the diner Pop and I had frequented for years was the service. I patted at my lips with a paper napkin, all the while aware I was being scrutinized. I cleared my throat.

"Um, what now? What's going on with *me*?"

"I listened to your show. Is there anything you want to tell me?" At my blank stare, he continued. "What's with the crank caller the other night? The last caller?" I was mystified and slightly excited for a moment.

"You listened to my show on the cruise ship? How did that work?" I didn't know anyone outside of the current affiliates in Connecticut and New York could tune in.

"Let's call it the miracle of modern technology," Pop said flatly. "What do your bosses say? Are they taking any kind of safety precautions?" I understood his reasons for concern. Three years ago, I was embroiled in a tangled web of lies and cover-ups when I sat second chair on a case of aggravated sexual assault and murder. My car had been vandalized, my home broken into, and my life threatened. Pop and his retired cop buddies had kept my witness safe for me, and I owed it to him to come clean.

"You're right, of course. The folks at Infinity are investigating, and the latest incident has been reported to the police."

"Your windshield? Yeah, heard about it. I was wondering when you were going to tell me." Wow, I had to hand it to him. The guy still had some serious skin in the game.

"I suppose someone from the station called to tell you?"

"I heard from dispatch right after we got in yesterday. Hell of a thing, Randi. Hell of a thing." I took a sip from my still-too-hot coffee and nodded. It *was* a hell of a thing.

"I'm being careful," I assured him. "Patrol will send a unit regularly to canvass the neighborhood. When I'm home, my car will be parked inside my garage and I'll turn the alarm system on. No, I really will. I mean it this time," I added when I saw him smirking at me. Pop and Sally had bought us a high-tech security system as a housewarming gift just over a year ago. Despite several reminders, we had yet to activate it. But now we would, if only to ease Pop's mind. I leaned over and took his hand. "I'm careful," I repeated, and I saw his face relax. He leaned forward and grabbed a coffee-stained menu.

"We ordering breakfast or what?" he asked. "I'm thinking a short stack and a couple over easy. Some bacon and more coffee. What about you? My treat." I gingerly took a menu and glanced at it briefly. The only changes to this greasy spoon over the years were the prices. They still had a section called "Fuel for the Working Man" and another called "Lite Fare for the Little Lady." I winked at Pop.

"This 'little lady' is going with an order of grilled cornbread and an iced tea." I repeated my order when a most-disinterested server ambled over a moment later. It was nearly a half hour before our food arrived. I used the time to fill Pop in on what was going on with Chase.

But of course, he already knew.

That night, *Miranda Nights* was the very definition of a shit-show. My rhythm was off and I couldn't seem to get it together. My callers and I continually tried to speak at the same moment, followed by the unavoidable result—the death knoll to a radio talk show: silence. By the time I realized there had been two or three seconds of dead air, which was significantly longer than you might think, I would start to talk at, you guessed it, the same time as the caller. During every commercial break, I tried to give myself a pep talk. Skip offered to bring me a coffee or a snack, but I declined. As soon as we were live, I launched into a monologue about the perils of do-it-yourself wills, but the trickle of incoming phone calls dried up all together. Skip came in and offered me the "get out of jail card," meaning airing a few best-of episodes he'd put together precisely for moments like these, and I was seriously considering it when the calls started coming in again. Before Skip was back in his seat in the sound booth, I took the first call.

"Good evening. You're live on *Miranda Nights*, and you're speaking to the host, Miranda Quinn. Do you have a question or comment for me and our listeners this evening?" There was a brief silence before the caller spoke.

"Good evening, Miranda. I'm Andrew, faithful listener and occasional caller. I tried the other night, but I could not get through. I hate when that happens, don't you? When you try to reach someone with, well, let's say an important message, and you can't reach them? Don't you just hate that?" It was the same guy, Peter, the pride-warning guy. The author of the gluttony message spray-painted on my windshield. My heart pounded in my chest, but I tried to sound calm and collected despite my unease.

"Sometimes, Andrew, when your message cannot reach its intended audience, it's time to come up with a new message or an entirely different audience. Just a thought. So tell me, what legal issue or concern did you want to discuss this evening?"

"Okay, right down to business. Good. I would like to get your expert opinion on forgiveness." Andrew/Peter was working on my last nerve.

"I'm afraid I'm not following you, Andrew. How does forgiveness relate to a legal information talk show?"

"If a person were to commit a crime and served his time to atone for that crime, do you believe he should be forgiven?"

"Well, it depends," I said.

"Spoken just like a lawyer," he said. "What does it depend on exactly?"

"The nature and severity of the crime," I said. "And the relationship between the criminal and the person whose forgiveness is being sought. Is it the victim of the crime? Or a family member of the criminal or of the victim? Also, the amount of time that has passed." I was warming up to the question. It was actually a good one. "Forgiveness might be a difficult ask for a victim of a recent violent crime, for example."

"Interesting, Ms. Quinn. I believe you've covered all the bases."

"Well, that's good to hear. Did you have any specifics to share, or is this purely theoretical?" I turned to see Skip signaling for me to wrap it up, but I turned my back to him and continued. "Have you perhaps committed a crime you're seeking forgiveness for?" A low chuckle rumbled through the phone.

"That is a discussion for another day. Meanwhile, be sure your own conscience is clear. Good night, Ms. Quinn." I saw Skip signaling wildly for me to wrap things up quickly, so I did.

"Well, folks, we are out of time, so I'll say good night, know your rights, and I'll be back Monday night to discuss all things legal. Stay safe." Stay safe? Where had that come from? Skip was looking at his controls, but I saw a ghost of a smile forming on his handsome face. I had been trying out different catch phrases to end the show. Last week, I had attempted to explain to him how all the on-air greats had a signature close.

"Walter Cronkite always said, 'And that's the way it is.'" Clearly, no sign of recognition, so I tried again. "And Edward R. Murrow? His was 'Good night and good luck.' It was wartime, so it worked." Still nothing. "Good lord, Skip. What are they teaching you in school these days? You're a broadcasting major. How about Paul Harvey? 'Now you know . . . the rest of the story.' You're messing with me, yeah?" Skip was not impressed with my examples.

"Just be yourself," he said. "Just say, 'Thank you.'" I tried one more time.

"How about 'I'm Miranda Quinn, and you're not.'" He shook his head.

"Oh please, never say that. It's just . . . No!" What? That was a classic. Damn Gen Zers!

CHAPTER 15

The next night, Eric had a late meeting with a client, so I settled in bed with a bowl of cereal, the beachy novel I had been trying to finish, and, of course, Hobie. I had just slurped the first spoonful when my phone buzzed. I grabbed it, assuming it was Eric with an ETA.

"Hey, sexy, I'm already in bed waiting for you." There was a silence on the other end of the phone, and I thought it was yet another in an increasingly frequent number of hang-ups when the caller spoke up.

"Randi, it's Dale." I have known Dale for over twenty-five years, when he first starting dating my bestie while we were still in high school. He and I are close, but other than occasional texts, it is not our habit to call each other. What was up?

"Hey. You okay? Is it Tracey or Chase?" He cleared his throat, his voice low and gravelly.

"No, yeah, I mean, everyone is fine. We're gonna meet with Chloe's folks tomorrow to clear the air. The school is sending Chase's work home with Flynn, and I think Tracey's found him a tutor. But it's not about him. He's fine. We're, um, fine." All righty, then.

"So what's up?" I asked.

"Can we talk?" That was exactly what we were already doing, but something was on his mind.

"Sure, yeah. Whatever you need." I looked over and saw Hobie had not only discovered my bowl of cereal, but was lapping away at the milk as well. "No. That's not what good boys do." Unperturbed, he continued enjoying my dinner, so I turned my focus back to Dale. "Sorry, he's being fresh," I said. "What did you want to talk about?"

"Um, can I come over?" Wow, again, not a thing we did. Get together without Tracey.

"When? Now?"

"Yeah, if it's okay."

"Sure. Come on over." He said he would see me in fifteen minutes and ended the call. What the hell? I hopped up and raced into my closet. The kimono-style robe I was wearing was not exactly family friendly, so I pulled on an ancient UCONN sweatshirt and a pair of shorts. My cereal now abandoned, Hobie had jumped off the nightstand and was circling around my ankles. "Sorry, bud, no time to cuddle," I told him and headed down the hall to the kitchen. I tidied up a bit before reminding myself it was Dale, and he wouldn't judge me for having a cluttered kitchen island. I waited on the front porch. It was a beautiful night, clear and breezy, and I hugged myself, glad for the warmth of my tattered sweatshirt. A couple of minutes later, Dale pulled up in his pickup truck. I walked down the steps to greet him. He leaned over and cranked the passenger window open.

"Eric's not here?" he asked, no doubt noting the absence of Eric's truck.

"Nope. Late client meeting," I told him. His face scrunched up as he considered his options.

"Why don't you hop in?" he asked.

"Okay. Or you come in and I'll make you coffee or an iced tea. Or a beer." He shook his head.

"Nah, thanks, but I'm good." He leaned over and opened the door for me, so I stepped up on the running board and climbed in. The closer I got to Dale, the more I saw how exhausted he looked. Deep, dark circles under his eyes, which were red-rimmed and cloudy.

I leaned over and patted his arm. "What's going on with you, my friend?" I asked gently. "Talk to me, please." Closing his eyes, he leaned forward, cradling his head in his large hands. From what I could see, he had lost weight since I had seen him a couple of weeks ago. A big cuddly teddy bear, he seemed shrunken. It was not just Chase's current situation hanging over their heads. Something was terribly wrong

"I screwed up, Randi," he mumbled. "Big-time." Recalling how Tracey had recently complained about their lack of a sex life, my mind immediately went there. Had he been having an affair? That would explain why he had been turning away from his wife in bed. Furious at the thought he was cheating, I spoke sharply.

"Have you met someone else?" I asked. "Are you cheating on T?" He turned to face me, a horrified expression on his face.

"What? No. I would never cheat on Tracey. Why would you ask me that?" He seemed surprised by my questions. I softened slightly.

"Well, you're here at night. Sitting with me in the dark, wanting to talk, and Tracey mentioned you two have not been, uh, intimate much. Or at all," I added. He shook his head sadly.

"Wow, she told you that, huh? I always forget how much you two talk. Christ, she must be really worried."

"If it's not someone else, what has you so upset? You can tell me anything. You said you screwed up. How?"

He groaned, looking even more miserable. "I'm afraid I'm going to lose the business. There's so much new competition, and the supply chain is royally fucked up. Even if I win the bid on a job, I can't be sure I can get it done on time cuz I can't guarantee I'll get the lumber I need. And don't even get me started on the labor supply out there. No one wants to put in an honest day's work anymore," he said bitterly. "I'm screwed," he concluded. "I've ruined everything."

Dale had started his construction company fresh out of high school. Ryan Builders had an excellent reputation for quality work and dependable service for the residential customers he served. He had weathered some tough economic times over the years but had always seemed to rebound. Could he really be looking at closing up shop?

"It's tough out there," I agreed. "But why is it so much worse right now? You keep hearing things are getting better. What's happened recently?" Dale looked away, unwilling to make eye contact with me. He shrugged.

"It's not all that recent," he said. "The last two years have been real ballbusters. I had to take out a loan to keep things afloat."

I was confused. "I'm surprised you got a business loan. I thought the banks were cracking down on them." Especially with a company whose only tangible assets were a beat-up truck and a lot of well-used tools and equipment. "How did you manage that?"

"It wasn't a business loan," he said. "I had to borrow against the equity in our house. It looks like we're going to lose it." Oh my God. Tracey's home daycare business would be at risk, and it was the only home Chase and Flynn had ever known. What had he been thinking?

"What the hell, Dale? What were you thinking, risking your house and Tracey's daycare? Does she know?" I asked, already certain she didn't, and he shook his head.

"No, but I think she might suspect something. I'm barely sleeping, and, well, you already know our sex life is circling the drain. She knows something is up."

"But she had to sign for the loan, yeah?" I had helped them refinance their mortgage several years earlier, and the house was in both of their names. Dale groaned again and shook his head.

"I didn't want to worry her. You know how she gets. I told her it was an equity loan to purchase a new vehicle for the business. She signed it, no questions asked." Because she trusted you, I thought, trying and failing to keep the anger I was feeling from bubbling up.

"You should have been honest with her," I snapped. "She would have understood. She's always had your back."

"Yeah, I thought things would turn around."

I let out a long sigh. There was nothing to say to make him feel any worse than he already did. Dale was a good man and a loyal friend, and he deserved my compassion. I moved closer and wrapped my arms around him. He slumped against me, and we sat for a while as the streetlights came on and the sky went dark.

I hoped Ms. Quinn had tamed that wild streak of hers when she married the architect, but apparently I was mistaken. Her behavior tonight was inexcusable. What decent married woman lounges around at night in a parked car with a married man? And with the husband of her supposed best friend? Lust is a sin, and those who sin must atone for their wicked behavior. I am afraid any thoughts I'd had that she was aware of her sinful existence and working at redemption were just wishful thinking. I am going to have to publicly expose her and her married lover.

I don't see any other way.

CHAPTER 16

Dale left after I made him promise to come clean to Tracey right away. He assured me he would, and I suggested we talk again early in the week. I was certain Eric would have some contacts or jobs for him. I wished he'd spoken up sooner, but I understood how proud he was and how much he hated to ask for help. Perhaps my stalker could warn him against the sin of too much pride.

When Eric came home fifteen minutes later, I was happily ensconced in bed with a fresh bowl of cereal and my book. He sprawled out on the bed next to me, and I put down the book but kept a close watch over the cereal. He rolled closer and kissed me, a long slow kiss that literally curled my toes. I was so grateful for this amazing man who loved me and supported every one of my crazy ideas. How had I gotten so lucky after a lifetime of kissing frogs? His kisses became more urgent, and, well, one thing led to another. Forty-five minutes later, I roused myself enough to see Hobie had once again appropriated my dinner.

Eric had rolled onto his side and was clearly down for the count. Tomorrow would be plenty of time to talk to him about Dale's business woes. I decide to skip my usual routine of brushing, flossing, and moisturizing for one night. I turned off my bedside lamp and snuggled in beside my sleeping husband.

In hindsight, all I can say is it must have been an extremely slow news day. Otherwise, why would a story about me and my allegedly unacceptable behavior be deemed newsworthy? Brian called just after six a.m. I struggled to comprehend what my agent was trying to say. As usual, his tone was snarky and sarcastic. Just the thing before coffee!

"So you're back at it, huh? I can't leave you alone for one minute and you're running around breaking up marriages." I stuttered my response.

"Wh-Wh-What are you talking about? It's Brian," I mouthed to Eric as he came in with a mug of coffee for me. He raised his eyebrows, and I shook my head—couples' shorthand for "What's going on?" and "I have no freaking idea." He deposited the coffee on the nightstand and, with a thumbs-up, mouthed, "I love you," and hightailed it out of the room. I took a sip before repeating my question. "Brian, what the hell are you talking about?"

"Have you seen the tabloids? No, of course you haven't out there in Bumfuck, Connecticut. Do they even sell newspapers where you live? Not that you can call these gossip rags newspapers. But still." I listened to him ramble on, figuring he would eventually get to the point of this early morning call. I had hired Brian to represent me when I was negotiating a contract for a TV show a few years back. I continued to work with him, and between my book deal, which had sold two hundred thousand copies in the first year of printing, and my radio show, it had been a mutually beneficial relationship. Minus the snark, that is.

"Are you even hearing me?" he asked, and I realized I had zoned out and missed the last minute or two of our one-sided conversation.

"Just tell me. What's wrong, and how can I fix it?" I asked.

"There are pictures of you in a parked truck in the woods embracing a man who is not your husband," he said simply. "Please tell me how I am supposed to spin this." I sat up straighter, nearly spilling coffee on myself. What the hell was going on? "From the angle, the photos were taken at fairly close range, and the unidentified man is possibly a lumberjack. He's kind of a beast." Someone had taken photos of me and Dale sitting in his truck. I had hugged him and held him close. That must be when the photo was taken. But why? And what reason would someone have to insinuate I was engaged in an illicit affair?

"This is ridiculous. We weren't in the woods. We were sitting right in front of my house. And he's no lumberjack. It's Dale Ryan, my best friend Tracey's husband." There was a sharp intake of breath on the other end.

"Well, as long as it's your best friend's husband," Brian said. "That's gonna be so much easier to explain. I guess that's what you do when you live in the boring burbs. Is it some freaky wife-swapping thing? Does Tammy hook up with Eric too?" I took another sip of coffee before I responded.

"It's Tracey, not Tammy, and you've actually met both her and her husband before. And no, sorry to disappoint you, but no swapping is going on. Not of wives or husbands or anything else. I'm not cheating on Eric. I have no idea why anyone would take pictures of me." But even before I said the final words, the realization hit me hard and fast, like a punch to the gut. It was my stalker again. The sin du jour must be . . . lust! "It's the stalker. The seven deadly sins guy. He's accused me of pride, gluttony, and now he has me lusting after a married man. Don't you see?" I finished weakly. There was silence on the other end, but I was too worked up to continue to defend myself. Finally, he cleared his throat and responded.

"Okay, I guess it makes about as much sense as anything does lately. And you're claiming it was just an innocent conversation in front of your house with a friend, right?" Without waiting for my response, he went on. "So was Eric or the wife nearby?"

"No, it was just the two of us. They're having some problems, and I tried to—"

Brian cut me off. "I don't want to know. Plausible deniability and all that. As long as I have your word there was nothing untoward about your rendezvous." I rolled my eyes at his penchant for sounding like an ancient dowager queen.

"Nope, nothing at all," I assured him. "Rated G, suitable for all audiences." He sighed and told me he would make some calls to clear up "this mess," and I thanked him. I slipped on a robe and hustled down the hall to the kitchen, where Eric was drinking coffee and reading the newspaper. From what I saw, there were no lurid photos of yours truly. I guess the New Haven papers had yet to hear of my transgressions. I pulled up a chair and filled Eric in on everything—Dale's business, our conversation, and the current media shitstorm. I've been involved in worse ones, but this could affect my best friends as well. I shared with him my suspicion it was the work of my deadly sins stalker.

Eric responded by grabbing his laptop and googling me. "Late Night Legal Floozy's Night of Sin," he suggested. "What do you think?"

"You're a laugh riot," I told him. "Seriously, consider a career in standup." He shook his head.

"Yeah, but I got a few thousand hits, and that's definitely you and the big guy," he said, studying the blurred images. "And . . . wait for it. All the media outlets are updating their stories. The unidentified paramour has just been identified. One photo reveals the logo on the driver's side door. Looks like you and Dale Ryan of Ryan Builders of Old Lyme, Connecticut, were caught *en flagrante*. Sorry, babe, but I will not be betrayed by any man, let alone one who's supposedly my friend. Who can I trust?" he added, and when I burst into tears, he leaned toward me and pulled me into his arms. I cried into his shoulder for a couple of minutes before I could talk.

"I hate when you do that. You make a joke out of something that's not funny. I hate that."

Eric nodded glumly. "It is one of my many charms that can be hard to appreciate," he agreed. I glared at him, and he shrugged. "I'm sorry, babe. I don't know what to say. It sucks. This guy is trying to discredit you, that's for sure. And poor Dale. This is not the publicity he needs right now. If he's already struggling to find clients, this'll be the last nail in the coffin of Ryan Builders."

My phone buzzed, and I glanced at the screen. Oh terrific. It was Tracey. Surely, she wasn't calling to warn me to stay away from her husband. That was just plain ridiculous. Still, it was going to be a truly sucky day. I just had that feeling.

I will not apologize for what I did. I had to expose the deceitful and fraudulent life the hypocritical Ms. Quinn is living. She needs to learn the error of her ways and soon. If she doesn't get the message from me, what will become of her? I have to continue my efforts. But maybe a gentler message next time?

Isn't it true you can catch more flies with honey than vinegar?

We'll just have to see.

CHAPTER 17

It had been a fairly insane weekend. The highlights? More photos and headlines detailing my late-night hookup as well as Tracey's tearful recap of the meeting with Chloe and her parents, which had been laced with awkward silences, punctuated by angry accusations, and ending with both teens tearfully promising to stay away from each other. On Sunday, Eric and I had taken the twins to Misquamicut Beach in Rhode Island to give their parents some alone time. Flynn and Eric bodysurfed while I walked on the beach and collected shells. Chase kept to himself, preferring to lie on a beach towel on the sand, hiding behind his sunglasses and a ball cap.

At one point, I made my way over and plunked down next to him. I waited patiently until he pulled himself up into a sitting position.

"At least I won't run into anyone from school out here," he mumbled.

"You're not back in school yet?"

He shook his head. "Nah, I'm still on suspension, and this is the last week of classes. Just as well, I guess." I waited until he continued. "Everyone hates me. It's bullshit, Aunt Randi. My whole school is sending photos and stuff. Chloe and me just got caught because some asshole leaked our photos and sent 'em to everyone. Her parents went apeshit. So did the school. Now they want to make an example of me. It's not fair."

"No, it's not, bud, but we still have to get you cleared." His eyes filled with tears, which he swiped at with his discarded T-shirt.

"But what's so wrong? I care about Chloe. Maybe I love her, I dunno. But what we had was special, private . . ."

"But it didn't *stay* private, and that's what we have to try to fix. Just lay low, yeah? And do what Justin tells you to do."

He said he would before adding, "Eric and Flynn are heading back here. Can we keep this between us? Our talk just now?"

I feigned confusion. "Talk? I don't recall any talk," I told him with a wink.

We stopped for fried clams and onion rings on the drive home. I saw a ghost of a smile on Chase's face a couple of times. All in all, it was a pretty good day.

On Monday, I caught up on emails from listeners before driving into town to treat myself to a mani-pedi. Tonight's show went fairly well, all things considered. I had messed up a few names—okay, several names—but overall the callers were bright and articulate and the entertainment quotient was high. I found myself clock-watching in the last half hour, certain my "special caller" was waiting for the right opportunity to pounce. But with less than five minutes to go, it seemed as if he was going to take a pass tonight. Through my headphones, I heard Skip letting someone know they were the last caller. The caller's name came up on my screen. James.

"Hello, James. This is Miranda. Do you have a question or a legal matter you would like to discuss?" Brief silence on the other end. Then a man's voice. The same one I had been playing over and over in my head for a week.

"Ms. Quinn. Nice to hear your voice. Thank you for taking my call," the man I knew as Peter and/or Andrew practically purred into my ear. I looked through the glass at an irate Skip, who appeared ready to disconnect the call and go to a commercial break. I looked at my screen, which said "trying to settle deceased parents' estate," and frowned. I shook my head at Skip and responded to my caller.

"James," I said. "Sounds like you have questions regarding your late parents' estate. First, let me say I'm sorry for your loss. Did either of your folks have a will?" I heard a low chuckle on the other end.

"Both of my parents are alive and well, and neither would have any kind of estate. If you'll excuse my French, dear old Mom and Dad never had a pot to piss in." I saw Skip slashing a finger across his throat, and I held up a finger to him. No, not that one. It was my pointer finger, showing I needed another minute. He shook his head at me, and I turned my attention back to my caller.

"I guess I'm more than a little confused by your call. Do you have a reason for phoning in tonight?"

"Not so much legal. Let's call it a matter of ethics." I ignored Skip's frantic gesturing and let the caller continue. "I've been trying to warn you about the dangers of repeated sinning. I've seen you give in to excessive pride and gluttony and, in the matter of your relationship with your best friend's husband, lust. What will it take to get you to repent?" I was about to tell him he could perform a highly impossible sex act upon himself but figured I could do one better. I'd done my homework.

"You are quite fond of quoting proverbs, aren't you?" Without waiting for his response, I hurried on. "How about this? 'Let he who is without sin cast the first stone.' Perhaps you're more concerned for *your* soul and not mine." A chuckle, followed by a long sigh. He seemed to enjoy this exchange, and

I saw Skip giving me the two-minute warning. "Well, I'm afraid that is all the time we have tonight. I would like to thank our sponsors from Grove Valley Granola for their support," I added, responding to Skip's gesturing with a box of the cereal. "James, I'm sorry I am not living up to your impossibly high standards. Thank you for calling. I—"

He cut me off. "Consider me your guardian angel. My role is to warn you when you give in to sin. I hope you were able to relax and recharge today, but remember: idle hands are the devil's workshop. And when you—" I quickly disconnected the call. Skip looked as annoyed as I felt but gestured for me to continue. To sign off.

"To those of you still listening, thank you for your support. Remember, it's up to you to know your legal rights, night or day. I'm Miranda Quinn. Over and out." I yanked off my headphones and flung them across my desk. Who was this guy, and why was he so hell-bent on saving me?

An hour later, I slipped into bed next to my husband. I felt chilled, and my hands were clammy. Skip and I had a done a debrief after the show. He would collect the call records and forward them to Sharon at Infinity. I didn't feel like there was much anyone could do, but at least we would have a roadmap to follow if Peter/Andrew/James escalated his efforts to help me redeem myself.

"Quinn, that you?" Eric asked, turning to face me. With the glow of the moon illuminating our bedroom, I saw he was smiling, still drowsy from sleep. I was relieved when he spoke up. I hadn't wanted to wake him, but I sure needed to talk to him. He usually listened to my show on tape the next day, so I was certain he hadn't heard tonight's last call. I made a quick decision to hold off on worrying him.

"Who is this Quinn of which you speak, good sir?" I asked with the world's worst Cockney accent. "I am merely a serving wench sent up to comfort my esteemed lord and master. How may I serve you this evening, good sir?" My hands explored the contours of his toned upper body, and he groaned in my ear, wrapping his arms around me.

"It's about time," he growled. "I thought I'd have to start without you."

###

It is quite entertaining that Ms. Quinn, who is an atheist or worse, feels she can match wits with me. The time and attention I put into my studies all these years would put her measly efforts to shame. And I guess it only makes sense the hardworking Ms. Quinn required time at the spa today. A little me-time. It must be nice. After all, the hours she spends yakking away on the radio have to be exhausting. And of course, all the hard work her overburdened husband puts in is just grueling. They both obviously need a break to recharge their batteries. Oh, puh-leeze. In my prime, I worked harder than both of them together, even on my worst days, when the demons made their appearance. If I hadn't been overwhelmed by them and the poor decisions I'd made as a result, it was unlikely I would have ended up where I did.

But then, who would save Ms. Quinn?

CHAPTER 18

The next day, I awoke before the alarm, allowing me time to enjoy a cup of coffee with Eric before he had to leave for work. After kissing him goodbye, I hurried off to take a shower. I was meeting with the assistant state's attorney assigned to Chase's case at eight, before he was due in court. I had worked with Ben Thomas once before and found him hardworking and fair. I hoped this whole mess could be cleared up with a frank discussion and perhaps some community service hours for Chase. As I was toweling off, I heard a familiar scratching on the door. I opened it just enough for Hobie to make his way through. He hopped up on the counter and began surveying the array of cosmetics I had assembled. All designed to make me look well-rested and dewy fresh. Not for the first time, I was happy to have a career in radio instead of TV.

After brushing my teeth, I dotted some concealer under my eyes and dusted my cheeks with a bit of rosy blush. I took my hair out of the messy bun I had been sporting, but after seeing just how out of control my shoulder-length mane had gotten, I twisted it back up. Maybe my next trip to the salon would be for more than just a quick trim. I was a low-maintenance type, and shorter hair might be just what I needed. I pulled on a sleeveless gray dress and grabbed my navy blazer and a pair of pumps to change into when I arrived at the police station. I gave Hobie a quick kiss on the head, and with a wave, I sailed out to my car. I had left it in the driveway again and figured if Eric had spotted any recent damage this morning, he would have told me.

I backed my minivan out of the driveway and headed toward the center of town. Three years earlier, I'd had to rent a car when my own was vandalized and ultimately totaled. I'd ended up with this van. I had kept it so long the rental place took pity on me and considered it a rent-to-own deal, and it made sense to just purchase it outright. I regularly vowed to trade it in, but honestly, what I drove was of zero consequence to me. And now I had a sparkling clean new windshield thanks to Peter/ Andrew/ James.

I was waiting at one of the few red lights in town when I glanced over and saw a note sticking out of the CD player. *Play me* was scrawled in childish script, and I saw there was a disc already loaded. What now? I held off since I was on my way to the police station. A couple of minutes wouldn't make a difference—unless there was some sort of bomb on a timer, in which case I was already dead. Get a grip, I told myself. This dude wants to scare you, or even save you, not kill you. I pulled into the only remaining visitor's spot, and after ejecting the disc, I hurried toward the entrance. I had plenty of time, so I wasn't rushing to meet Ben. It was more of a feeling that I needed to get inside, where I would feel safe.

I was greeted warmly by Mike, the desk sergeant, before being hugged by my dad's most recent partner, a tall and lanky cop named Ed "Monty" Montgomery.

"Tell Dez I'm looking forward to learning all his favorite fishing spots," he said. "I put in my papers and expect to see a lot of my old pal and soon." I didn't bother reminding Monty how Pop was a newlywed and his time spent fishing had been reduced considerably since the nuptials. These days, he and Sally were more likely to walk on the beach or take day trips and have lunch at spots all around Connecticut and Rhode Island. I had never seen Pop happier.

"Will do," I promised. "Which room did Ben Thomas reserve this morning?" It was a small station, and everyone knew everything going on under its roof.

"I'm heading that way," Monty told me. "C'mon, follow me." I walked through the door he held open for me and found Ben in the first room on the right. I thanked Monty and assured him I would fill my dad in on his upcoming retirement and turned to greet Ben. Short and round, he had a receding hairline and five o'clock shadow, even at this early hour. He was a nervous sort, at least around me. Initially, I had assumed it was because I had been fired and he had replaced me. But that was over five years ago, and he was still skittish. I always felt like it was my responsibility to put him at ease.

"So, Ben, I was hoping to put this to bed today. Can you give me an update? Where are we regarding Chase Ryan?" Ben cleared his throat, shifted around in his chair, and seemed intent on studying the tips of his shoes instead of making eye contact with me. This was not good.

"Well, the situation is a bit more serious than we had been led to believe. Our investigators have found many graphic images. I'm afraid—"

My breath caught, and it took me a second before I could speak. I cut him off.

"How many are we talking about?"

"Oh, thousands," he said. "Mostly photos, but videos too." What? If that were true, Chase could be charged with a felony carrying a mandatory sentence of . . . I immediately went on the offensive.

"How is all of this just now coming to light?" I asked. "Why wasn't I informed of this evidence?"

Ben finally met my eyes, and I noticed how tired he looked. If he put in anywhere near the same number of hours I had when

I was on the job, it was understandable. But if the workload was that punishing, why pursue a case against a teenaged couple playing doctor? Don't get me wrong. If I thought Chase's girlfriend was coerced in even the slightest bit, I would be all in favor of prosecuting him. I may have changed the kid's diaper — well, actually, I only helped the one time — but sexual assault wouldn't be tolerated, not on my watch. It was an unfortunate coincidence Chase had just turned sixteen when the sexting began, whereas his girlfriend was five months younger. If they were both sixteen, Chase's actions would not be criminal in the state of Connecticut. But Chloe was a minor and technically could not give consent. The metrics could not be any worse.

"Well, technically you are not the attorney of record on this case," he said. "Um, Mendez, yes, Justin Mendez is, and I am waiting for him to return my call so I can let him know. I'm speaking with you today out of professional courtesy. But from now on, I'll need written approval from the Ryan family and from their attorney before I can divulge anything further."

"Of course, I realize this is irregular. It's just hard sitting on the sidelines while my friends are going through all of this." Looking relieved at my response, Ben nodded slowly.

"I can only imagine how difficult it must be. But, Miranda, you know the drill. You've got to trust the process. Justice will prevail." Yeah, I knew that, but for whom?

"I do. Have trust and all," I lied smoothly. "But honestly. Off the record. What are we talking about here? Worst-case scenario, six months' community service?" Ben shook his head, and I gulped. "What, then? Time in juvenile detention? What is it? Why are you still shaking your head?"

"Off the record? You need to prepare your friends. If Chase is found guilty, he could spend the next ten years in prison." All the oxygen in the room seemed to disappear as I sat stunned, trying to come to terms with what I had been told. This was as bad as anything I had allowed myself to consider.

How could I tell my best friend her son might be incarcerated until his twenty-sixth birthday?

###

I thanked Ben for his time and wished him well in court. I headed to the detectives' trio of cubicles and was relieved to see Dennis Reynaldo was at his desk. He looked up as I approached, but nothing about his facial expression or body language showed how he felt about my dropping by. I guessed I would find out soon enough.

"Good morning, Detective," I said warmly. "How are—"

He cut me off, looking back at the pile of paperwork in front of him. "I have no updates for you, Ms. Quinn. And since you are not the Ryans' attorney of record—"

It was my turn to cut him off. Two could play at this game. "I am not here in any official or unofficial capacity regarding Chase Ryan," I assured him. "The attorney they hired is more than competent. I'm here for an entirely different matter." He looked up, his steely glare softening.

"How can I help you?" he asked, attempting a tight smile. I motioned to the empty chair to my left.

"May I?" I asked, and he nodded almost imperceptibly. What a grouch. Did he hate on everyone, or was I just the lucky beneficiary of his mood today? I chided myself for not bringing coffee or donuts or both. I pulled up a chair and sat to face him.

"You're busy, so I won't take up too much of your time," I said sweetly. In response, he shifted in his seat, looking bored and a bit put out. I hurried it up.

"I'm the host of a late-night talk show," I began. "It's a call-in show. We discuss legal issues, talk to guest experts, and I answer legal questions and provide resources—"

He frowned and interrupted me. "I'm familiar with talk radio, Ms. Quinn. What is it exactly you're looking for my help on?" I took a deep breath and told him.

"Two weeks ago, I had a caller named Peter. He was kind of creepy. He mentioned my recent success and my marriage and warned me that pride cometh before a fall." Reynaldo was still listening, so I continued. "Then I was out to dinner with Trace— um, a friend, and when we came out, someone had spray-painted a message on my windshield. It said how gluttony was a sin, which is ridiculous since I'd had a salad for dinner and not even a bite of dessert. It's all in the police record. My husband called it in. And now he's moved on to lust." He looked at me, a question in his eyes. "Oh yeah, so we started calling him the deadly sins stalker. You know, pride, gluttony, lust . . ." I counted off on my fingers.

"Greed, envy, wrath, and sloth," he concluded. I nodded, happy to not have to struggle to recall them by myself.

"So I was sitting in a car with a friend, a male friend. He's actually my best friend's husband. Dale Ryan?" I saw just the beginning of a smirk. What the hell was that? "Anyhoo, some photos of the two of us appeared in a couple of newspapers and online insinuating . . . well, suggesting we are having an affair." Reynaldo was about to speak, but I stopped him. "And then he calls in to my show again, this time calling himself Andrew, and he tells me how he's trying to help me, to repent, I guess, for my sins. But he called again, and this time he gave his name as James. It's gone beyond creepy. It's downright menacing." The detective seemed deep in thought before he began peppering me with questions.

"Has this man threatened your life, any type of bodily harm?"

"Um, well, no."

"Has he entered your residence or your workplace?"

"It's one and the same. My husband built me a studio. . ." He was frowning again, and I tried to keep my answers brief and to the point. Gosh, you would actually think I understood the process of interrogation. "No, he did not. Just my driveway."

"I'm assuming you have recordings of his calls or transcripts?" I nodded, suddenly remembering the latest threat I'd received. I fished the disc from my bag and placed it in front of the detective.

"There. This was in my car this morning. With a note, which I must have left in the car. It said, 'Play me.'"

Reynaldo looked at it and slipped on a pair of gloves before he picked it up. "So you took it from your car, tossed it into your bag, and dug it out just now. Is this how you treat evidence?"

I flushed, embarrassed at what I must look like to a seasoned law enforcement professional. I shrugged in response, unable to defend my actions. "Did you play it?" he asked.

"No way. I wanted to wait for you," I assured him, and he smiled. A genuine smile, the first I'd seen on him.

"Then let's get to work," he said.

CHAPTER 19

The next hour reminded me why I had loved being a prosecutor. The search for the truth. The pursuit of justice. Until the last few minutes, when we played the CD after it had been thoroughly analyzed for any traces of DNA or fingerprints. That's when it all fell apart. Any credibility I'd had with the detective was completely gone.

Late in the afternoon, Eric and I were sitting on the patio, drinking iced tea. I was binge-eating handfuls of stale caramel corn from a holiday tin. Please don't ask which one. Initially upset the stalker had entered my car, Eric was trying hard not to laugh but failing miserably.

"So it was 'Walking on Sunshine'? Katrina and the Waves from the 80s? That song was on the CD the deadly sins guy left for you?"

I glared at him. "Yes, it was. But you're missing the point. He broke into my car. My unlocked car, but still. It was a warning." Eric tried to hide his grin.

"Well, yeah. Maybe he was warning you about the dangers of walking on sun—"

"Don't say it," I told him. "And let's not forget when it was dusted for prints, the only fingerprints were—"

"Yours," said Eric. "So let me get this straight. You're answering a definitive no to the question: and don't it feel good?"

I couldn't believe it. "Screw you, Eric. If you won't take me seriously, I'm not talking to you." I started to leave before turning back and grabbing the tin of popcorn. "You can go to hell!" I went back into the house, wanting to slam the door behind me, but my hands were busy holding my dinner. I would not be dining with my husband or anyone else this evening. I heard him say, "I'm sorry, Quinn," but I ignored him and went down the hall to our bedroom. Oh, finally a door I could slam. I put the tin on my nightstand, turned, and slammed the door with all my might. The sound was satisfying until I realized it was unlikely that he heard it from outside.

I was already in a comfy pair of sweats and a T-shirt, so I plopped down on my side of the bed, grabbed the remote, and settled in for a pity party for one with a collection of sitcoms from my childhood. *Growing Pains, The Wonder Years, Saved by the Bell,* and *The Facts of Life*. A simpler time, for sure, but not without its share of preteen angst. At first, I fumed at Eric's lack of empathy for what I was dealing with, then gave my jumbled emotions over to the trials and tribulations of a young Fred Savage and his sweet girlfriend, Winnie. I had left my phone in the kitchen and thoroughly enjoyed watching TV with no interruptions. After a while, there was a knock, followed by a turn of the knob, and Eric's face poked around the open door. He looked upset and sounded concerned.

"Babe, you need to take this," he said, crossing the room to hand me my phone. "It's your dad."

The doctor's face was grave, and despite his obvious youth, it was clear he was confident in his initial findings.

"Mr. Quinn, I'm sorry, but your wife did indeed have a mini-stroke earlier this evening. When she was admitted, it appeared she was merely dehydrated, but the scans confirmed it." I squeezed Pop's hand and asked the question plaguing me since arriving at the hospital three hours earlier.

"What can you tell us, Doctor? Is Sally going to recover fully?" As I had feared, he shook his head in response.

"We have no way of knowing for sure. I'll run some additional tests, and we'll know more when we see how she responds. Since Mrs. Quinn is in no immediate danger tonight, I recommend you go home and get some sleep. We can regroup in the morning." As he was clearly eager to get going himself, I thanked him and turned to Pop.

"You heard the doctor. Let's get you home, okay? I'll call Eric and—" I turned in surprise at the sound of my husband's voice.

"I never left. I wanted to give you some space. I've just been hanging out. Did you know the cafeteria has three kinds of soft serve?" I grinned at his attempt to inject some levity into the situation. It was a habit of his I loved—except when it thoroughly pissed me off.

"Did you hear that, Pop? Let's go home, and when we come back in the morning, we can check out the ice cream." His face darkened, and he shook his head forcefully. Clearly, no promises of frozen dairy goodness would sway Desmond Quinn from his post.

"No," he said clearly. "You two run along. I'm going to stay here tonight." Eric sat beside him.

"I hear you, Dez, but Sal's going to need you at the top of your game tomorrow. Why don't we—"

Standing up suddenly, Pop seemed to lose his balance for a moment. He grabbed the back of the chair and regained his equilibrium before he spoke up.

"I understand all that, but I am trying to tell you I'm not going home. I'm staying, and I'll call you when I have something to report." His tone brooked no argument, so I hugged him and told him to call me anytime during the night.

"Hang in there, Dez," Eric said and squeezed his hand. Pop nodded and sank back in his chair. We trudged toward the exit, and when I turned back, he was leaning forward, his head cradled in his hands. He looked small and broken, and for a second I considered running back to him. Eric held my arm and led me to the exit.

"C'mon, babe. Let's let him have some quiet time. We'll come back in the morning with coffee and breakfast sandwiches."

I teared up. "Without waiting for him to call first?"

"Sure thing. He'll be glad to see us." He squeezed my arm as we entered the elevator, heading to the parking garage.

On the way home, I turned to him. "I'm sorry about before. I just felt like you weren't taking me seriously. Sometimes . . ." He looked over at me. The glow from the dashboard illuminated his face, and seeing his smile warmed me to my core.

"I always take you seriously. It scares the hell out of me you're in any sort of danger. I crack stupid jokes because I don't want you to see how scared I actually am."

I nodded slowly. "I get it, I do. But it's okay for you to worry. You don't always have to be all brave and manly for me."

"Fuck brave and manly, babe. This guy has taken things to the next level, and now it's our turn. We are going to amp up the security right away. Cars will be locked and in the garage. All the doors and windows will be locked and double-checked morning and night. I've been looking at state-of-the-art security systems online and have calls in to a couple of places. This has gone on far too long. I'm done playing nice."

Wow, he was deadly serious.

"Thanks, babe. I appreciate it. You're right; it's time for us to take action. Let's just keep all this between us, okay? No need to get Pop involved. Or his cronies." I smiled, remembering how they had watched out for Becky in the days leading up to the trial where she had been a key witness.

"You got it. And don't worry, I'll let you know next time I'm scared shitless. Hell, I won't even have to use my words. I'll just be curled in a fetal position, sucking my thumb," he promised. I groaned in response.

Where had this crazy, sweet, silly man been all my life?

A lack of a sense of humor is hardly a sin, but even Ms. Quinn needs to find a reason to smile every once in a while. A cheerful song from the 80s with a catchy chorus? Where is the harm in that? Yet another lesson I apparently must press upon her: Stop and smell the roses! She needs to pick up on the messages I am sending and think long and hard about whether her sinful behavior is worth the price of eternal damnation.

What is she waiting for?

CHAPTER 20

The next morning brought good news on Sally's condition. Pop phoned early to report her stroke would have no long-term effects and that she would be released later today.

"Don't bother coming to the hospital," he said. "We'll be busy with discharge papers and all that. I'll call you from home when she's up for a visit, yeah?" I told him to give her a kiss from me and placed my phone back on the nightstand. I shared the good news with my sleepy husband, who squeezed my arm, made a kissing noise, and fell back to sleep. I lay on my back, certain that thoughts of Sally, Pop, Tracey, Chase, and the deadly sins guy would prevent me from sleeping, and I was right. Twenty minutes later, I rousted myself from bed and, after a quick kiss on the top of Eric's head, padded down the hall to the kitchen.

Hobie greeted me in his usual fashion, a cross between "Good Morning, Human" and "Feed me, I'm famished." As I made a pot of coffee, filled his water dish, and opened a can of foul-smelling (at least to me) salmon shreds in gravy, he wound his way around my ankles, purring loudly.

"This one's got kale," I said as I placed his bowl in front of him. He gobbled it up in a couple of minutes and walked away, licking his chops. "You're welcome," I called after him. I poured myself a mug of coffee and, after a quick glance confirming the patio furniture was coated with dew, plopped down on the couch. I looked around the open-concept room flowing from the large eat-in kitchen. I had never been much of a decorator, preferring comfort to style, but I'd had the good fortune to marry a man with the brain of an architect and the soul of an artist. It was a lovely home, sleek and efficient, with warm, homey touches and brilliant splashes of my favorite oranges and reds. I could not imagine what it might take to get me to consider spending any amount of time in some soulless corporate condo in the city. I would quit my job before I would allow that to happen.

I tried to picture giving up my radio show. It wasn't that difficult since I had only been on the air for a few months. I still had my podcast and could resurrect my blog if I wanted to. *Miranda Writes* had been my salvation a few years back after I was axed from the DA's office, and the advertising dollars my brand generated had allowed me to live a comfortable, if somewhat frugal, life. Then came the TV show offer, the book deal, and now, the radio show. Yes, I would keep talking about the law in whatever format I had available, preferably from the comfort of my home.

With my professional future decided, my mind slipped back to the issues of the day, the ones that had caused me to vacate my cozy bed and watch the sun come up from my vantage point on the couch. God, it was still ridiculously early. I wished, not for the first time, I was more like Eric, who could compartmentalize. He was always encouraging me to focus only on the situations where my actions could affect the outcome, and I tried, I really did. But I was a worrier. That's what I did.

I figured there was at least one area where I could make an impact, and that was my radio show. I poured more coffee and grabbed my laptop. I was deep into researching articles on lawsuits involving excessive sentencing at the judicial level when Eric came into the room.

"Morning, babe," he called out as he headed to the coffeemaker. He lifted the pot and sniffed suspiciously. "Good God, woman. In what decade was this coffee made?"

I smiled apologetically at him. "Sorry. It is pretty old. Want me to make another pot?"

Eric shook his head as he poured stale coffee down the drain. "I got you covered," he said and began scooping grounds into a fresh filter. "Did I hear you right? Sal's getting out today?" I shared what I knew and suggested we plan to bring them dinner tonight. "How about Thai?" Eric suggested. "It's not your dad's favorite, but he's pretty easy. Just like his daughter," he added with a wicked grin.

"Ha ha. You're a riot. But why don't I make something?"

Eric looked unsure how to respond. My lack of culinary skills was legendary, but I had a few tried-and-true recipes in my wheelhouse. "How about a pot of low-sodium homemade chicken soup and a fruit salad for dessert?" Sally would need to watch her diet more carefully from now on, and it wouldn't hurt for Pop to reduce his salt intake as well. "That way, they can heat it up when they're ready to eat and have leftovers for lunch tomorrow."

Eric came over to sit next to me. He lifted my feet onto his lap and sighed contentedly. "Sounds great. What are you working on?" I wriggled my toes and grinned at him.

"Looking up some background on punishment and excessive jail sentences for my next show. Oh crap, I just realized it's tonight. I've been up since 4:30. It's going to be a long-ass day."

"Hmmm. If only there was some way of getting some rest during the day . . ." He snapped his fingers. "I've got it. How about a nap?"

I frowned in his general direction. "I'm not a napper. If I lay down this afternoon and actually fall asleep, I'll be all drowsy for my show. I'll just power through with caffeine and maybe a walk on the beach? Do you have time?"

He considered the question and nodded. "Sure thing. How's about I pour us a couple of travel mugs and we pick up some donuts at Francesco's and head to the beach?" I swung my legs around and hopped up.

"You had me at donuts," I called over my shoulder. "I'll be ready in a jiff." Carbs, fat, and caffeine: Breakfast of Champions. I would need all the help I could get, what with work, grocery shopping, cooking, and phone calls to Tracey, Justin, and Brian before dropping off dinner to my folks, making it home in time for my show.

CHAPTER 21

Sally was lying down when we arrived at the condo late that afternoon. Her son Jake and his wife Meg had already visited, bringing a veggie casserole, and a turkey meatloaf. Pop assured me the soup and fruit looked delicious and they would enjoy it when she woke from her nap. He looked exhausted, so we turned down his half-hearted invitation to stay and visit.

"I need to prep for my show, Pop," I said. "I'll call you in the morning to check on a good time to drop by."

He rubbed his forehead wearily. "Don't let that deadly sins bastard monopolize your show tonight," he said. "Tell Skip to cut him off."

I told him we were on high alert and not to worry. But I knew he would. He was a worrier, just like me. My mom had been the one to focus solely on the positive. An enviable trait, for sure.

Eric and I drove home as the sun set. It was a beautiful June evening, and just for a moment I resented the fact I had to get home and go to work. It would be a perfect night to go for a stroll on the beach or walk into town for an ice cream at Tessie Lou's. My husband, the mind reader, spoke up.

"I realize we had donuts for breakfast, and I can only assume you had a bowl of cereal for lunch," he began. Guilty as charged. "What do you say to me dropping you at home so you can go through your notes and I'll swing by Tessie Lou's and grab us a burger?" At my dubious expression, he hurried on. "Or I'll grab a burger for me and pick you up a shake?" I brightened at that and nodded happily.

"No whipped cream," I reminded him as he pulled into our driveway.

He placed his hand on his heart. "I promise to remember," he told me gravely and leaned in to give me a quick kiss. "I'll be back as soon as I can." I waved and walked toward the house, already hearing Hobie scratching at the door. As I turned the key and pulled the door toward me, a slip of yellow paper fluttered to the ground. I picked it up and entered, dropping my bag on the credenza. I assumed it was a notification of a delivery that couldn't be completed, but as I opened it, I felt a chill and an overwhelming sense of dread stopped me in my tracks.

Time to repent, Ms. Quinn. No more excuses! D

I locked the door behind me and leaned against it, trying to control my breathing. D? Now he was signing his notes? Who was this guy, and what exactly was our connection? What had first seemed like some disturbed rando now felt deeply personal. How and when had our paths crossed? My first thought was of my years as a prosecutor. A mostly successful one. They didn't call me "Quinn for the Win" for nothing. First thing tomorrow, I would call my former boss, District Attorney Rick Cooper, and ask him to assign someone to review all the convictions I had won during my tenure and cross-reference them with prisoners released in the last few weeks. A quick glance at my watch showed I had only twenty minutes before my show was to air. Suddenly, my phone buzzed, and I heard banging on the basement door. The call was from Skip, and I figured he was also the one at the door.

I ran down the stairs and opened the door to my flustered sound engineer. He came in and dropped his backpack on the floor.

"My key doesn't work," he said. "Are you locking me out or something?" I recalled how I had turned the dead bolt on the door the other night as an extra precaution. I should have unlocked it when I reviewed my notes, my usual pre-show ritual. But not tonight.

"Sorry, Skip. I forgot I'd locked it. We went to drop off dinner for Sally and Pop, and I am running late tonight."

"What's up with your folks?" he asked, and I told him about Sally's emergency room visit. Before he responded, I waved him off.

"I've got to grab my notes, and you should get set up," I told him as I dashed back up the stairs. Hobie cornered me in the hallway, clearly irate his dinnertime had gone unnoticed. "Sorry boyo," I told him. "Your dad will be home any minute, and my adoring fans are waiting." I finished up in the bathroom, grabbed my notecards from the front hall table, and headed back downstairs, grateful once more for the invisibility of the radio.

I had only a few minutes to organize my notes before getting the three-minute warning from Skip. My milkshake would have to wait, I realized sadly, as Eric would never interrupt me when the red recording light was on. Once more, I focused on my breathing, trying to get the yellow slip of paper out of my mind. Tomorrow, we would begin the search for the crazed fan determined to shake up my life. Tonight, we would talk about punishment. A fitting topic, for sure.

The show was going well. There were at least half a dozen callers on hold at all times, and everyone seemed to have an opinion on tonight's topic: Does the Punishment Always Fit the Crime?

Roughly half the callers felt most prison terms, fines, and sentences were justified.

"You kill someone or rape someone, you should sit in jail for the rest of your sorry-ass life and think about how you screwed up," said Anne, a first-time caller from New Haven. Most of the remaining, more irate callers, were convinced judges handed down heavier sentences to people of color, and the evidence I had seen over the years supported those claims. I made a note to pull together updated statistics and find well-qualified experts to interview on an upcoming show. The more radical callers complained prison sentences were far too light and that more convicts should be put to death.

Susan from Danbury said her neighbor had killed his wife and had to only serve six months in lockup. "He had money, her money, and he must've paid off some judge or someone to get out so soon. They should have given him the chair," she said. "Money talks, bullshit walks," she added, and I cut her off quickly.

"Well, it sounds possible that justice wasn't served in that situation," I conceded. "Who else has a comment on too-lenient sentencing?"

The next couple of callers shared their opinions that convicted criminals got off far too easily and that "a slap on the wrist" was insufficient for most crimes committed. Frank from West Hartford reported his ex-wife had gotten away with attempted murder just a few months ago. "She got off scot-free," he complained bitterly before admitting her intended "victim" was a garter snake that had scared her.

Skip kept busy fielding calls and screening callers while I listened, corrected, cajoled, and responded, certain a call from "D" would sneak through. My suspicions paid off at the start of the fourth hour. Right after a commercial break, I took a call from John.

"Good evening, John. You're on the air with Miranda Quinn. We're talking about whether the punishment always fits the crime. Do you have an opinion to share?" There was silence on the other end, and I felt my heart start to pound. Skip looked ready to disconnect the call when the caller spoke up.

"Well, of course I do, Ms. Quinn." It was my stalker. He spoke smoothly, and for the first time I detected a faint accent. Brooklyn, maybe, or the Bronx? "I think most crimes go unpunished, that's what I think." He chuckled but did not sound the least bit amused. "And those that do, receive punishment that is woefully insufficient. An eye for an eye, that's my motto. If you steal, lose a hand. If you trespass, a foot. If you fornicate with your neighbor's wife, well, I'm too much of a gentleman to tell you which body part should be eliminated, but I'm sure you catch my drift." I felt bile rise in my throat and tried to focus on my breathing.

"I appreciate your call this evening. You should stay tuned to see what callers will have to say about your rather unorthodox punishments."

Again with the chuckle. "Hardly unorthodox, Ms. Quinn. Look back through history and see for yourself. It might alter some of your own flaming liberal views."

It was my turn to chuckle. I shouldn't bait this psycho, but it gave me a kind of perverse pleasure to do so. "A flaming liberal? Wow, John, I've been called a lot of things, but . . . well, actually, I believe I have been called a flaming liberal. You might be on to something."

"And what should your punishment be, Ms. Quinn?" he asked, sounding more heated. "You are not above reproach, am I right? You've been prideful, given to excess, and have acted lustfully with a man who is not your husband. What do you imagine is a suitable punishment for all of that?" Skip looked like he was ready to disconnect the call, but I held up a finger. No way was I not going to respond to his accusations.

"You sound as if you have an issue with my lifestyle and choices, John, or is it James? Andrew? Peter? D? Tell me, if my personal life is such a disaster, why would you waste your time listening to anything I have to say?"

His response was immediate. "Because I need to save you, and I am the only one who can. If I fail, if you reject my attempts to help you redeem yourself, I will watch you burn in hell for your sins. How does—" Skip disconnected the call and switched to a commercial break before he hurried out of his control room.

"Randi, are you okay? Geez, he has like a hundred different voices. I am so sorry."

Removing my headphones, I leaned back in my seat and stretched. I shook my head. "Skip, it's not your fault, okay? This guy is obsessed, off the deep end. I'm going to call the district attorney's office tomorrow. We need to find him. This is getting out of hand."

Skip looked skeptical. "What can the DA do? I'm not sure— hold on, the private line is ringing." He took the call. "Hello, this is Stephen Hansen, lead sound engineer for *Miranda Nights*," he said. "Okay, uh-huh, yeah, I guess. Okay, I'll tell her. Well, if you think that's best. All right. Thank you. Good night." Although I heard one side of the conversation, I wasn't in the least bit surprised when Skip turned to me wide-eyed and shaky and shared the news.

"That was Sharon. We're off the air effective immediately. They'll announce a schedule change beginning tomorrow. We're both getting paid for now, but the sponsors don't like the hostile environment the deadly sins guy has created."

"They said that? They called our show a hostile environment?" I asked incredulously. This was bullshit. This guy was affecting my career, my livelihood. I would call Sharon in the morning and talk to Brian as well. Surely, we could keep this hiatus to a few days, a week tops. I managed a smile in Skip's general direction.

"You, sir, have earned yourself a paid vacation for the foreseeable future," I congratulated him. "Why don't we talk on Monday, see where we're at, yeah?"

"Are you going to be okay?" he asked, and I felt a lump in my throat. Why were the Hansen men so damned sweet and thoughtful?

"Your uncle is here with me, Skip. I'm far from alone. And I've got Pop, okay? I'll be fine, and we'll try to get away for a couple of days. You should think about going somewhere yourself." Skip blushed and studied his feet, suddenly unable to make eye contact with me.

"Maybe I'll head to Florida for a few days. I can get a pretty cheap flight, don't you think?" I nodded in agreement as I tidied my workspace.

"Yeah, sure. But what's in Florida, besides sandy beaches, sunshine, and Mickey Mouse?" I asked.

"Um, yeah, I thought I would check on Becky. See how she and Jesse are making out, catch some rays . . ." His voice trailed off when he saw me staring at him, my mouth hanging open. "No, wait, it's not like that. We're just, um, friends, and we've been talking, so why not?" Nonplussed, I continued to stare at him. The thought of my sweet twenty-year-old nephew and my twenty-four-year-old former witness, a single mom with a checkered past, was quite a lot to take in, especially after all the drama from the last couple of days. But still . . .

"I can transfer you some air miles," I said with a smile. "But before you make any plans, can we talk about this a little more?" Skip nodded and gave me a quick hug.

"Thanks Randi. You're the coolest." He slipped his backpack over his shoulder and left the studio. I immediately locked the dead bolt behind him. The coolest, huh? I was fairly certain my husband, my brother-in-law, and his wife would feel differently when Skip shared his plans with them.

I double-checked the locks and made my way upstairs. I poked my head in the fridge and found my milkshake waiting for me on the top shelf with a note.

Drink me, it said, so I did.

That call did not go as I had hoped. I am wondering if Ms. Quinn is simply beyond help at this point. I have tried to be subtle, to deal with her privately, but SHE REFUSES TO LISTEN TO ME. I will try once again to get her attention, but I admit my patience has worn thin and my hopes of saving her are all but gone. I am trying with all my might to show my love of all God's creatures by trying to assist Ms. Quinn in the process of her redemption, but my options are limited.

What on earth can I do?

CHAPTER 22

The next morning, after voicing my concerns about cancelling the show with both Sharon and Brian, I placed a call to Rick Cooper, the New London County district attorney. Even if there was little to be done, it would help to talk about the situation with an experienced and neutral third party. He answered on the first ring.

"Rick Cooper," he said, sounding just as I remembered. Professional but also impatient. Kind of like, "I am here to help, but let's hurry this along."

"Rick, it's Randi Quinn," I said. "How are you?"

"How can I help you, Ms. Quinn?" came his speedy reply. I had been hoping for a bit more warmth, as our last time working together had resulted in a serial rapist and murderer getting convicted and sentenced to life behind bars. I had worked tirelessly alongside him in a consultative fashion, and the ensuing notoriety had been the primary factor causing the cancellation of my TV talk show. *How soon we forget.*

"I need your help with something. Is there a time we can talk? Like today?" I waited while he considered my request.

"I was due in court at nine, but it got pushed back to eleven. Can you be here in an hour?"

"Yes, of course. Thank you. See you soon. I appreciate—" He had ended the call.

I raced for the shower, nearly colliding with my dripping husband, who was wearing only a towel and a big grin.

"Slow down, hot stuff," he cautioned. "What's your rush? I've got—"

"No time," I told him. "I'm going to meet Rick to ask him about my, um, stalker." Eric frowned and watched me as I discarded my T-shirt on the floor along with a pair of panties and turned the shower back on.

"What happened last night? Did he call in again?" From behind the shower curtain, I brought Eric up-to-date on the note I had found and the threatening phone call as well as the news my show was off the air for the time being. I hoped I sounded calm, almost blasé, and was glad he couldn't see the worry pasted all over my face. After I rinsed off, I stepped out of the shower to find Eric holding a towel for me and looking downright furious. I dried off, not sure what to say to break the ice. I didn't have the chance.

"Randi, this has gotten way out of hand. This guy is seriously unhinged. Why didn't you tell me about this last night?"

"I'm sorry, babe. After Skip left—and oh, believe me, have I got a juicy bit of gossip for you—I drank my milkshake and then came to bed. You were sleeping so soundly I didn't want to wake you."

"And this morning?" Eric asked, clearly still pissed.

"I got up and made coffee. You were still asleep, so I placed a call to Rick. I figured I might catch him before court. And I did," I added brightly. "So that's why I am rushing to meet him right now. I won't be long, and I'll fill you in on everything. I think Mr. Deadly Sins might be someone I locked up back in the day. I'll ask Rick to check for recent parolees." I pulled on a pair of black pants and a white shirt and gathered my hair into a ponytail. Perfect, all I needed was an apron, and I was ready to wait tables at just about any chain restaurant. "This'll have to do," I mumbled to myself after taking a quick look in the mirror.

I turned to see Eric sitting on the edge of the bed, looking less angry. "Babe, this guy is just trying to push my buttons. I'm not in any real danger, okay?"

Eric snorted in response as he got up to pace, counting off on his fingers. "He has accused you of being prideful, lustful, and a glutton. He's followed you, vandalized your car, come to our house, and threatened you with hellfire and brimstone. He got your goddamn show canceled, for Christ's sake."

"Don't forget his taste in 80s music," I quipped. Uh-oh. Too soon. The glare I got was positively glacial. I grabbed my bag and shrugged into a gray blazer. "I'm sorry. I know you're upset, and I promise I'm being careful. I'll fill Rick in on everything, see if he has any ideas on how to proceed, and I'll come right home."

He shook his head. "I'm driving you. I want to hear what he has to say." He was already pulling on a pair of chinos and grabbing a shirt. "You're buying breakfast afterward," he said, and I agreed. We poured to-go cups of coffee and hurried out the door. I called out a goodbye to Hobie. His dish was half-full from last night, and we would only be a few hours at the most. I squeezed my husband's arm.

"Thanks for having my back," I said.

"I love your back and your front, and your sides are pretty choice as well," he said. "I'll always have your back, babe. Just promise me you're being cautious." I kissed him on the cheek, and we drove to New London in companionable silence.

CHAPTER 23

We parked in the lot next to the New London Courthouse and made our way inside. Rick had already requested a visitor's pass in my name, but the guard insisted on calling upstairs to verify Eric would be allowed as well. Permission granted, my "plus-one" and I took the elevator up to the sixth floor. I was disappointed the receptionist I had met the last few times I had visited was not on duty. I had privately referred to her as Cruella de Vil, due not just to the shocking white stripe in her angular black bob but also her icy-cold and haughty personality that I found quite intriguing. Where had her self-assuredness come from? But there was no sign of her today. An older woman, a Ms. Crowley, greeted us warmly and told us Mr. Cooper's administrative assistant would be out in a minute to guide us to Rick's office. I wanted to say I had worked in the building for nine years and my office had been right next door to Rick's, but I just thanked her and turned back to Eric.

Suddenly I heard: "Ms. Quinn? The district attorney will see you if you'll follow me." It was Cruella!

"Okay, sure thing. This is my hus—" but she had already taken off down the hall, so I signaled to Eric, and we hurried to catch up to her. When we were just a few feet behind her, I called out, "Actually we have met, you and I." She turned and gave me an appraising glance, taking in my too-snug black pants dotted with fluffs of gray kitty fur, my slightly wrinkled button-down, and a dated polyester-blend blazer.

"No," she told me with a shake of her head. "We haven't." Eric took my arm to stop me from arguing with her, and I took the hint. She was clearly more memorable to me than I was to her. We stopped just outside Rick's door, and she gave it a sharp rap.

She turned the knob and swept inside. "Sir, a Ms. Quinn and a Mr. Hansen are here." She looked at the oversized silver watch on her wrist and frowned slightly. "Your 9:05 appointment," she drawled, calling attention to our tardiness as she did. My former boss stood and nodded.

"Thank you, Katrina," he said briskly, and she turned on her heel and left. I thought the temperature in the room might have gone up several degrees as the door closed behind her but kept my thoughts to myself. Rick came around from behind his desk, crossing the room to greet me. He was a small, no-nonsense man and one of the smartest people I knew. "Miranda," he said, "it's been too long." He grasped my hand in his and shook it enthusiastically. "Good to see you." He turned to Eric. "And Mr. Hansen, yes? I've heard good things. It's nice to attach a face to the name." Eric's hand was pumped next. Who was this effusive and charming man? Elections were two years away. I smiled at Rick.

"Good morning. Thank you for seeing us on such short notice."

Rick ushered us over to a cozy seating area in the corner of his cavernous office. We took seats on the plush loveseat and he perched on the matching chair directly across from us.

"What can I get you? Some coffee, tea?" We both declined, and I sat forward.

"We'll get right to the point. I have a radio talk show, *Miranda Nights*." He nodded, so I continued. "A couple of weeks back, I had a caller at the end of the show. He called himself Peter and told my sound tech he had a legal question. But his real reason for calling was his concern for my conceit, my excessive pride." Rick scribbled some notes on a yellow legal pad before studying me with a frown on his face.

"Did he threaten you in any way?" he asked, a note of concern creeping in.

"No, nothing like that," I said. "It was more creepy than sinister. More 'I know who you are and I know what you've done' than 'I'm going to find you and kill you.'" Eric winced at this, but it was an accurate statement, so I hurried on. I described the notes, the message scrawled on my windshield, the unflattering and misleading social media posts, and the comments made in the subsequent calls. "So far, we have pride, gluttony, and lust. That's three of the seven deadly sins." By the time I was finished, both men were staring at me. I guessed Eric was unnerved at hearing the chain of events in their entirety while Rick just looked concerned . . . and confused.

"Other than vandalism, for which I'm sure there were no witnesses, technically no laws have been broken," he began, but I cut him off.

"That's true. But unofficially, I was hoping to get a list of the offenders I sentenced over the years, starting with those who have been paroled in the last couple of months." A frown crossed his face as he appeared to briefly consider my request. He shook his head.

"I would need a court order. Parolees have a right to their privacy and—"

"We need your help," Eric said. "Miranda's show is on hold. The threats and the tie-in to the deadly sins are escalating. I'm afraid of what he'll do next."

Rick nodded sagely before he continued. "I understand, Mr. Hansen. I do. But let's back up a step, shall we? Miranda, the first caller referred to himself as Peter. Is that correct?" I told him it was, and he went on. "And the next was Andrew? Then James?"

"Yes, and then John," I said. "But what does that—"

Eric nearly jumped out of his chair. "The disciples. Jesus's disciples."

Rick looked as if he would like to high-five my husband. "Indeed. There were twelve of them, representing the twelve tribes of Israel." The two men grinned at each other, but I was still in the dark. Apparently, whatever I may have been taught in my catechism classes at St. Francis of Assisi had not resonated with me.

"What are you saying?" I asked. "Besides spouting proverbs and warning me against the seven deadly sins, my fanatical fan also fancies himself as one of Jesus's spokespersons? Like, he has a message to give me from God?" Both men nodded.

"Yes, pretty much," said Rick. "I think we should narrow our search to cases with a religious tone, maybe warnings or threats similar to the ones you've received."

"That works," said Eric. "How can we get that type of information?"

Rick closed his eyes for a second, deep in thought, before sitting forward with a look of glee. I had rarely seen him smile, but now he was positively beaming.

"We pull names from the files, and I'll put a couple of law clerks on it. Tell them it's part of discovery, to assist with a case that's pending. Piece of cake," he said with a note of finality. We spent another fifteen minutes or so talking logistics until Katrina knocked sharply on the door before opening it and poking her head in.

"Sir, I'm sorry, but you . . ." I gathered my things and stood, smiling reassuringly at Katrina.

"No worries. We have taken enough of your time. Please keep me posted, and I'll let you know if anything else comes up." I was deliberately vague, as Katrina appeared quite curious about our discussion. Not today, Cruella!

Eric and I shook hands with Rick and headed for the elevator. There were no familiar faces among the staff sitting at cubicles in the center of the large space, and I didn't recognize anyone in the windowed offices running along the entire length. I had been gone for over five years, so it wasn't too surprising. I thanked Ms. Crowley, who smiled back as she answered a ringing phone.

"Who's your friend?" asked Eric as we waited. "The one with the stripe in her hair?"

I squeezed his hand and grinned at him. "Why, that was my good pal Cruella de Vil. I'm sure I mentioned her to you."

Eric shook his head. "No, I would have remembered her."

"One of your favorite Disney gals?" I teased. "I always thought you were hot for the Little Mermaid."

"Ariel is a total babe," said Eric. "Red hair, green eyes. What's not to love?"

"I have reddish hair and green eyes," I reminded him.

"But no tail," Eric said mournfully. "And that's a deal breaker."

The door slid open, and we got in. "Empty, just the way I like my elevators," he said, pulling me into his arms and kissing me. After a quick smooch, I pulled back.

"I'm sorry," I said. "For all this . . . drama. It seems to follow me wherever I go. And now you're involved."

Eric gave me a quizzical look. "I'm all in, babe. You have to know that. For better or for worse, yeah? We've just got to figure out who this guy is and why he's targeting you." He gave me a quick squeeze as the door opened onto a crowded lobby.

"I'll work on the tail thing," I said as we made our way to the exit.

CHAPTER 24

"Where do you want to go for breakfast?" I asked Eric as we drove out of the courthouse lot. "Do you want to stay downtown or head closer to home?"

"Let's hit up Mystic. We always say we'll go there, but the weekends are too crowded and . . ."

"Sure, let's go," I said. "I'd love to stop in at Bank Square Books. See if they have any copies of *Miranda Writes* for me to sign. And then we can browse, find something new to read this weekend." I'd had a successful signing at BSB when my legal advice book was published last year. I hadn't stopped by in months.

"Sounds like a plan," Eric said, and we drove to the lovely town of Mystic. I had lived there with Adam a gazillion years ago and had always imagined I would end up there again one day. But Old Lyme had been closer to Eric's New York office before he put up a shingle of his own, and we both had family there. It was home.

The parking gods smiled upon us this morning, and a prime spot became available when a huge SUV pulled out in front of us. Within minutes, we found a table out on the sidewalk of a bustling café, and after a quick perusal of the menu we placed our orders: a ham-and-Swiss omelet for Eric and cinnamon crunch French toast for me. Our server poured us coffee from a steaming pot, which she (Bless her!) left on our table.

"This is nice," said Eric. "We should do this more often."

I nodded enthusiastically. "But without the first stop at the courthouse," I added.

Eric studied me from over the rim of his mug. "This has been an awful lot to unpack. Do you want to talk about it?"

"No, not really. This is a delightful break from all of that. Let's just enjoy ourselves."

And we did.

After breakfast, we made our way to my favorite bookstore. *Miranda Writes: A Consumer's Guide to All Things Legal* was prominently displayed in the window and on a table labeled "Local Authors" near the front of the store. I took a quick peek and saw each one was already autographed. Based on my last several royalty checks, the most recent of which would not have even covered today's breakfast tab, I knew sales had stalled out. Although the possibility of a sequel had been discussed in the early days of high rankings and significant royalties, I had not been privy to any recent discussions. I had been keeping notes of topics I would cover if I were asked to write a second edition, but to date I had barely compiled a couple of pages' worth of ideas. Not nearly enough for an entire book, and I was fine with that.

"Are you finding what you're looking for today?" a sales clerk whose laminated nametag identified her as Molly asked me, and I nodded.

"Yes, thank you. Oh, is Carolyn in today?" I thought I should at least say a quick hello to the store manager.

"No, I'm sorry. It's her day off. Can someone else help you?"

I shook my head. "I just wanted to check in, say hello. Can you tell her Miranda stopped by?" I fished out a card from my bag, but Molly stopped me.

"We all know who you are," she said with a grin. "I'll tell her." I thanked her and headed to the mystery/thriller section, my favorite genre after beachy romances. "And you have a very devoted fan, Miranda," Molly called out. The news should have cheered me, but I felt a sense of dread welling up instead.

"Oh, who is that?" I asked, trying to sound casual and only mildly interested in her response. Molly's youthful face screwed up in deep concentration.

"Um, he said his name was Dante," she said. "Yeah, Dante."

D! It was him. I was certain. "What did he look like?" I asked, trying to hold on to a shred of nonchalance. "Do you remember?"

"No, I'm sorry. I never actually met him. He usually calls late in the day."

"And what does he want?" I asked, all traces of indifference a thing of the past. Damn, if only Molly could shed some light on the identity of my number-one fan, but that was apparently too much to ask.

"To tell you the truth, I think he's just a sweet guy. Kind of lonely. He asked if I've tuned in to your radio show. I haven't, sorry. Talk radio," she gave an involuntary shudder, "not for me."

"Yeah, I get that," I assured her. "Um, what else does he say?"

"He asks if you've come into the store lately, if your book is selling well, if you're working on a sequel. You know, fan stuff." Yeah, I knew. Man, this guy was hell-bent on screwing with me.

I drew in a breath and tried not to look as freaked out as I felt while I watched Eric walking toward us. His arms were full of books, no doubt the latest historical titles from the nonfiction section. I spoke quickly, trying to keep my voice low.

"Molly, this is important. Did he say anything else?"

She appeared deep in thought when it hit her. "Oh yeah, he said you needed to be saved. Isn't that so weird?"

Weird? That a man who wanted to save me was going by the name of an Italian poet and philosopher from the thirteenth century? It was the very definition of weird. Who was this guy?

CHAPTER 25

I stood by while Eric waited in the short line at the registers to pay for the books he had chosen. As we walked to the car, I listened as he raved about the excellent selection of titles and the knowledgeable staff.

"Let's go back there again soon. Was that the store manager you were talking to?" He opened the car door for me before running around and hopping into the driver's seat. "Quinn, what's up? You look kind of pale." As much as I hated to spoil what had been a nice day until this point, if you left out the part about visiting the courthouse, I had to tell him.

As we drove home, I filled Eric in on what Molly had said about "Dante," and I told him I would call both Rick and Infinity to let them know as well.

"As soon as we get home," Eric made me promise, and I said I would, but only if we changed the subject for the rest of the drive. He agreed.

"So we've talked about it, but what do you think about getting everyone together?" I had been lost in thought and missed most of what Eric had said.

"What's that now? Getting everyone together?" I asked.

"Well, yeah. I'm thinking your dad and Sally, my brother, John, and Tricia, Sally's son, Jake, and Meg and her daughter, Julie, and Brad. That's ten with us."

"And Tracey and Dale. An even dozen. Oh, and can't forget Clem. A baker's dozen." Jake and Meg's daughter Clementine was eighteen months old and the absolute apple of my dad's eye. Dez was a wonderful grandfather, just as I had always known he would be.

"Okay, let's do it. I say sooner rather than later. This weather won't last forever." He was right about the weather. July and August were usually hot and humid, and I hoped to eat dinner on the patio, with a cool breeze keeping things comfortable.

"Remember how I bought all those twinkly lights at the end of the season last year?" I asked. "We could hang those and set up a bar on the patio. But what about food?"

"That's a no-brainer. I vote yes. Let's definitely plan to serve food."

I groaned. "What food exactly?"

"Let's keep it simple. Burgers and hot dogs. Oh, what about the Ryan kids? We should invite them, yeah?"

"Then we need to ask Skip and Sarah too," I said. "And by the way, there's nothing simple about them. Just for the record."

Eric glanced my way for a second, his face a mask of confusion. "I'm glad to hear you don't think my niece and nephew are simple. Seriously. It means a lot." Now it was my turn to be perplexed.

"What are you talking about? I didn't say either of them was simple. They are two of the brightest, most together kids I know. I was talking about your menu suggestion." At Eric's blank look, I hurried on. "Everyone says, 'Oh, burgers and dogs, so simple.' But are they really? Don't even get me started on plant-based products. And all those condiments. Rolls or lettuce wraps. Tomatoes, onions, pickles. And don't forget the sides. It's a minefield." I was shaking my head when he leaned over and patted my arm gently.

"Someone's been giving this a lot of thought," he said. "How about chicken?"

"Barbecue sauce or not? Marinade? Thighs, drumsticks, breasts? Cutlets, bone-in?"

"Okay," said Eric briskly. "Let's table this discussion for now, yeah? We don't even have a date yet."

"The next couple of weekends are free. I'll call Pop and see if they have a preference. And we can figure out the food."

"Sounds good," he said with a grin and reached out for my hand. We rode like that, hand in hand, until we pulled into our driveway. Or, correct that, attempted to pull in. There was a mountain in the way!

Eric backed out and parked on the street before jumping from the truck and striding over to the mountain of . . . mulch? Someone had dumped a lot of orangey-brown matter in the driveway, making it impossible to enter the garage. But who and why?

"Did you order—" I began before Eric turned to me, furious.

"What do you think?" he asked, and I knew Dante had sent another message.

My suspicions were proven correct when I found a note jammed in the doorway along with a creepy stuffed toy. A sloth?

You know what they say about idle hands, Miranda. Get to work. D

There was no question which of the deadly sins was being warned against today.

"Sloth," I called out to Eric, but when he turned to face me, I saw he was on his phone. He gestured rather strenuously, and I assumed it was one of his employees. I moved closer to hear his side of the conversation.

"I need you to send some guys over here with shovels and a couple of trailers. It looks like, I dunno, fifteen yards, maybe twenty. It's covering most of my driveway. Yes, I'm certain I didn't order any mulch. And call all of our suppliers in the area, okay? Someone has to remember taking an order for a mulch delivery to this address. No, there's no paperwork, no invoice. Just a shitload of orange crap and I need it gone." He ended the call and looked at me. "Have you called the cops? Infinity?" I shook my head.

"It's sloth. The sin du jour," I said. "He wants me to get to work." Eric shook his head and started for the door. "I'm gonna change and get started on that pile. Tim is pulling some guys from the Taylor house and sending them over. Can you call the police and take a few photos before we start?" I said I would and, grabbing my phone, headed back outside. What a mess! The smell made my eyes water, and I quickly took a dozen photos from every angle.

I skipped 911 and placed a call to the desk instead. While a major nuisance, this would hardly classify as an emergency, and as a cop's kid, I knew the difference. Mike picked up on the first ring.

"Mike, hey, good morning. It's Randi Quinn."

"Good morning to you, Randi. What can we do for you this fine day?"

"We just came home from breakfast and—"

"Oh, sounds great. I'm starving. Where'd you go? Center Grille?"

"No, we went to Mystic, to a little—"

"Well, look at you, Miss Fancy Pants. Too rich for my blood."

"I hear you, but we had to be nearby this morning for an appointment, so it—"

"A doctor's appointment? Are you pregnant?" Damn, I should have called 911 after all.

"No, not pregnant. But listen, I need a cruiser to come by my house, 157 Birch Lane, and take a statement. Right now, if possible. We received a delivery, and we're having it removed, but I want to make sure there's an official report on file." He must have picked up on the severity of my tone because suddenly he was all business. He repeated the address and said a cruiser would be dispatched immediately. "Thank you," I said and ended the call as Eric joined me wearing a pair of ripped jeans and a vintage *Stop Making Sense* Talking Heads T-shirt. Man, he was pissed off.

"Did you make the calls?" he asked, and I told him an officer was on the way.

"Now I'm going to call Infinity," I added.

"Tim phoned around, and it looks like your stalker ordered the mulch from Rousseau's Landscaping to be delivered this morning." At my hopeful expression, he held up a hand. "Don't get too excited. The order was placed by phone. Some company I've never heard of. Inferno?"

Dante's Inferno. Seriously?

"That could be anyone," I moaned. This nutjob always seemed to be one step ahead of us. But maybe . . . "Can we actually use the mulch?" At Eric's blank look, I hurried on. "There is that area out back between our yard and the Donnelans' that could use a little mulch, don't you think?"

"You're saying we should treat this as a gift of some sort? Like we wanted it?"

I was warming up to the idea. "Yeah, it's like 'In your face, psycho.' Anything you dish out, we can take."

Eric frowned as he considered my suggestion. "Sure. Waste not, want not? I guess when the guys show up, I can have them bring it out back. After the police report, that is." And right on time, a police cruiser pulled up behind our car, followed closely by two pickup trucks towing empty garden trailers. Eric went to talk to his guys, and I approached the officer as he exited his car. Not someone I recognized from Pop's time on the force, but that was just as well. I was not up for small talk and catching up this morning. Dante had ruined my good mood. I just wanted to put all this behind us.

CHAPTER 26

An hour later, I was waiting on hold to order a half dozen pizzas. Tim and a couple of his guys had joined Eric, then Dale and Flynn had showed up, and now there were six of them transporting and spreading mulch. In hindsight, I thought it looked hideous, and the idea my stalker was possibly watching us deal with the mess he'd caused made me slightly crazy.

"Where are your paper plates?" Tracey's voice caught me unawares. I had been lulled into a dreamlike state while listening to an acoustic version of "Afternoon Delight" by the Starland Vocal Band, which sounded even worse without the lyrics. Go figure.

"Athena's Pizzeria," came a human voice, and I pointed to the cupboard for Tracey's benefit and placed my order. "Forty minutes," I was told, and I ended the call.

"What are we doing for drinks?" Tracey asked, and we headed to the garage, to a fridge always stocked with beer, seltzers, and soda. The doorbell rang, and I heard my dad's voice.

"Randi? What's going on?" he bellowed, and I froze. Damn, I should have known. Pop was as tuned in to the town as he had been during over thirty years on the force. I had never gotten away with anything during those years, and there was no reason to believe I ever would.

"Pop, we're in the kitchen," I called back and turned to see him walking toward me. He was not a big man, but his confidence and "take no bullshit" demeanor had worn down many a hardened criminal over the years. I melted immediately as I hugged him.

"I meant to call you," I snuffled into his shoulder as Tracey piped up.

"Hey Dez, it's actually my fault. Randi asked me to call you, and I totally spaced. I was just about to . . ."

Pop fixed us with a steely gaze. "Tracey, you're as bad a liar today as you were at fourteen when the two of you got hauled into the station after trying to buy cigarettes at the Park & Go. Something about a homework assignment on the effects of smoking, wasn't it?" Tracey blushed and suddenly became fascinated with the floor tile.

"Sorry, Mr. Quinn," she mumbled. Pop turned his focus on me.

"And as for you," he said, "what kind of lunatic sends twenty yards of mulch and a stuffed toy to a radio host?"

Now it was my turn to hang my head. "I honestly don't know," I admitted. As he paced, Pop caught sight of the flurry of activity in the yard, with shirtless men carrying shovels and pushing wheelbarrows in the blistering sun. He turned to me with a smile, a quite welcome one, I might add.

"So you're laying down the mulch. That ought to get that lowlife's attention."

"I guess. Sal didn't want to join you today?"

He shook his head. "I told her I was heading out to do a few errands. I didn't want to upset her with all of this, you know?" No, I didn't know. Sally was one of the toughest, strongest women I had ever met. Since when was there anything she couldn't handle? Pop wouldn't meet my eyes, no doubt sensing he had revealed too much information.

"Spill, old man. You said Sally was doing fine since you brought her home. What's going on?"

"She *is* doing well," Pop protested. "She's just a little fragile right now, and I didn't want to worry her." Fragile? Were we actually talking about the same woman? I studied him closely and, based on the stubborn set of his jaw, decided I had grilled him enough for one day. I knew that face well. It was the same one I frequently saw staring back at me in the mirror.

"Okay, so are you going to join the parade of shirtless guys out there or help us girls in the kitchen? I'm looking for a cooler with ice so we can load up some drinks to go with the pizza that's on its way."

Pop grinned and gave me a mock salute. "Cooler and ice coming up," he announced and headed to the garage. I looked at Tracey, who was stacking paper napkins and plates in neat piles.

"Seriously, a homework assignment on smoking?" I asked. "That was the best you could come up with?"

CHAPTER 27

That night, I sat in bed reading as Eric and Hobie slept soundly beside me. It had been a good day. The yardwork was completed, the pizza devoured, and all of our helpers had gone home early. The yard looked okay, I had to admit, and I hoped Dante had received the message we would not be threatened by the likes of him, whoever he was. Besides, I had other people to think about, specifically Chase and Sally.

Tracey and I'd had the chance to catch up during lunch and, according to her, Chase's legal situation was still in limbo. As far as she knew, there was no additional evidence in the state's case against Chase. I was certain Justin and his associates were digging into similar cases and reviewing the charges currently pending. When it came to Sally, I was relieved my stepsister, Julie, was planning on spending time with her mom this weekend and had promised to report any unusual or concerning behavior. It never hurt to have a fresh pair of eyes to gauge how things really were.

I finally gave up on my book, which was failing to hold my interest. I switched off my nightlight and snuggled into the covers, grateful for the life I had. Other than being stalked by a crazed fanatic and worrying about Chase and Sally, my life was pretty freaking perfect. I soon fell asleep, lulled by the dual snores of my bedmates, and slept soundly. The next morning arrived quickly with a whole new group of troubles, which redefined the crap sandwich that was now my life.

By mid-morning, I was ready to throw in the towel, pack it in, and wave the white flag of surrender. Things had gone haywire in every direction, and there was no end in sight. It all started when I checked my email. Eric had risen early before crossing the yard to his office, a tricked-out utility shed with a mini fridge, a large drafting table, and all the technology anyone could want. As I scrolled through my inbox, I found several messages from friends, extended family, and former colleagues. All were upset, some deeply concerned and some downright hostile. In a nutshell, I had been hacked, and apparently everyone on my personal contact list had received an email from me asking for "forgiveness and understanding" as I dealt with a myriad of financial, professional, personal, and marital problems. Oh, and apparently alternate-me had also asked for money and, in exchange, provided a link to a lot of porn. The subject line said it all: Please Forgive My Sins!

Holding my laptop in one hand and my coffee in the other, I raced across the yard and, reaching Eric's door, hollered for him to open it. He had been about to come find me as he had also received a copy of my plea. Eric said he would call the police to report on this recent development while I emailed everyone apologizing and assuring them I was fine and there were no problems for anyone to be concerned with. That generated a new crop of emails expressing relief and understanding, including one from Sally:

Damn mother-f*ckers!! Why can't they leave good, hardworking folks alone? Oh, and call your dad, please!

After changing my password, I was about to call Pop when Tracey called.

"Hey, T. Sorry about the email. I think it's been taken care of." Silence on her end, followed by:

"What email? What are you talking about? The police called, and they want to talk to Chase again. Today at eleven. They've got the feds involved." I was shocked into silence for a moment before I could respond.

"Did the photos get sent out of state? That could be why—"

Tracey shrieked in response. "I don't know. I don't know anything anymore. Chase is barely talking, especially not to me. My husband is avoiding me, and your friend Justin hasn't returned my last call. So IDK. Beats the shit out of me." I looked at the clock: 7:55 a.m. Tracey had recently begun offering Saturday morning hours to allow working parents to catch up on chores and errands. I had thought my friend was crazy to work so much, but there was definitely a demand since several of her clients had taken her up on the extended hours.

"Aren't you getting ready to open your doors?" I asked, deftly changing the subject.

A loud sniff, followed by a long sigh. "We're, um, cutting back. Well, closing for a week or so. It was Justin's suggestion, just until everything calms down. A few families have already canceled, and I spent last night calling the other ones. It was . . . hard."

What the hell?

"I thought things were going okay. You said—"

"I didn't want to bother you. You have your crazy fan and all that mulch and poor Sally in the hospital. It just seemed like I should be able to handle it."

"No, that's not the way this works. You tell me whatever you want, T. If I can't handle it, that's on me. So what's happening?" My own problems forgotten for the moment, I listened to Tracey's recount of the hate mail, phone calls, and social media posts in the last eighteen hours. The gist of the attack was the unsuitability of a licensed daycare provider housing a sexual predator under the same roof. Her voice broke as she repeated her last words.

"A sexual predator. Chase, my boy. It's . . . just too much." She broke down and sobbed into the phone. I let her cry, making what I hoped were soothing sounds before switching gears.

"Okay, so I'll call Justin and make sure he gets his butt to the police station at 10:45 at the latest. I will pick you both up at 10:30. Tell him to suit up—nice pants, shirt, and tie. Shoes, not sneakers." Tracey was parroting my words back to me, clearly getting the message. This was serious. "Tell him to stay off social media, no phone calls, no computer. Got it?"

Tracey let out a long breath. "Got it. Thank you."

"I'll see you in a couple of hours," I promised. "Try to relax, okay? And eat something. Get Chase to eat too." She promised she would, and I ended the call before I'd had the chance to ask about Dale. Where was he in all of this?

I saw I had missed calls from Pop, Sally, and my agent, and my mailbox had forty-seven unread messages. By the time I had returned calls, gotten hold of Justin, and responded to a half dozen of the emails I thought were most pressing, I realized it was time to jump in the shower and get ready to leave. Minutes later, I pulled my dripping hair into a ponytail and slipped into a dress and my go-to black pumps and grabbed my bag and a black cardigan. I raced out the door and headed for the garage when I remembered. Eric. I had a husband to talk to, to bring up-to-date. If anyone could calm me down in moments like this, it was him. I made my way through the side yard to the office. I couldn't avoid viewing the freshly laid mulch in all its' orangey-red glory, and I realized I still hated it. Plus it smelled funny.

I called Eric's name as I approached, and a split second later, he stuck his head out.

"Hey, you, what's up?"

"Are you busy, or can I come in?" I asked, just a touch of exasperation in my voice.

He cleared his throat. "Hmmm. I'm not sure my wife would like it if I entertained sexy women like yourself in my man cave. She's really jealous."

I had married the world's biggest goofball, of that there was no doubt in my mind. But he read a room like no one else, and he picked up on my anxiety quickly. "Babe, I'm sorry. C'mon in. I was on a conference call lasting over an hour, and now I am trying to pay some bills. Oh, and I got an invoice from Rousseau's for the mulch. Seven hundred dollars, for the record. Nice, yeah? What's going on?"

I filled him in on the call from Tracey and told him we were meeting with the FBI in thirty-five minutes. He offered to drive me, but I told him I was fine. And I was, more or less. Or at least I hoped I would be after I'd seen what the feds had on Chase Ryan.

###

Straight out of central casting, Agents Turner and Robinson were well-groomed and professional, but they didn't mince words and wasted no time explaining to Chase exactly what kind of trouble he was in. According to them, the FBI was investigating the charges against him and would decide fairly soon if they would pursue federal charges in addition to those already filed by the state.

Justin explained to Chase that sexting could be considered a crime under federal law. The Prosecutorial Remedies and Other Tools to end the Exploitation of Children Today (PROTECT) Act of 2003 made it illegal to produce, distribute, receive, or possess with intent to distribute any obscene visual depiction of a minor engaged in sexually explicit conduct. Possession of such material—without intent to distribute—was also a crime under the PROTECT Act. Federal law also criminalized the act of causing a minor to take part in sexually explicit conduct in order to depict that conduct visually. Parents who allowed this behavior could also be prosecuted.

"Wait, does that mean Chloe can be charged and my parents too?" asked a pale-faced Chase. When Justin nodded, tears welled up in his eyes.

"But federal prosecution of juveniles for sexting is unlikely," said Justin. "The Federal Juvenile Delinquency Act mandates juveniles should be prosecuted in state—not federal—courts."

Agent Robinson replied that all of this was speculation and that their investigation had just begun. But if Chase were convicted of a class A misdemeanor, it was punishable by up to one year in prison, a fine of up to two thousand dollars, or both. Justin responded by reminding them that, in most cases, sexting crimes were handled by the juvenile courts, providing punishments including a warning, a fine, probation, or a commitment to the Department of Children and Families custody for up to eighteen months.

My heart went out to Chase, and I wanted to hug him and tell him Aunt Randi would make it all better. I had to settle for holding Tracey's hand and watching her son get read the riot act. She stifled a sob by burying her damp face in my shoulder, and when Chase turned to look at her, all he could see were her heaving shoulders and the back of her head. I tried to smile and was about to mouth, "It'll be okay," but he frowned and turned away quickly.

"Is my client under arrest?" Justin asked almost as an afterthought when it seemed things were winding down and the agents had said all they needed to. We were completely shocked when Agent Turner responded with a nod.

"Yes, he is." He opened the door to the tiny conference room and two uniformed OLPD officers entered, approaching Chase and instructing him to turn around with his hands behind his back. Tracey let out a whimper as she watched her son comply with the officer's request.

"Chase Ryan," the older one said, "you are under arrest for the unlawful possession and distribution of child pornography, a class A misdemeanor in this state. You have the right to remain silent; anything you say can and will be used against you in a court of law. You have the right to an attorney, and if you cannot afford an attorney, one will be provided for you. Do you understand these rights as I have read them?"

"Yes, I guess," he mumbled before turning to his parents, trying hard not to cry. "Mom?"

"It's okay, sweetheart. We'll have you home before you know it. Right, Aunt Randi?" There was no guarantee a judge would grant bail today, as it was a Saturday, but what could I say?

"You betcha, bud. Don't worry," I said with as much confidence as I could muster.

Justin whispered something in Chase's ear, which I had to assume was a strict reminder to not talk to anyone, as Tracey sagged against me in tears. Chase appeared numb, looking straight ahead as he was led away.

CHAPTER 28

Miraculously, the on-call judge granted that bail be allowed in Chase's case. After going to the bail bonds office in nearby Niantic, Dale, who had shown up right as we were leaving the police station, arranged bail. Chase was free to go home with his parents. I wanted to ask Tracey if she would be okay, as the tension between her and Dale was palpable, a living thing that could crush them both. I wanted to ask Dale if he needed a loan to cover the expense of posting the bond, and I wanted to ask Justin what I could do to help, but I never had the chance to ask these questions. The Ryans left the courthouse and headed to the parking lot and Dale's truck. Justin was on his phone and gave me a distracted wave as he got into his late model two-seater and sped off. I stood there wondering what I should do or who I could call. Eric would be at one of three different job sites, and Pop and Sally had her daughter, Julie, visiting. A definite no on Brian, as I did not feel like getting a lecture today.

On a whim, I called my stepbrother, Jake. I liked him and we got along well, but similar to my relationship with Dale, it was more of a group thing or a "we'll pick up some wine and be there in an hour" type of texting friendship. But right now, I needed to talk to someone, and Jake had drawn the short straw.

"Randi, how're you doing?" he asked, and we spent a few minutes catching up: the increased traffic with all the beachgoers, the need for an upcoming date for all of us to get together, Sally's health scare and his daughter Clementine's apparent genius IQ and certain path to the White House. I hoped Clem would not be the *first* female in the White House, but I agreed with his assertion that she could do anything she put her mind to. I listened patiently while he brought me up-to-date on all of her newly earned skills, her sense of humor, and her incredible vocabulary. "I swear, she's going to be reading any day now," he added, and I had to chuckle. I had never spent much time around kids, except for the Ryan twins, but I was certain at eighteen months Clementine was at least a couple of years away from reading. "So what's up? I'm sure you didn't call me to hear your niece is a child prodigy, did you?" I have to admit, when he referred to me as his sister or Clem's aunt, I got a kind of thrill. I'd never had siblings, and after my mom died it was just me and Pop for the longest time. It was so nice to be part of a new, blended family.

"I just wanted to hear your voice, bro," I told him. Suddenly, I didn't want to bitch and moan about work, or the lack thereof, and Chase's arrest. Jake had only met Chase a handful of times, and as far as work went . . .

"Tell me what's going on with the show. Mom says there's some psycho who's been rattling your chain. What's up with that?" he asked.

"Yeah, some fanatic is convinced I'm going straight to hell, and he's chosen himself to redeem me. He's called in a couple of times." And spread lies on social media, hacked my email, requested money and sent porn to all my contacts, defaced my car, delivered a ton of mulch and a creepy sloth toy, and . . .

"Great email this morning," Jake said.

"Oh, you liked that, yeah? Tell me, was it the plea for money or the porn that did it for you?"

"Oh, the porn for sure. But hey, you say the word and I'll teach him to not mess with my sister," Jake said firmly. I had to smile at the thought of my mild-mannered stepbrother getting physical with Dante.

"So what, you're an accountant by day and a masked avenger by night?"

"Sure, as long as I can get my eight hours of shut-eye. Why not?"

I smiled again, thinking this call had been exactly the right one to make.

"I'll let you get back to it," I said. "Talk with Meg and your sister about getting together at our place. Maybe . . ." I thought ahead, trying to picture the calendar on our fridge. "Let's try for two weeks from today."

"That's the 27th," Jake told me. "Will do." We said our goodbyes and ended the call. A few minutes later, I pulled into the garage and went into the house. Hobie welcomed me home by rubbing himself around my ankles and purring loudly.

"Who's my good boy?" I asked. "Is it you?" He responded by sidling over to his near empty dish and pushing it toward me with his nose. "What do you want? Hobie, use your words." I had a running bet with Eric I could train our cat to meow when he wanted to be fed. So far, he only complied when Eric wasn't around to hear. On cue, Hobie meowed loudly and pushed his dish even closer. "Sure, when Dad's not here, you can sing for your supper." Silence. I bent and grabbed his dish and filled it with his favorite kibble. I freshened his water dish and left him to enjoy his meal in peace.

I went out and grabbed the mail, tossing most of the flyers and requests for donations in the recycling bin. As I entered the kitchen, an envelope caught my eye, and I turned it over. It was heavy ivory stock with my name and address in a lovely calligraphy font. Odd, no return address. I slid it open and went to pull out the card and immediately threw the whole thing in the sink. It was crawling with dozens of tiny insects, and the message was written in what looked like rusty, dried blood.

Even sloths need to eat sometimes. Don't forget to share. D

"I'm fairly certain sloths eat leaves, Aunt Randi. They're herbivores. Bugs make no sense."

"You're missing the point," I told Flynn. Poor kid, he clearly wasn't accustomed to dealing with hysterical women, but when both Eric and Tracey failed to answer their phones, I called the Ryans' house and got Flynn.

"Oh wait, I just googled it, and yeah, apparently some sloths eat bugs. Pretty rare, though. I'm just saying—"

"Where's your mom? She's not picking up. Or your dad? Is he around?" I wasn't looking for a scientific explanation. I wanted someone to tell me it would all be okay. "Oh no, bad boy," I yelled at Hobie. "No, not you Flynn. It's Hobie. He's climbed into the sink and is trying to eat the bugs. Oh my God, a few of them are still alive." I dropped my phone and turned on the faucet to get the bugs down the drain, soaking my cat in the process. Wow, if looks could kill! He stalked off after flipping his wet tail in my face.

"Aunt Randi?" Flynn sounded worried. "Are you okay?"

"Yeah, sure. Right as rain. Tell your mom to call me when she gets back from . . . Where did you say she went?"

"She and my dad packed a snack and headed for the beach. Soundview, I think. You can find them there." What? Was that good news I just heard? A walk on the beach and a snack? Possibly wine and some of those cheese straws Tracey frequently whipped up. And grapes. Yes, definitely good news!

"Thanks, bud. I didn't mean to bother you. Um, all good, then?"

Silence for a moment, then Flynn spoke up. "Is Chase gonna go to jail? My folks won't say, and he's acting like a zombie. No one is talking and I just . . . I need to know, you know?"

Sure, I did. "Oh, sweetheart, I'm so sorry. It's got to be so tough on you. All I can tell you is he has a terrific lawyer. I swear, Justin is one of the absolute best."

"As good as you?" he asked in a small voice. Oh, this poor sweet kid. My heart broke for him. What must he be thinking?

"Even better than me for cases like these. And we're doing everything we can to make sure the truth comes out, okay?" It wasn't much, but there was nothing more I could tell him.

"But lawyers are expensive. And Dad seems worried, not just about Chase, and now with the daycare closing . . . Will we lose our house?" he asked.

"Don't you worry that fantastic brain of yours, do you hear me? That will *not* happen, I promise. Just try to focus on schoolwork."

"Umm, it's summer," he replied.

"Oh yeah, of course. Hey, did you get the job at Tessie Lou's?"

"Yup. Mom didn't tell you? I start tomorrow. Twenty-five hours a week and all the ice cream I can eat." Free ice cream? If that was a perk of the job, count me in.

"Okay, so work hard and always have a mocha shake ready for me cuz I will stop by frequently and without warning. And help at home a bit, yeah? Dishes, laundry, you know the drill."

"I will, Aunt Randi. Thanks. I love you."

"Love you too, boyo," I said with a catch in my throat. We said goodbye, and after running the garbage disposal and disinfecting the sink, I went off in search of my fur baby to tell him I loved him as well.

CHAPTER 29

The bugs were gone, and I put the envelope and card in a Ziploc bag in case there were fingerprints or DNA that could be preserved. I wasn't holding my breath, however. I was more certain than ever Dante was highly intelligent, and it was *not* his first rodeo. I shared the gory news in a text to both Brian and Rick Cooper, wanting to bring them up to speed. Even though no laws were technically broken, I called the police and left a message for Detective Reynaldo. Doing so would also alert my dad, and I didn't feel up to dealing with his questions right now, but it was important if we were going to build a case against my stalker. Then I called Tracey to tell her all was fine and that I was sorry to have dumped my drama in poor Flynn's lap. She responded with an invitation to come over for breakfast in the morning, and I accepted.

Before ending the call, I asked, "How was your visit to the beach?"

"It was mmmm, so nice," she said and promised to tell all in the morning. Feeling relieved, I left the phone on my nightstand before heading to the kitchen.

By the time Eric got home an hour later, I had put a pot of water on to boil, opened a box of pasta, and doctored up a jar of sauce with sauteed mushrooms and a hastily diced green pepper. I had asked Alexa to play R.E.M. and was enjoying the sounds coming through the built-in speakers.

"Dinner in ten," I called out when he came in through the back door. He crossed the room quickly and pulled me into his arms. His voice was taut, and his embrace was unyielding.

"Jesus Christ, Quinn, you scared the crap out of me. I've been trying to get in touch with you since you called earlier. I finally called the Ryans and got hold of Flynn. He told me what happened. Are you okay?" I pulled back to see his dear face.

"I'm fine, babe, honestly. It was scary as hell at first, but most of the bugs were already dead, so it wasn't all that bad, I guess." Wow, I didn't even believe me, and Eric was clearly not convinced either.

"This is bullshit. Don't sugarcoat it for me. I'm scared as hell, and I know you are too. This guy is escalating. And the time between these messages of his is getting shorter. We are going to have to hire security, and I'm going to get that system your folks gave us installed tonight. We can't just sit here waiting for this lunatic to strike again." Everything he said made perfectly good sense, but I hated to admit just how scared I was. I fell back into his arms.

"You're right. We need to protect ourselves. Should I see if Rick can recommend any security firms?"

Eric nodded his agreement. "It can't hurt, I guess. But for now, I'll start working from home more often."

"Okay. I'll go drain the pasta." I wished I would hear a snappy comeback, like, "Is that what the kids are calling it these days?" but Eric was already on his knees, digging through the front hall closet looking for the housewarming gift we had never opened.

I dished up two bowls but wasn't sure if I would actually enjoy it. Eric joined me at the table a couple of minutes later and sprinkled grated parm on his dinner.

"This is great, babe." I nodded and tried to swallow my food, but I had a lump in my throat, and my savory sauce tasted like glue.

"So after we eat, we'll see if we can secure the premises?" I asked, trying to sound cheerful. Eric agreed, and we ate silently, neither one of us with much of an appetite.

After about an hour of me trying to read the directions, which appeared to be written in every language besides English, to my increasingly frustrated husband, our security system was up and running and our homestead was indeed secure. We had a keypad, base station, four sensors—one for each doorway—a motion detector, a camera to record all sorts of shenanigans, and a video doorbell.

"And the best part is we can control all of it on our phones," Eric said, clearly enthused. Hearing I would have one more reason to monitor my phone every freaking waking moment of every freaking day warmed my heart. Not!

"My joy knows no bounds," I told him disconsolately. "I'm going to bed." I fell asleep quickly, but I woke up after only a few hours. No longer even pretending to let go of the problems facing me and everyone I loved, I finally gave up trying to fall back to sleep. I grabbed the top book from the pile on my nightstand and padded down the hall, Hobie following closely. I made myself comfortable on the couch, and several hours later that's where Eric found me. Sound asleep.

"Didn't you say you were having breakfast with Tracey?" he whispered, and I woke to see him perched next to me on the couch.

"What time is it?" I mumbled, still half-asleep.

"It's almost eight. Hobie's been fed, and you'll love this. After you went to bed last night, I walked the perimeter of our yard with no lights on. Louise Donnelan apparently likes to parade around in sexy lingerie late at night. Who knew? I'm going to catch up on some work in here instead of the shed while you're gone. And how would you feel about me inviting Louise to swing by?"

"Sure, why not?" I told him as I stood and stretched. "I like it when you play well with others."

"If you wore some naughty knickers or edible underwear, I wouldn't have to."

I managed what I hoped was a saucy wink. "We can shop online later, together. It'll be fun," I purred. "But this afternoon, let's do something, yeah? Just us. Go for a drive or rent those electric bikes. What do you say?"

"Sounds like a plan," agreed Eric. "Right now, how can I help you get out the door? I hate to keep Louise waiting." What a goofball!

"Can you rustle me up a coffee to go first?"

"You got it," Eric replied, and after a quick kiss he headed for the kitchen while I made a dash for the shower. Ten minutes later, I kissed him goodbye, grabbed my travel mug, and left for Tracey's house.

"Have fun on your playdate. Remember to share," I called over my shoulder.

"You know I will," he promised.

CHAPTER 30

The Ryans lived in a raised ranch in one of Old Lyme's older neighborhoods populated with young families and featuring large lots. Years earlier, Dale had transformed their two-car garage into a roomy play area with a bathroom and a kitchenette and created a large fenced-in outdoor space. Normally bustling with a dozen little kiddos, even for a Sunday, it appeared abandoned and forgotten. Surely, this would all be over soon and Tracey could open up again. I went to the front door and knocked once, then let myself in as I had been doing wherever Tracey lived since we had become best friends in second grade.

"Hello," I called out. "I'm empty-handed and starving, so I hope you didn't forget I was coming." I followed my nose to the back of the house, where the aromas of freshly brewed coffee and something spicy and fresh from the oven greeted me.

"C'mon in," Tracey responded, and she crossed the room to give me a hug. "I made pumpkin bread, and sorry, it's from a mix. I got delayed this morning and didn't have time." I took in her tousled hair and glowing complexion. Combined with a big goofy smile, there was no doubt in my mind how she had been delayed and with whom.

"You got laid," I said, and she shushed me, failing to look upset, instead quite pleased with herself. "You did," I added in a stage whisper, and she nodded, blushing and looking exactly like the seventeen-year-old girl who had admitted to me nearly twenty-five years ago, "We did it, Ran. Dale and me. We did the deed." I went to high-five her, but she had started cutting thick slices of bread and setting out plates, so I poured myself a coffee and sat at the breakfast bar. I looked around the room. "And Romeo? Where has he gotten off to this morning?" Again, with the blush. Oh my!

"He's out back, taking inventory on his tools. He's been booking jobs right and left. Ever since your husband put in a good word or two, Dale's been getting calls and keeping busy. Real busy," she added with a wink. "Didn't Eric tell you?"

I tried to think back on our last several conversations, most of which focused on the warnings from my stalker, Chase's arrest, and Sally's health. I had told Eric about Dale's predicament but didn't know he'd offered to help. Typical of my guy, I thought proudly.

"Yeah, well, that's just great," I told her and blew on my coffee. I studied the plate she placed in front of me. "Got any cream cheese?" I asked, and instantly a tub of it appeared.

"Anything else?" Tracey asked. "Champagne? Eggs Benedict? Um, crêpes Suzette? Your wish is my command. We owe you and Eric big-time." I tried to protest, but Tracey had more to say. "You found Justin for us and helped with the bail hearing and everything. I don't know how to thank you." Her large brown eyes glowed with unshed tears. God, I loved this tiny woman. I pulled her into a hug, then released her just enough to study her closely.

"You have been beside me every step of the way since we were seven years old. I could not ask for a better friend. You don't owe me a thing," I told her. She hugged me again, and I felt her relax against me. There were no words, and we stayed like that for a moment, and I relaxed as well. When she pulled away, I saw a smile and a gleam in her eyes that had been missing for weeks. "Welcome back," I said with a smile of my own.

"Let's eat this bread before the Three Musketeers invade us," she suggested. I hadn't heard her call Dale and the twins that since forever. That must have been some walk yesterday and some pretty terrific make-up sex as well.

"So spill," I demanded after wolfing down the first slice of bread. Mix or not, it was delicious. "I can only assume you talked, yeah?"

She nodded enthusiastically. "Uh-huh, we did. He told me everything about the business and how worried he had been. And how Eric had referred him for several projects. Oh yeah, and you told him he had to talk to me, to come clean. I guess I need to thank you for that too."

"Well, you saw the photos. You know all about our *special* relationship." I batted my eyelashes, attempting to look seductive despite my bleach-stained cargo shorts and a faded Counting Crows *August and Everything After* T-shirt. She swatted at me playfully.

"Those photos were the beginning of the end for my daycare," she said with a frown. "No, the middle of the end. Chase was the beginning."

"The beginning of what?" Chase asked as he entered the kitchen, yawning and wearing a pair of low-riding board shorts. He scratched his bare chest and sniffed appreciatively. "Is there more coffee?" Tracey moved faster than I had ever seen her, and I've seen her move fast more times than I can count. She poured a mug of coffee, added a healthy dollop of creamer, and pushed it toward him.

"Sit, sit," she said. "Your Aunt Randi and I are just catching up. Want some pumpkin bread? Fresh out of the oven."

"It's fantastic, Chase. You should have some," I said. When he nodded, Tracey sawed off two slices from the quickly shrinking loaf and offered cream cheese and butter. Chase picked up the bread and took a large bite, chewed thoughtfully, and nodded.

"Yeah, butter, please," he mumbled. Tracey beamed at her son and began spreading swirls of it on the bread. I think she was so happy he was out of his room and actually eating something that she would have whipped up a three-course meal for him on the spot. He took a bite and gifted us with a hint of a smile. "Thank you. It's good."

The three of us sat companionably together, drinking our coffee and eating bread. It felt like old times, more or less, until I opened my big fat stupid mouth.

"So what have you been up to? Flynn was telling me about his job . . ." Tracey glared a warning at me and Chase clammed up. Literally shut down before our eyes. He pushed back his stool and stood up. "No. I just mean, now that school is out. Are you, um . . . ?" Out of Chase's line of sight, Tracey was shaking her head at me. Chase flushed dark red and started for the door, head hung low and shoulders slumped. This whole mess had aged him. He looked broken. I spoke sharply to get his attention. "Bud, listen. Everything is up in the air, and I'm sure finding a job or acting normal is not anything you can focus on right now. But believe me, this will not define you. Okay? We're going to make sure the truth comes out and you are not judged any more harshly than necessary. This is a dark time, probably the darkest you'll ever face. But your family is behind you. You've got Justin and you've got me. You were caught doing something stupid, yeah? We'll figure it out, okay?" Chase turned, and I saw tears running down his face. His sweet face he had to shave once a week at most. His large brown eyes, so like his mother's, were damp and red-rimmed. "Oh, sweetheart," I said and held out my arms. He fell against me, and it was all I could do to keep us both upright.

His thin body shuddered with sobs as he cried over and over, "I'm sorry. I'm so fucking sorry." I held him and patted his back, making sounds I hoped were soothing. Finally cried out, he pulled away, still unable to meet my eyes.

"I *am* sorry, Auntie. And, Mom, you too. God, I really fu—messed up. It all just got away from me. One minute I'm hooking up with my girl and the next I'm being arrested as a sex offender. I just don't get it." He shook his head in amazement, his brown hair long and unkempt and nearly covering his eyes. "I'll do whatever you say and whatever Justin says too. He's cool. He's a good dude. And Dad wants me to work with him this afternoon. I figured I would ride my bike over to the job site. It's near the high school."

"That sounds like a great idea, sweetheart," Tracey said. "I'll pack you a lunch if you like. And don't forget your sunscreen."

Chase smiled at his mom and asked her to chill. "I'm just going over for a while. See what's what. Don't get too excited, okay?"

Chastened, Tracey shrugged. "Sure, whatever you say."

Chase, who now towered over his mother, kissed her on the top of her head and nodded at me. "I'll let you two get back to whatever," he said, and with a wave he strode out of the room. From my perspective, he looked a lot less broken than he had just minutes earlier.

"What *were* we talking about?" I asked Tracey.

"Hmmm. Maybe it was the time you let Jimmy Porter get to second base by telling him, 'You can go to second base if you want to, Jimmy.'" I spurted coffee out of my mouth and nose as I erupted into laughter. I was fairly certain I'd actually uttered those exact words.

"And I didn't even know what second base was back then. I'm not even sure I do today."

"That actually explains a lot," Tracey said wryly. "How about I make another pot of coffee and we can plot the demise of your deadly sins guy?"

"Sounds like a plan. And, oh, we're calling him Dante these days. As in Inferno," I said as I liberally spread cream cheese on my third slice of still-warm pumpkin bread.

CHAPTER 31

A few days later, I got a phone call from Brian. It seemed the folks at Infinity were growing impatient, and they wanted to see me ASAP. I understood their frustration. A show in which they had invested heavily had been on hiatus for two weeks after less than four months on the air, and the affiliates were getting restless. Add in the fact they wanted the show to go live from their Manhattan studio a minimum of four nights a week, and there you have it. A disaster in the making!

"Do you think they'll fire me?" I asked Brian. Silence. "Seriously, Bry? What do you think?" All I heard in response was chewing. "What are you eating? Falafel or an empanada?" His favorites, as I recalled. God, I could murder some NYC street food right now.

"I'm multitasking. It's not just for women anymore. Fifty-third and Lex," he said, and I heard a car door slam. "Okay, where were we?"

You called me, I wanted to scream, but I kept my cool. More or less.

"You were about to tell me *Miranda Nights* would go live tomorrow night and Infinity has no issues with my doing two nights a week from my home studio forever."

Brian let loose with a deep-throated chuckle. "Still got that wide-eyed optimism, don't you? They can take the girl out of the country, but they can't—"

"Brian," I shouted. "Give me a heads-up, please. I need to know what I'm walking into. You owe me that much."

"Sorry, and I will. It's just talking with you reminds me of conversations with my older sister, and I find it hard sometimes to dial down the snark factor."

I let out a long breath. "Brian, Focus."

"Okay, here's what I know. Their priority is to get *Nights* back on the air right away."

"Tomorrow?"

"No, more like next week, Monday. They need to contact the affiliates, create some new promo spots, yada, yada. I'd plan for next week. Now as far as how often the show airs and where it's broadcast from, what can I say? We've had the discussion, and nothing's changed."

"Worst-case scenario?"

"If you don't agree, they'll stop all on-air promos and won't sign any new affiliates. They'll let the timer run out on your one-year contract, and in just over eight months *Miranda Nights* will be six feet under with barely a whimper."

Damn. "When do they want to meet?"

My meeting with Infinity was scheduled as a luncheon for the next day. I talked with Eric, and we decided to make the most out of the trip, aka command performance. We would drive to his former office in New Rochelle in the morning. He planned to hang out at the firm, and I would take the train into Manhattan and meet with Brian and the Infinity execs, aka firing squad. Then I would take the train back to New Rochelle. We would dine at a Brazilian steakhouse Eric raved about with his former colleague Rob and his wife. After a nice dinner, we would spend the night at Rob and Amanda's and drive home the next day. If

I got fired at lunch, at least we would have a fun night out with friends. Eric arranged for one of the guys in the crew to watch our house while we were gone. I thought it was overkill, but I had been underestimating Dante all along, so I agreed.

That night, I started looking through my closet for a work-appropriate outfit and a pretty dress to wear for dinner. Eric plopped down on our bed and watched me with mild interest as he thumbed through a dog-eared copy of *Architecture Today*.

"That's nice," he said when I held up a midnight-blue cocktail dress.

"Maybe for Manhattan, too much for New Rochelle," I countered. I kept digging.

"Don't be dissing the City of Homes," Eric protested. "That dress would fit right in."

I smirked and kept considering, before rejecting, other dresses.

"Says the man who owns a dozen pairs of pressed chinos," I said.

Eric spoke to Hobie, who had just sauntered in.

"Do you believe this?" he asked. "My wife, for whom cargo shorts and concert T's are a daily uniform, is questioning *me* and my sense of fashion." I held up a summery green dress with cap sleeves and a scoop neck.

"Thoughts?"

He pretended to consider my choice. "I think it will look even better crumpled in a heap on the floor of Rob and Amanda's guest room tomorrow night," he said with a grin. I crossed the room and curled up next to him.

"If it's any consolation, I think you have fantastic taste," I whispered in his ear. "You can dress me anytime you want, but I prefer it when you undress me." Hobie scampered out of the room, and packing was postponed until much later that evening.

CHAPTER 32

The next day, at 1:00 on the dot, I walked across the large and graceful lobby of the Ritz-Carlton Hotel and gave my name to the hostess at the entrance of the dining room. She looked at her impressively large computer screen and hit a few keys before looking up and beaming at me.

"Of course, Ms. Quinn. Your party has been seated, and they are expecting you. Follow me, please." I trailed along behind her as we made our way across the elegantly appointed room, noting the abundance of crystal, heavy damask tablecloths, and fresh flowers. I had to hand it to my employers. If they were going to fire me, they had chosen a lovely place to do it.

"Here we are, Ms. Quinn. I hope you enjoy your meal." Everyone stood as I made my way to the only empty seat at a table set for five. Brian reached me first. He leaned in to give me a brotherly hug.

"It's all good. Smile for God's sake. You look like you're heading to your own execution," he whispered, and I drew back. "Alan, head of operations, here's our Miranda," he announced. "And, Miranda, you've met Infinity's Talent Acquisition Director, Sharon." I smiled in recognition. "And I don't think you have met Edward Wallace yet. He's the Eastern Division Vice President for Infinity Holdings. Edward, meet your newest voice of late night, Miranda Quinn." There were a flurry of handshakes and a couple of air kisses before we all sat. I unfolded my napkin, placed it in my lap, and took a sip of water.

"It's nice to see you all. And to meet you, Edward. Thank you for inviting me today. I love any opportunity to come into the city." Too late, I realized the opening I had just created.

"Well, that is one reason we wanted to talk with you, Miranda," Edward said smoothly. "New York is the hub for the entertainment industry. Wouldn't it make more sense to move the show here? And you as well?" I looked around for something to shove into my mouth—besides my foot—to delay answering, but nothing edible was on the table. Brian interjected, and I flashed him a grateful smile.

"Before we get in too deep here, I suggest we place our orders. What do you think?" he asked without waiting for an answer. He passed me a menu and I studied the choices quickly. Grilled halibut was the catch of the day, and it came with a side of steamed asparagus. Perfect!

After we ordered, Edward jumped right back in. No talk of the weather, today's headlines, or sports. He wanted to talk about *Miranda Nights* and nothing else.

"Tell me more about the caller of yours that has shut down the show," he said. "How close are the local police to catching him?" There was a touch of impatience in his voice, and I took another sip of water and tried to collect my thoughts.

Alan jumped in, attempting to move the conversation along. "That's apparently part of the problem, Edward," he said. "There's not much local authorities can do. Technically, the SDS guy, oh sorry seven deadly sins," he amended after receiving a blank stare. "His actions, until now, amount to a case of criminal mischief punishable by a slap on the wrist and a fine. So there's not a lot to be done at this point."

Edward looked exasperated at the news but controlled himself with slow, deliberate speech.

"So, Alan, as head of network operations for New York Metro, can you please tell me who is investigating this fiasco?" he asked. "Have they identified him? What do we know about this man?"

I figured I should address the question. "My former boss, the district attorney for New London County, is looking into it," I assured him. "His office is reviewing case files as we speak. We believe the stalker, who refers to himself as Dante, may be a recently released convict I put away when I was in that office. Any court proceedings with religious overtones are being pulled."

Edward looked intrigued as he leaned toward me. "This sounds promising," he said. "Do any cases come to mind?"

I shook my head.

"I'm scheduled to meet with some of the staff in a couple of days. The last names will be redacted, but they have already identified half a dozen cases that seem promising." Our server approached with an overloaded tray, and for several moments the conversation ceased as we ate. I nibbled at my fish, convinced I would be back on the hot seat the minute I dug into my lunch. But other than comments about the quality of the food and its preparation, talk was limited, so I enjoyed my meal. After plates were cleared and coffee was served, I felt myself getting anxious. I had been hydrated, well-fed, and properly caffeinated, so it was likely time I was the one who got grilled. Edward took his time before speaking, adding a hefty dollop of cream to his cup and stirring it slowly. He cleared his throat. *Here we go.*

"Please keep us posted on the status of this caller," Edward said. "Let's plan, barring any additional delays, to start back live on," he consulted his watch before continuing, "next Monday, the 22nd." That date had already been determined, but everyone nodded as if he had just made an executive decision. "Now, let's address the most pressing issue before us. Regardless of where

Miranda Nights originates from, it is critical we increase the number of nights it airs. I understand your hesitation," he added, holding up a hand to silence my protest. "But our affiliates and our sponsors are demanding more shows. As are your listeners. We *are* in the entertainment service, Miranda. And we all must sacrifice for the greater good."

Brian cast me a warning look, no doubt certain I was about to respond with some snarky retort. Please, I was a professional, and I was raised to be polite and to never bite the hand that fed me. If I were to respond, I would have focused on the fact that whatever sacrifices Edward was making, surely they did not include sitting in his basement until midnight and waiting for an unidentified stalker to send another message or threat. But this *was* my job, and I was paid well for doing it. It was time I faced up to the responsibilities that came with it. I smiled and nodded enthusiastically.

"I understand, I do. Here's what I propose. Give me a month, once the show starts up again. If all is going according to plan and Dante has been identified and stopped, *Miranda Nights* will go live three nights a week."

Quickly recovering from surprise at my announcement, Brian spoke up. "And that would naturally precipitate a salary increase of fifty percent as well as a new contract."

"For me as well as for my studio technician, Stephen Hansen," I added.

"And moving the show to New York?" Edward asked. I shook my head.

"Baby steps, Edward," I responded with what I hoped was a note of finality, and he nodded. Alan conferred with Brian, Sharon typed notes into her phone, and Edward smiled happily and called the server over.

"Champagne?" he asked us, but we all shook our heads. I needed to get going, and everyone else wanted to get back to work *without* a champagne buzz. "Just the check," he said with a touch of regret, and minutes later Brian and I were walking toward the exit after a final round of air kisses and handshakes.

"Well played, grasshopper," Brian said. "I thought you'd blown it when you started out talking about how much you love New York. But you recovered nicely. Even though you caved on the number of shows. Hubby is gonna be mad at you."

I shrugged. "It was easier to offer three than to come down from five, and anyway, you realize all this depends upon our stopping Dante. Crap, I hate that moniker. It makes him sound romantic, almost. He's a stalker, plain and simple."

"Oh, I heard that. So if he isn't apprehended, you can stick to your two shows a week. No harm, no foul."

"Talk about a silver lining. And all from my home turf," I reminded him.

"I can't believe you shot him down." He held up a hand and with a dramatic flair crooned, "Baby steps, Edward."

"Thank your sensei, grasshopper," I said. "And now I've got to get to the station so I can hop on the 4:10 to New Rochelle."

Brian looked confused. "And why on earth are you dining in New Rochelle when all of Manhattan awaits?" he asked.

"Don't diss the City of Homes, bro," I said. "I have it on excellent authority they have a Brazilian steakhouse that is to die for. *Ciao*," I said with a wave and took off on foot to catch my train.

CHAPTER 33

I spent the thirty-five-minute trip to New Rochelle responding to routine emails and exchanging texts with Skip. He had returned from five days in Florida with Becky and her son, Jesse, and all I knew from his mom was they had spent a day at Universal Studios and had a blast. I couldn't tell how Tricia felt about Skip's relationship with Becky, and I wasn't about to bring it up myself. I had already told him we were starting up on Monday, but now I had to tell him I had committed both of us to a third night on air each week. And of course, that would mean a fifty-percent pay hike as well.

Wow, that's huge. Do you think they'll reimburse me for mileage? If not, NBD
Yes, start submitting miles with your time sheet each week. Speaking of which . . .
Sorry, I owe you like 3 weeks' worth. Will catch up, I promise.
No worries, Skipper. U good?
Sure

The telltale dots appeared, and it looked like he was going to continue, but they disappeared. Hmmm. I typed quickly.

How're Becky and Jesse?

Good
You had fun, yeah?
Yeah

Suddenly, it was like pulling teeth trying to get him to share anything.

Want me to stop asking about Becky?
Yeah I guess
Okay. See you on Monday night. 7:30 okay? We can go over a few things. Work things.
Sounds good TTYL

What had happened down there in the "happiest place on earth"? Had Becky rebuffed his advances? Had he rebuffed hers? Yeah, no way *that* had happened. Maybe things had been hot and heavy and he didn't want to be in Connecticut without her. What if he just missed her? I could always call Becky, certain she would be less evasive, but I did not want to be that person yakking away on the phone in a crowded railroad car. I would have to be patient for now, *not* one of my strongest qualities.

Ten minutes later, I emerged from the station to find Eric double-parked and waiting for me. I had already texted him that the meeting had gone well but had neglected to tell him an additional one of "his" nights would soon belong to Infinity. He was all sorts of enthusiastic about his day, which he'd spent meeting with the partners of his old firm.

"They have more work than they can handle," he said. "And it looks like there may be an opportunity . . ." He trailed off, and I studied his dear, familiar profile as he maneuvered us through the heavy traffic of the surface streets leading out of downtown. I had only been here a handful of times, but despite my comment to Brian defending the city, I had to admit it didn't appear to have all that much to offer in the way of fine dining. But there was still the promise of tonight's steakhouse.

"What type of opportunity?" I asked. He shrugged and glanced over at me briefly.

"They want me back, Quinn. As a *senior* partner." He was attempting to sound casual, but the way he was grinning and gripping the steering wheel, I could tell he was excited. I had not seen that coming.

"That's fabulous! I mean, as long as it's what you want, it's fabulous. And it is what you want, right?" He nodded vigorously and was now beaming with pride. I was so happy for him, but I was still confused.

"But how would it work? You were a partner, and when you left a year ago, they bought you out. And now?"

"I'm going to pay back the money, and I'll be back in. One of four senior partners. Named partners," he added, and I gave a little shriek.

"Wow! Andrews, Colby, Dolan, and Hansen." His enthusiasm was contagious.

"Sounds good, huh?" It did. Except . . .

"Um, so will you need to get a place here? Commute on weekends?" We had just had this conversation and had both agreed we would not do this very thing. But unless Eric wanted to commute three or more hours a day, it was the only viable alternative. Damn. He looked at me in surprise.

"No way, babe. We just had this—"

"I know we did, so how?"

"We're expanding into Connecticut. I'll be in charge of the team based there. I can work from home for now, but I'll need to find office space, and we'll be hiring more people. I was thinking I would talk to Dale to see if he's interested."

"You sure got a lot more done today than I did. All I did was eat halibut and manage to not spill."

Eric studied me for a second. "And negotiate a third show."

Crap. "Who told?"

"John shared the news. I called him while I was waiting for your train to arrive. He said Skip told Tricia, and she told him, and here we are."

"I'm sorry. I was going to tell you."

"It's okay. We knew it was bound to happen eventually, and three nights is still better than four."

"Yeah, I guess. But hey, speaking of Skipper."

"Were we speaking of him?"

"Sure. So . . . what do you think of his visit with Becky?"

"I dunno. They went to Universal Studios and had fun. That's about it. Why? What do you think?"

"I think there's an age difference which won't make a difference in ten or fifteen years, but it's enormous right now. She's a wonderful young woman whom I truly love, with a lot of baggage and a kid. And there's sweet, innocent Skipper."

Eric was silent for a moment, but his brain was working overtime. "Does Skip know about Becky's past? Has she been open with him about the drugs and her time as a prosti—"

"Sex worker. Yeah, apparently she has. Remember, they were hanging out a bunch before she and her sister moved to Florida? He had given her a ride home from the party after the trial, and they were each other's plus-ones to our wedding and Pop and Sally's too. I thought they were cute together."

Eric smiled. "Yeah, they make a good-looking couple."

"And Skip told me he thought she was a great mom, and it was a big deal since she'd had such a hard time growing up. Being homeless, her mother's problems, and how Becky had turned herself around. He sounded proud of her."

"Well, if Skip doesn't have a problem, then neither do I," said Eric.

"What about John and Tricia? And Sarah. What do they think?"

His tone was gentle, but firm. "I think if it were important, we would have to ask them to find out. But for now, let's trust Skip and just let it be, yeah? Thanks to you, he'll be making bank this summer before he heads back to UCONN. Still has two years to go to get his degree. He won't have a lot of free time to head to Florida for another visit anytime soon."

I had to agree with him. "You're right."

Eric cocked his ear toward me. "What's that now?"

"I said you're right, okay? Wait, are we here?" The Dolans had moved six months ago, and I hadn't been to their new house yet. "Damn, I should have brought a plant or something. A housewarming gift."

"Relax, Quinn. We sent them one of those fruit baskets that's mostly chocolate when they moved in. It was a big hit. And dinner tonight is on us since we have so much to celebrate. So relax. We're good." I saw our friends coming down the walk of their huge Georgian Colonial. It was time to forget about work and stalkers and have a nice evening.

CHAPTER 34

The steakhouse was as good as Eric had promised, and I sent a photo of a sizzling platter of churrasco beef to Brian with a caption: *The steak is divine. Wish you were here. XO.*

The four of us had a wonderful evening, and Amanda, who had just found out she was pregnant, had no problem serving as a designated driver. I hadn't realized she was nearly a decade younger than her husband, and they had apparently been trying to start a family for the better part of a year.

We toasted the coming addition to their family, my new contract, and Eric's rejoining the firm. He and Rob were the two youngest senior partners, and despite our promise to limit work talk, the two men had a lot of ideas for the continued expansion of Andrews, Colby, Dolan, and Hansen. We arrived back at the Dolan's around ten, and I turned down the offer of a nightcap, kissing Eric good night. I fell asleep quickly, and although it felt like only a few minutes, according to the bedside clock in the plush guest room, it had been an hour since I had gone to bed. Eric was shaking me awake.

"We have to get home. There's a problem," he said, and despite the wine fog I'd been floating on, I jumped up and started getting dressed. The more he told me, the more I hurried. It was bad.

Our home had been broken into, and the main living area had been trashed. At first glance, nothing appeared to be missing. Our recently installed security system had sent an alert to Eric's phone, plus Tim had called him just minutes later. According to Tim, his guy had been driving past the house every hour or so, and just before 11:00 p.m., he saw the front door was wide open and heard the alarm going off. He had immediately notified the police and then Tim, who had called Eric. The intruder had gained access by breaking a window in the guest bathroom. Tim was the one to notice something *was* missing. Hobie!

One hour and fifteen minutes later, we pulled into our driveway. Before the car was actually in park, I jumped out and went charging into the house. There were so many emotions whirling in my brain, no longer fuzzy after being woken up after an hour of sleep. Mainly, I was goddamn furious. This psycho had to be stopped. Being the daughter of the most popular cop on the force, even five years after his retirement, clearly had its perks. The house and yard were crawling with officers as well as off-duty and retired cops. I saw a few familiar faces as I raced around, trying to make sense of what I was seeing, before Pop's former partner, Monty, grabbed my arm and pulled me in for a quick hug.

"Dez is out there," he told me. "He got here only minutes after the responding officers showed up. When he found out your kitty was missing, he organized a search team to comb the neighborhood to look for him."

Eric arrived in time to hear that last part, and he wrapped his arms around me.

"Don't worry, babe," he whispered. "This is Hobie we're talking about here. He got spooked and ran off to hide. He's probably halfway up a tree in a neighbor's yard, waiting for the coast to clear."

I snuffled into his shoulder, only slightly mollified, coming up for air just long enough to whimper.

"What if he t-took him?"

Eric shook his head adamantly. "The deadly sins guy? No way. First off, we don't even know for sure it was him . . ."

"If you're trying to make me feel even worse, you're doing a great job. The thought there are two crazies out there instead of just one? Not very comforting," I said.

"Yeah, you're right. It's most likely him, but why would he take our cat?"

I counted off on my fingers. "To terrify me, to prove he's untouchable, to pay me back for some perceived injustice I caused him? To teach me a lesson? All of the above?" I shook my head miserably. Somehow, someway, I had wronged this guy, or at least he felt I had. But who was he, and what did he think I had done to warrant this level of payback? Even if he hadn't taken Hobie, he had to know that open windows and doors were like an engraved invitation to a scared feline. Although Tim had told Eric he had searched everywhere, I crawled around looking under beds, behind the dryer, on top of cabinets, anywhere Hobie could be hiding. But he was gone.

Walking around the neighborhood calling Hobie's name seemed foolish, as there was already a search team out there, and besides, I was dead on my feet. So I did what I did best. I started a pot of coffee, unearthed some lemon squares from the freezer, and set them out to defrost. It was drizzling and unseasonably cool for June, not a great night to be outside. My poor kitty! Although he had apparently spent his formative years homeless and on the streets, he was now thoroughly domesticated and rarely even stuck his nose out the door. I needed to do something, so I cracked a dozen eggs, added a splash of milk, a couple of handfuls of grated cheese, and some diced onion and green peppers. The least I could do was offer Pop and his crew a hot breakfast when they came in with Hobie. I nibbled on a frozen lemon square and tried to channel some positive thoughts. Eric stuck his head in the door, startling me out of my funk.

"Babe, the police chief wants to talk with you. Want me to bring him in here?" I looked around before nodding. The kitchen was the only place to have a quiet conversation.

"Okay, sure. Um, any news?"

Eric shook his head sadly, and I wiped at my eyes before greeting Bob Cronin, Old Lyme's police chief. Pop had respected him and had worked alongside him as beat cops back in the day. He was a big, beefy guy with a permanently flushed complexion and a terrible comb-over.

"Randi, darlin'," he said as he made his way over to me. "Don't worry about a thing. That chump left more clues behind than a dalmatian has spots. We'll catch him real soon. You have my word."

I forced a smile. "Thank you for coming out, Bob. It means a lot."

"There's nothing I wouldn't do for Dez, and you too, of course."

"Do you want some coffee? I just made a fresh pot," I said. "And I have a plate of Sally's lemon squares." He nodded enthusiastically, and I poured him a mug and pushed the plate toward him. I joined him at the breakfast bar, still nibbling my pastry.

"Your mom is a great baker," he said after swallowing half a square. "Ah, your stepmom, I mean. But Nora was too," he added. I laughed at that. Despite her best and continued efforts, my lovely mom had been a disaster in the kitchen. And in my case, the apple hadn't fallen far.

"Sally is a wonderful cook," I agreed. "Pop has actually put on a pound or two since—"

"I'm still at my fighting weight, my girl," said Pop as he entered the room. "Cronin, you old SOB. Since when do you make house calls?" Other than the fact he was thoroughly drenched despite the ancient yellow slicker he wore, the first thing I noticed was he was empty-handed. No Hobie. He turned toward me, a grave expression on his dear, lined face. "I'm sorry, Randi. No sign of him. I'm sure he's found a dry place to hide out, or he's charmed his way into someone's home. You'll get a call from a neighbor first thing tomorrow. I'd bet money on it." I sure wanted to believe him, and I forced another smile. All I could think of was curling up in bed and not having to smile or talk, but this was not the time to give in to my despair.

"Get dried off, old man, you're dripping all over my kitchen," I told him. "Then sit and have a coffee. I'm about to make eggs." My dad went in search of a towel and a place to hang his wet jacket. Bob smiled at me.

"I could eat," he said.

A short while later, Pop, Bob, Tim, Dennis Reynaldo, and one of our neighbors were sitting around the kitchen table, working on a third pot of coffee. The lemon squares and eggs were long gone along with half of a sour cream coffeecake our backyard neighbor Louise had sent over with her husband. Yes, the lingerie model also baked! Eric and I were keeping up with the demand for coffee, and I finally had the chance to ask him the question that had been bugging me.

"Where's the guy from tonight?"

Eric studied the room full of men. "You'll have to do better than that," he told me.

"The one who was here tonight. The guy who called this in."

"Oh yeah, um, it was the new guy."

"What new guy?" I asked suspiciously.

"One of Tim's men," he said. "He needed to expand, what with all the work I was generating. Now, with going back to the firm, we'll need to hire even more."

"What is his name, and where is he?"

"Yeah, it's Mick. And I sent him home. I figured we wouldn't need him tonight with all of this," he said, gesturing around the room.

"What do we know about Mick?" I asked.

Eric scratched his stubble and thought for a moment. "He's a little older than most of the crew. Single, I think. Lives over in Milford or Bridgeport. Why? What's up?"

"It just seems odd he didn't stick around. Just heads for home . . ."

Eric looked exasperated. "Jesus, Quinn, it was well past midnight when I told him to leave. What do you expect?"

"I expect when someone is being paid to watch our house, they actually watch the house. And have we called Elinor to see if everything was fine when she came to feed Hobie earlier?"

"No, *we* haven't called because it's four in the morning, Miranda. I will call her when it gets light, okay? And besides, you know Elinor. She has our numbers. She would have told us if anything was wrong. You're clutching at straws . . . or looking for someone to blame," he added.

I had to agree with him, but right now I didn't have the energy to continue this conversation. I hugged him briefly and whispered that I was going to lie down for an hour.

Our bed felt as good as I had hoped it would, despite missing my two bedmates, and I fell asleep quickly. When I woke a couple of hours later, the rain had stopped and rays of bright sunshine were streaming in.

CHAPTER 35

I threw on a terry-cloth robe and belted it tightly as I stumbled down the hall to the kitchen. I half expected the crowd from last night would still be there, but the table was empty, and the countertops were bare and wiped clean. There was coffee left in the pot, and it smelled fairly fresh, so I poured myself a mug and wandered out to the back patio. Where was Eric? Had they found something, or had everyone gone home?

"Randi! Good morning," I heard a familiar voice calling and watched as Louise Donnelan, neighbor, lingerie model, and coffee cake baker, emerged from the row of bushes separating our yards. I shielded my eyes from the sun.

"Hey, Lou," I called out. We weren't exactly the sort of friends that dropped in on each other, but she had sent over half of a coffee cake, so . . . "How are you doing?"

"The better question is, how're you doing? Carl filled me in on the break-in. You must be terrified." More furious and pissed off, but yeah, terrified too. I nodded in agreement, and she perched on the lounge chair closest to mine, leaning in conspiratorially and speaking in a low voice. "Did they take anything?" *Besides my peace of mind, good humor, and feelings of safety and security? Besides all that, you mean?*

"It doesn't look like it. It was scary, for sure. But now I'm most worried about Hobie. My cat," I added as she fixed me with a blank stare. "Didn't Carl tell you what he was doing last night? Searching the neighborhood for our cat?"

"Hmmm. Oh yeah. The cat. Still haven't found him?" She looked around the empty yard, as if expecting Hobie would magically appear. I shook my head.

"No, but speaking of which, I should head back inside and make some calls." First, I wanted to find Eric and get an update. He must be exhausted, having been up for over twenty-four hours. Next I would call Elinor to double-check Hobie had been present and accounted for when she'd crossed the street to feed him last night. "Thank you for the cake. It was a real hit."

"No rush on getting the plate back to me," she said with a wave. "Have a great day." Thoughtful, for sure, but definitely a space-cadet. I went inside to find my phone, realizing I had several unread texts.

From Eric an hour ago: *At the police station now. Checked the cloud. Nothing helpful. Home soon. Don't worry. XOXO*

The cloud? Somewhere in the recesses of my puny brain, I recalled Eric telling me any camera footage would automatically go to cloud storage, but that would be just from the front door, wouldn't it?

From Elinor, about forty minutes ago: *So sorry about Hobie. Eric called to ask me. All was fine when I left at 7. (sad face emoji, heart emoji, cat face emoji)*

From Sally, ten minutes ago: *Your dad is laying down for a bit. Thinking of you both. Hobie will find his way home, you'll see. (Heart emoji) Sal*

From Brian, five minutes ago: *M, need to discuss the deets on the new contract. Phone moi, B*

My phone rang as I went to put it down. Tracey.

"Hi, T," I said. I couldn't imagine who had shared the news from last night with her.

"Oh my God," she said. "Dale ran into Tim getting coffee this morning. Are you okay? What do you need? Did Hobie show up yet?"

I let out a long sigh. "Yeah, I'm okay, pretty much. I don't think I need anything, but no, no sign of Hobie yet." My voice caught on his name, and I struggled to keep myself from crying.

"I'm on my way," she said and ended the call before I could ask her to stay put. But there was nothing I could have said to stop her. Tracey had always been there for me; when my mother died from cancer, when my college and law school workload threatened to do me in, when Adam and I split and I lost my job as a DA. I could always count on her. So I started a fresh pot and went to brush my teeth. I threw on a pair of shorts and an R.E.M. *Automatic for the People* T-shirt and re-entered the kitchen as I heard voices. Eric walked through the door with Tracey, the two of them gabbing away. I looked first at Eric.

"Anything?" I asked him. He shook his head and came over to give me a hug.

"Sorry, babe, no sign of him."

I wiped at my eyes with the hem of my shirt. "When you said there was nothing on the cloud, what did you mean?"

"The only thing the doorbell camera picked up was Mick walking up the steps and looking into the open door. But we already knew that." I shook my head, frustrated. Freaking technology. "Sorry, babe. I'm gonna call around and find a better system with live monitoring. I should have done that from the start."

I went to him and pulled him close. "It's not your fault, Eric. Don't beat yourself up, yeah? Hey, you," I said, finally turning to Tracey. She hugged me as well and then drew back to study me closely.

"You look like hell," she said before turning to Eric. "And so do you." She was right. Eric looked exhausted. At least I'd had a couple hours of sleep.

"Who wants coffee?" I asked.

Eric shook his head. "I'm going to catch a few z's," he said and started to leave before turning suddenly. "Oh, and before I forget, I asked Tim about the new guy, Mick. He just joined the crew last month. It turns out he was a cop in New London years ago. There was some kind of problem with an arrest he made. But he paid his debt, did his time, and his recent references are spot-on. Thought you'd want to know," he added, kissing me on the cheek and giving me a quick squeeze. "Wake me for any reason," he murmured. "See you, Trace," he called out and headed down the hall.

"What was that all about?" Tracey asked, a frown on her pretty face as she poured herself some coffee. "Who is this guy?" Unspoken was her follow-up question. *And why do you care?*

"I'm not sure. But the one night we're away, the new guy, who apparently has a record, shows up to find the house broken into. It's just a weird coincidence and I—"

"Don't believe in coincidences," Tracey finished for me. "So what are you saying? The person who was supposed to watch your house is the one who broke into your house?"

"Well. When you put it like that, I guess it sounds pretty lame."

Tracey chugged the last of her coffee. "Let's see what we can do to clean up a bit, yeah?" She peeked into the living room. "Holy hell, it's not good. Yeah, let's check with the cop out front and see if we can make some headway in here."

I checked the damage myself and shuddered. "Let's go for it." Maybe the physical activity would provide an escape, if only for a short while, from the dark and twisted thoughts swirling in my head. It felt like the answer to Dante's real identity was right in front of me, but everything was too blurry to see it clearly.

CHAPTER 36

The young officer stationed out front admitted he wasn't sure if the crime scene that used to be my living room was cleared for us to be in there. I went back inside and called Chief Cronin, and he confirmed all the evidence had been collected and carefully catalogued.

"Clean up the mess," he said. "No word yet on the perp. We're continuing the search. Don't worry, Randi." I was trying to stay positive, but it was a challenge. A small town, overstretched police force was out looking for a man of no known age, no physical description, driving an unknown vehicle somewhere unknown, who had already proven himself to be fast, clever, and nothing short of invisible.

Armed with a vacuum cleaner, a mop and dustpan, and several large trash bags, Tracey and I were making some headway on the mess when Eric joined us. After a quick nap and a shower, my husband appeared ready to take on the world. Bright-eyed, alert, and up for anything. At moments like these, it was hard to love a man like that, but I did. The broken glass from the bathroom window got swept up and thrown away along with half a dozen throw pillows that had been gutted, the down filling ground into the area rugs and littering the tabletops. After that, there were a few books and magazines scattered around and a vase of fresh-cut flowers that had been knocked over. It could have been worse, I thought. It was just stuff, things easily replaced. If only Hobie were here.

Around noon, Pop and Sally came by with grinders from Fortuna's, and we ate outside on the patio. Eric produced a pitcher of iced tea, and for a while it was a lovely midday break. I had very little appetite, which was to say I couldn't quite finish my entire roast beef and cheddar sub. I picked at the remains, thinking how much my fur baby would have enjoyed nibbling. Lost in thought, I was surprised to see Sally jump up and start waving.

"Hobie, you good boy! C'mon, Hobie cat!" Pop and Tracey joined in as Eric bolted across the yard. I watched as my handsome gray tiger emerged from the bushes at the far end of the yard. He sprang toward Eric, who scooped him up and shouted to me.

"It's our boy, Quinn. Hobie's back!"

I dissolved into tears and raced toward them, overjoyed at the sight of my kitty. I hugged them both, and together we made our way to the patio. I noticed something new and studied the red leather collar Hobie was wearing. What the hell? Since he was an indoor cat, we never made him wear a collar, but this one was brand new and secured tightly around his neck. I unfastened it, and as I did, a tiny slip of folded paper fell to the ground. I bent to pick it up and unfolded it. I felt a wave of panic hit me as I read the message.

Only eight lives remain! Time to repent. Dante

Somehow my shaky legs got me back to the patio, where I slumped into my chair, hugging myself to control the shivers that had overtaken me. Pop put down my plate of shredded beef, cheese, and bread, and Hobie dove in as if he had missed several meals instead of just the one. After he gobbled his food, he sat back licking his chops and looking quite pleased with himself.

After a moment or two of his standard post-meal grooming, he sauntered to the door and waited to be let in. One night out of the house had been plenty for my buddy. He ignored his food dish, which was nearly empty, and drank some water before jumping up to the top of his cat tree, where he circled around to get comfortable and fell fast asleep.

Eric noticed it first. My out-of-character silence and blank gaze.

"Hey, babe, he's back. It's all good. You okay?" Wordlessly, I passed him the tiny note, and as he read it, his eyes grew wide and his face contorted into rage. "What the fuck?" he shouted, and Tracey and Sally, who had been chattering away, looked up in surprise. Pop came back outside from the kitchen, a concerned look on his weathered face.

"What's the matter?" he asked, and Eric waved the note around and read it out loud. Pop called the police station, and Eric offered to call Rick. Tracey and Sally checked Hobie for any signs of injury or abuse. I knew they wouldn't find anything. Dante wanted to scare me, and he had succeeded. I honestly didn't feel he would harm me, but I couldn't exactly explain why. I guessed if he wanted me dead, he'd have figured out a way by now. He was still toying with me, like a cat with a mouse. My cat. Jesus, when would all of this end?

A short while later, Tracey announced she needed to go, prompting Pop and Sally to get ready to leave as well. I turned down Tracey's invitation to dinner, claiming I wanted nothing more than a quiet night at home. I heard Eric telling my folks the same thing. It had been a long and eventful two days, and I hadn't called my agent back or thought for a single moment about the upcoming show on Monday. I would put some time in tomorrow getting caught up, but for today, I wanted to be home with my guys.

Eric had a different vision for the rest of the day. He announced his need to spend time in his backyard office, catching up on paperwork before heading over to a couple of job sites.

"Tim has been doing all the heavy lifting," he told me. "I want to get him thinking about what kind of role he'll want to play once I go back to the practice. I have the approval to hire him on full-time if he wants, or he can stay an independent contractor. I'll fill him in and give him the afternoon off to think about it. Depending on what he wants to do, I'll schedule some time with Dale as well." He kissed me and started toward his truck but paused and turned to face me. "The chief has scheduled an extra patrol car to cruise by regularly, and the window guys will be here any minute. You gonna be okay?"

I assured him I would lock all the doors, activate the alarm, and only let in the uniformed repair crew.

"One thing, babe," I added as he prepared to leave. "Check out this guy Mick. Find out all you can about him, yeah?"

Eric nodded, knowing it was pointless to question my gut instincts. "Will do, Quinn. Thinking burgers later?"

I groaned in protest. I had been eating my feelings since we had arrived home late last night.

"To be determined," I said with a wave and watched the window guys pulling in as Eric backed out of the driveway. The three-ring circus that was my life would not be pulling up stakes and heading out of town any time soon.

Several hours later, Eric and I were dozing in front of the television while Hobie purred happily between us on the couch. I absentmindedly stroked his speckled belly and tried to make myself care which of the three McMansions the young couple would choose for their forever home.

"Number two," murmured Eric. "Less distance to work and an open floor plan."

I rousted myself into a sitting position and considered their options. "Number one. They don't need a fifth bedroom, and that one already has a fenced-in yard for their dog."

We watched as the next scene showed the two of them frolicking with their border collie in their fenced-in yard. Decision made.

"You win," said Eric.

"Yay me," I said. "Can we go to bed now?" And although it was barely past eight, we did.

###

I almost hated to let the little guy go, but I am hardly in any position to take care of a cat. Maybe after all of this is settled, I will look into adopting one. I hope Ms. Quinn appreciates the new collar I bought for him. I hadn't planned on taking him last night, but he was scared and looked like he was ready to run, so I grabbed him and stashed him in my car. Then I went back into the house to take a last look around and figured I had done enough damage for one night. We drove back to Bridgeport, him meowing like crazy. I almost pulled over to let him out, but I had to make sure Ms. Quinn knew I was the one who had taken him, didn't I? So I got him home and poured him a bowl of cereal with milk and went to bed. The next morning, I loaded him back in the car and stopped at Target to buy him a collar. Why hadn't he already been wearing one? That's how you protect the ones you love, isn't it? I finally let him go a couple houses away from his house, so I wasn't able to watch the joyful reunion or her reaction to my note.

I smile, thinking of the joy, and the fear, Ms. Quinn is experiencing right about now.

CHAPTER 37

After a good night's sleep, I spent the morning in my office, a small room next to the studio in the basement. I phoned Brian, and after filling him in on the events of the last couple of days, we discussed the details of the revisions to my contract as well as Skip's. We were no closer to catching Dante, so the actual start date for my third weekly show was undetermined. I had only one genuine concern about the terms Infinity had sent over.

"I want to maintain ownership of the rights to the show's name," I insisted. I had almost lost the use of the name *Miranda Writes* when my TV show was canceled, and although I had no immediate plans to use *Miranda Nights* for anything other than this show, it was mine, damn it.

"That's nonnegotiable."

"I'll let them know," agreed Brian. Hmmm. He wasn't fighting me on anything. As my agent, it was his job to fight *for* me and to protect my interests, but our long-ingrained habit of squabbling over just about anything usually won out.

"What's up with you today?" I asked. I got a long sigh in response. I waited another second until he spoke up.

"Taylor wants to get a place out in the Hamptons for the summer. I brought it up months ago when there was loads of inventory, but Taylor couldn't decide. Now that it's a go, the prices are ridiculous and the places we've looked at online are dumps."

Talk about first-world problems, but still . . .

"Does, um, Taylor have a preference?" I asked, but the question I wanted to ask was if Taylor had a preferred gender. Brian had been peppering bits about Taylor into our conversations for months now, and I had quickly noted he never used gender-identifying pronouns. I didn't care who loved who, but Brian was a friend, and I wanted to meet this person to get to know them. If my radio show got pulled, I wouldn't need "agent Brian" any longer, but I wanted to think I would still need "friend Brian."

"No, and that's what is driving me crazy. It's all 'Well, this one has the extra bedroom, but this one is more central to the shops and restaurants.'"

"Who's writing the check?" I asked rather bluntly. After all this time, I did not know how Taylor made a living, but I suspected Brian was supporting them both to some extent.

Wrong.

"Taylor will. Family money and all that." So Taylor had a trust fund. Interesting.

"Tell Taylor a decision needs to be made and nothing good will be available after July 1st. But it doesn't hurt to check for cancellations either. A lot of couples get cold feet or break up, and they lose their deposits. There may still be some hot properties out there. But act now. Tell Taylor," I concluded. See, I could talk without pronouns too.

"Thanks, Randi. I'll do that. Anything else, or are we good?"

"We're good. I would love to meet Taylor someday," I said lightly.

"Oh, you will. Taylor wants to meet you too. Hey, and I'm glad you got Hobie back," he added and ended the call. I sat back in amazement. Brian had not only assured me I would get to meet Taylor but also brought up my cat? What parallel universe was this?

I spent the rest of my morning responding to emails and outlining my next few shows. It had been nice to have a break these past two weeks, but I was raring to get back on the air. If only there was some way to ensure HE couldn't get through, I would be even more excited. I called Skip to remind him of our agreement that as soon as either of us suspected the caller was Dante, the call would be ended and we would immediately go to a commercial break.

"We should both listen for any more disciples' names," I added and, after referring to my hand-written list, recited, "Simon, Phillip, Nathaniel, Levi, Thomas . . ." Ugh, I could barely read my own writing. "Umm, Matthew? Judas, oh yeah, definitely Judas." Skip agreed the name Judas was an immediate red flag and said he would see me on Monday.

I hoped cutting off Dante would benefit us. He wanted airtime and my attention. By thwarting his efforts, we might draw him out in the open and catch him in a big dramatic finale. Chiding myself for all the thrillers I had read and watched over the years, I realized he could be even smarter than I'd given him credit for. We might be in for a long haul, and I needed to be prepared for that.

It was time to take a break for lunch, so I went upstairs and grabbed a yogurt from the fridge. I went outside and sat on the patio, enjoying the sunshine. Hobie was nestled high on his perch, sleeping soundly and enjoying the tangy, salty breeze through the screen that separated us. I relaxed a bit, daydreaming about places I wanted to go with Eric. Sedona, Arizona, was at the top of the list. Those desert Jeep tours looked like so much fun! I also wanted to visit Ireland again. I'd been to Dublin back in my twenties, and it was definitely a vibrant and lively city, but this time I wanted to see the countryside and the southern and western coasts. And Northern Ireland too. As soon as things settled down, we would need to make a plan. I wondered if Pop and Sally would be interested in going with us. Eric had driven on the left during a semester abroad in England, so we could rent a car and go exploring. Pop's mother had been born in Ireland, and he had spoken several times over the years about his desire to visit Tralee, the small fishing village she came from. If not now, when? Time to seize the day and go!

I would have loved to spend more time outside, but I'd neglected to put on sunscreen and was getting drowsy. I decided to go to the grocery store and stop for an iced coffee. I drove to the center of town, found parking, and filled my cart with a few necessities and a good-looking sirloin for tonight's dinner. I added a few ears of corn and the makings for a salad before dropping everything back into the car and crossing the street to Tessie Lou's.

"Welcome to Tessie Lou's," came the cry as I pushed my way into the delightful air-conditioned comfort of the old-fashioned ice cream parlor. If you hadn't lived here for most of your life, like I had, you might not remember this used to be a bustling Blockbuster back in the day. It was fairly empty, as it was past the lunch rush and before the midday break time. I joined the relatively short line of waiting customers when I heard, "Hey, Aunt Randi," and there was Flynn, wearing a starched white apron and an old-time straw hat. And a beautiful smile.

Not wanting to embarrass him, I stopped myself from complimenting him on his snappy uniform and just said, "Hey, bud. Good to see you." He beamed at me and took an order from a harried mom of two toddlers. I waited my turn and was about to order my coffee when he presented me with a mocha shake prepared by one of his co-workers. No whipped cream, no cherry. Perfect. "How did you know?" came out before I recalled telling him to have one ready whenever I showed up. And he had remembered!

"On the house," he told me, taking money from his apron pocket and ringing up the sale. I didn't expect him to spend his valuable tip money on me, but I thanked him and stuffed a ten-dollar bill into the communal tip jar when he wasn't looking. I drove home with the windows open, blaring Don Henley's "Boys of Summer" at top volume while taking sips of my shake. All was right with my world until I approached my driveway and watched a dark-haired man walking through the side yard. Was he visiting Eric in his office? I doubted it since Eric's truck was nowhere in sight and I didn't expect him home for hours. There was something vaguely familiar about the man, and as I drove closer, I turned down the volume on my radio and stuck my head out the window.

"Excuse me. Can I help you with something?" He turned and looked at me before sprinting toward a beat-up four-door sedan parked a few houses down the street. He got into the car, and after a couple of false starts, the engine fired and he drove away. What the hell was that about? Had I just seen Dante? Was that the devil who had been warning me and lecturing me and scaring the bejeepers out of me these past weeks? I felt a small thrill as I copied the last four digits of his license plate. XT23. A white Toyota Camry circa 1995 registered in Connecticut; unless the car or the plates were stolen, there couldn't be all that many left on the road. I sipped my shake, feeling strangely calm. Thinking back to the first car I ever owned when I was seventeen. A baby-blue 1995 Toyota Camry. Take that, Dante!

CHAPTER 38

My first phone call was to Chief Cronin, who complimented me on my fast thinking and excellent detective skills.

"You're a chip off the old block, Randi. Cut from the same cloth as Dez Quinn himself. You should consider a career in law enforcement," he told me. I stifled a laugh, deciding not to remind him I was forty-two and a bit too old to consider that kind of career shift. Although if I tanked my radio career . . . He promised to look up the car's registration for an owner's name and put out an APB on the vehicle. "I'll call Dez," he added, which told me although he couldn't share details of a criminal investigation with a mere citizen such as myself, it would be perfectly okay to discuss the case with a retired and well-respected member of the force. I was fine with that. Next I called Pop, filling him in on the details and telling him to expect a call from Bob. Then I called Eric, who sounded relieved our stalker was one step closer to being identified. He said he would be home by six, agreeing it was a perfect steak night.

"Oh yeah, remind me to tell you about Mick," he said. "He called out today." Then, talking to someone nearby, I heard, "Sounds good. Give me a minute." Turning his attention back to me, he said, "Got to go, babe. See you soon," and ended the call. Having no time to worry about a missing employee, I called Tracey and then my stepbrother, Jake. After I told him what had been going on, he asked me to keep him posted and offered to call Julie and fill her in.

"You lead such an exciting life," he teased me. "The high point of my day was watching Clem try to comb my hair."

"Sounds pretty good to me," I said. "Working remotely sure has its perks."

He agreed and added, "And tell me what we can bring to dinner next Saturday."

Damn, planning a dinner party. One of the many things I had told Eric I sucked at and with good reason.

I started browsing online menu ideas and suggestions for decorations before I realized my throw pillows needed to be replaced as well, and that was the rabbit hole I had traveled down by the time Eric came home. Shortly after we had eaten our fill of steak and grilled corn, he got around to sharing Mick's full name. The surprising thing was I knew who he was. I had seen him in a courtroom ten years earlier and again, more recently. Unless I was mistaken, it had been when he was sneaking across my lawn before speeding away in his Camry just three hours ago.

"Daniel McMurphy," I breathed, not sure exactly how to process this new piece of information. A name from the past checking several of the boxes in my head. An axe to grind and a debt to settle with me? Check. Medium height and build, dark hair, and probably a few years younger than me? Check. Some religious overtones to his case? Hmmm. Nothing I could recall. McMurphy was a former New London cop who I had convicted on sexual assault charges and sent to prison ten years earlier. It had been my first big case, and a real feather in my cap. It was the case that essentially made my career and destroyed his. I hadn't thought about him in years. And now he was back, recently paroled, living in a halfway house in Bridgeport and working a construction crew my husband had hired, going by the name of Mick.

I can't believe how close I came to getting caught today. I thought she recognized me, but the stuck-up bitch never made time for screw-ups like me back in the day. Apparently, nothing's changed. Early in my time on the force, I had helped her make a case or two. I took real good notes on every arrest I made; they were airtight. A monkey could have secured convictions on the perps I arrested, and when I testified in court, the jury believed me. They took one look at me and thought, Now there's a decent, hardworking cop. I was young, clean-cut, and honest.

Yeah, lawyers like her appreciated me, or at least they should have. None of them would ever say a simple "thank you" outside of the courtroom. Put a note in a guy's personnel file saying how valuable he was. What a responsible, dependable civil servant. Or even cut the same guy a little slack the one time he gets caught doing something wrong. But no, not her. That conceited know-it-all was too busy to help me out the one time I messed up. You would have thought after her attorney boyfriend dumped her and she lost her job in the district attorney's office, she would have been less cocky. Or when her TV career ended before it even began. But she was still too big for her britches and far too good for the likes of me. Seriously? After all, her father was a cop. Not even in a city like New London. Small time, all the way. Just who does that high-and-mighty bitch think she is?

During my time in prison, I had time to reflect, to make up for my behavior those last couple of years on the force. To make amends with those I had caused harm to. Of course, being locked up meant I had to do all this in my head. I had to picture the women I arrested and apologize. I mumbled the words under my breath, and my cellmates thought I was batshit crazy, but it was important to me. I had taken advantage of those girls, some of them real young, too young for what I made them do. I had used the same line over and over, and it worked almost every time. "What would you do to not get arrested right now?" Most of the dumb broads were hookers anyway and got on their knees faster than you could say "Who's your daddy?" Of course, I arrested them anyway after we finished our transaction. Soliciting, disturbance of the peace, possession. Sometimes I added resisting arrest or assault of an officer to the charges. They were pissed off, but it's not like I could just let them go. We live in a civilized society, and if you break the law, you gotta pay the price. I was saving them from a life of sin, if you think about it.

I got caught eventually, and I asked my lawyer to talk to Ms. Quinn, to remind her I had testified for her in court, helped her to win a few cases. I even wrote her a note. She could've thrown me a bone for old time's sake. On the day of sentencing, I was watching her, waiting for her to speak up on my behalf for a lighter sentence. But she looked at me like I was something she would pay someone else to scrape off her shoe. When she spoke, it was like hearing a pond freeze in front of you. Pure ice, that evil bitch. Thanks to her, I got the max, ten years in prison.

Those years I spent in lockup changed me for the better. The first year was worse than I ever could have imagined. A locked-up cop is a dead man walking. I had the crap kicked out of me every time I turned around. The worst beating was by an inmate who found out I was the cop who had sex with his girlfriend before arresting her for possession. I couldn't walk for days, and my ribs never fully healed. But after a while, it got better. Not great by any stretch, but I didn't have to watch over my shoulder all the time either.

But eventually, I found my people. A group of guys who had been through hell and back but who had been saved by the love of our Creator. At first, I sat in on the twice-a-week meetings cuz I was bored and had nothing better to do. And they gave you cookies, and my sweet tooth finally got some relief. Mostly, I just sat there stuffing my face, listening to these sad, pathetic losers tell their tales of woe. "I was abused," "My parents didn't love me," "I got in with the wrong crowd," blah, blah, blah. Grow up, I wanted to say. Stop blaming everyone else for your problems. Start taking some fucking responsibility, would you?

After a few weeks, I was eating fewer cookies and actually listening to these guys. Their stories, their miserable lives. And Kevin, the guy who ran the meetings? He had served his time, got clean and sober, and was certified as a lay minister. He was giving back and wanted to help us. Giving myself over to a higher power didn't seem like a bad idea. I became a cop to protect people, and who protected us better than our Creator? No one, right?

I am a new man, better now that I know the power of His love for me. Since I got out, I have lived simply and honestly. But the one thing I'll never do? Forgive Miranda Quinn for sending me away for all those years. I cannot do that. I have tried to help her repent for her many sins, but I think she is a lost cause. I hope I will be forgiven for what I need to do.

Sorry, not sorry, Ms. Quinn, as Tony, who works days at the Grab 'n Go, would say. It's not like I didn't warn you.

CHAPTER 39

I had thought it would be much easier, less stressful having identified my stalker. There was an APB out on his vehicle and plainclothes detectives watching his rooming house and the convenience store where he worked on weekends. According to the store manager, McMurphy had asked his hours be cut back temporarily to help rebuild a family member's home destroyed in a fire. For the last three weeks, he'd worked for Tim and Eric and even watched my home, earning overtime pay.

McMurphy would need to show up at one place or the other, even if he thought we were on to him. I should feel relieved, right? But honestly, now that I had a name and a face and even a motive, none of it consoled me. Before, he was just a faceless, nameless, angry zealot, a crazed religious fanatic convinced I was a sinner in need of redemption. But now? He was an actual flesh-and-blood guy, a former cop, for God's sake, who had testified on the state's behalf in a handful of fairly low-stakes cases. Rick had sent over a file with some basic info on him, and I vaguely recalled a clean-shaven rookie cop on the stand a couple of times. He had been nervous but credible, which made it even more shocking to see him only a couple of years later up on charges for the aggravated sexual assault of a suspect shortly before taking her into custody. The evidence against him was irrefutable; he'd been caught red-handed—an open-and-shut case.

According to his file, he was thirty-eight, but the man I had seen looked older. Prison records showed he had been a model prisoner after a rocky first year. I'd heard stories of what inmates did to former cops in prison and could imagine what a hard time that had been for him. After he had joined the men's Bible group, he seemed to find some inner peace and a sense of community. And a desire to save evil sinners . . . like me.

I had an excellent conviction rate during my time in the DA's office and had been responsible for countless criminals getting sent away, so I guess it was not out of the realm of possibility one of them would seek me out looking for revenge. But why now, and why him?

###

Justin left me a message to meet him on Monday morning at a coffee shop in Old Saybrook. I tried to call him back to invite him to our house for breakfast but couldn't reach him, so I drove a town over and entered the bustling restaurant. He had not said why he wanted to meet, but I assumed it was to catch me up on Chase's situation. Maybe he would tell me all charges had been dropped! The smell of freshly ground coffee was exhilarating as I looked around and spotted him in a corner booth. I slid in across from him with a satisfied smile.

"Good morning. I love this place," I said. "I had forgotten the Buttercup Café was here. We used to—"

"Miranda, we need to talk," Justin said, silencing my chatter. I looked at him and saw his mouth was drawn into a thin line and his eyes were ringed in red and sported deep bags I swear hadn't been there last week. Oh crap.

"What's up?" I asked. He started to say something when our server ambled over with two menus and two glasses of water.

"Anything to start?" she asked with a welcoming smile. "Our coffee flavor of the day is buttered pecan, and our—" Justin cut her off as he'd done with me.

"Two black coffees and please leave the menus. We'll let you know when we want to order." She placed the menus in front of us and turned to fetch our coffee. I thought he'd been rude as I watched him rearrange his menu to leave room for the mug that quickly arrived. I did the same, and we waited while our no-longer-bubbly server poured us each a cup and left without a word. By now, I was worried. The out-of-the-way location felt almost sinister, guaranteeing neither of us would run into anyone we knew. What the . . . ?

"We're in trouble," Justin said and took a quick sip of coffee, patting his lips with a bright yellow napkin. Yes, I was beginning to see that.

"Tell me," I said, and he cleared his throat and began.

"As you know, the feds have had possession of Chase's phone, laptop, and tablet. Turns out he has close to seven thousand images stored between the three devices."

"Seven thousand?" I whispered.

"Pictures, videos of naked minors, some engaged in sex acts with adults and some with each other." I felt bile rise in my throat and grabbed my glass, swallowing some water quickly.

"B-But how?" I stammered when I could catch my breath. "He's a kid. He's only had the phone for a year or so." I remembered how the long-suffering twins would beg me to intervene on their behalf since they were the only twelve, thirteen, fourteen-year-olds without their own phones. How had Chase accessed that much porn? Tracey and Dale were loving parents, but they were fairly strict. The twins had limited tech time until fairly recently.

Justin looked pained as he spoke. "It's bad. I've seen worse, but it's bad. Kids today have access to an unfathomable number of sites from across the globe. It's nothing more than a keystroke to download dozens of images in seconds. Hundreds." He shook his head in disgust. "It's so far out of control, and most kids don't even know what they are storing and how they got it."

"But if that's true," I interjected, "how can they make the charges stick? What if Chase just admitted that he'd had no clue what was on there? That he'd accessed none of them?"

Justin took another sip of coffee and shook his head sadly. "Because there is proof files were opened on his laptop, and oh yeah, he told the feds he had."

Again with the bile and again with the water. I drew in a deep breath and tried to let it out slowly. "When? How did this happen? Does Tracey know?"

Justin raised an eyebrow and studied me closely. "It was last night, and no, she doesn't. They asked Chase to come in to answer a couple of quick questions, and I said I needed to be present. Dale waited outside, and after Chase and I agreed to be recorded, I announced my client was under no obligation to answer questions and I would inform him when questions were appropriate or not. Everyone agreed, and not one minute later, the agent—Turner's a real piece of work, by the way—he says, 'Well, we found lots of sexual images on your computer. Did you know they were there, and did you view them?' I tried to stop Chase, to tell him not to answer, and he waved me off. Like, 'Oh, it's okay. I got this.' He said, 'Yes, I knew they were there, and I saw them.'" Justin threw up his hands and was about to continue when I stopped him.

"But he didn't mean all of those downloaded images. The imported ones. He meant the ones of him and his girlfriend. Goddamn it, Justin. That's a bullshit question. There's no good way to answer it. If he said, 'No, I didn't know, and I didn't see them,' he would be lying because he obviously took those of himself and Chloe. You should have—" I stopped myself, but it was too late. Justin was furious. He spoke in a low, even tone, but I suspected he would have preferred to just walk right out of the restaurant after telling me to fuck off.

"I did everything to protect him short of having him fitted for a muzzle, but he's gonna serve some time. Even if I can get that question thrown out—too vague, too nebulous—they are gonna find another way to nail him. And no, his parents don't know their son confessed. I don't think even Chase knows what he's done. But I have to talk with them. Today. I wanted to meet with you first to come up with a plan. But if you're not on board—"

"Of course I'm on board. And I'm sorry. I didn't mean to blame you. Freaking kids—one minute you can't get them to say a word, and the next they won't shut up. You're doing a great job. It's way bigger than I had ever imagined." Justin nodded, but I had hurt his feelings. I wasn't sure what he was charging my friends, but I was certain it was considerably less than his standard rate. I needed to be certain he was still on our side. "Let's order, yeah? And figure out our next steps. We'll pay a visit to the Ryans about noon. I'll tell Tracey that Dale needs to join us on his lunch break. Chase too. How's that sound?"

"You're buying," he told me as he looked around the crowded space. "Now let's see if I can get our friendly server back. If I didn't piss her off too much," he added with a grin. Rude behavior all forgotten, our breakfast arrived minutes after we ordered, and we talked and ate and drank more coffee until we felt fairly confident that we'd ironed out our next steps.

Then Justin got a call that changed everything.

CHAPTER 40

A couple of hours later, Justin and I sat in the Ryans' living room with three of the four family members present and accounted for. Justin got things started by sharing the high points of last night's meeting between the assistant state's attorney, the two FBI agents, Chase, and himself along with the impact Chase's answers might have on the future of the case.

"Why the hell did he . . . ?" Dale began, while Tracey begged to know, "Chase, why do you have all that filth on your phone?"

Justin may have had a wonderful track record as a criminal defense attorney, but he could also pinch-hit as a referee, asking everyone to calm down, to be quiet. Dale was still mad. Tracey looked confused, and Chase appeared to be shaking in his proverbial boots as his lawyer continued.

"The question was deliberately vague, and we will get it thrown out." He whispered something to Chase, who shook his head adamantly. He whispered two more questions and got equally vehement responses.

"No way," Chase said, loud enough for us all to hear.

"I have my client's assurance that although he answered in the affirmative, the images in question were, to his way of thinking, those he and Chloe took in the privacy of his—" At Dale's glare, he changed course. "And further, he did not know of any other sensitive material on his phone, tablet, or laptop. He is not in the habit of visiting porn sites, and if he were to," Chase shifted awkwardly in his seat and turned nearly scarlet, "he would download none of it because of the viruses and spam attachments they would contain." Chase leaned over to whisper something to Justin, who nodded. "And because he has more important things to do, like study so he can get into a good college," he finished with the ghost of a smile. Dale groaned audibly, and I refrained from rolling my eyes as Justin continued.

"Anyway, I got a call a little while ago, and based upon my conversation, I can almost guarantee the feds will pull out of this case entirely after what I have to tell them," Justin said, looking pleased with himself. Well done, my friend, I thought as each of the Ryans began peppering him with questions. That's when he told them how he had hired an IT expert his firm used to comb through files duplicated from Chase's computer. Parker was a professional hacker who dug and dug until she found proof of what Justin had suspected all along. The triple X videos and images were well hidden and difficult to access. They had arrived as unwelcome guests on Chase's computer and had never been acknowledged by him. He had inadvertently clicked on a link he came across on one or another social media sites which acted like a Trojan horse, delivering the images right to his virtual door. And possibly, so had tens of thousands of other kids around the world.

"So what I'm telling you is there is strength in numbers. If Parker finds what I'm paying her to look for, Chase won't be prosecuted for possession if we can prove it's that widespread. We just need a few more days."

"This is fantastic news," I agreed. Young people all around the world had an abundance of free porn at their fingertips, whether or not they wanted it. Yay us! Then I thought of something.

"But didn't you say the state has evidence files were opened on Chase's computer?"

Justin nodded briskly. "Yes, but they haven't shared which files were accessed, and I'm going to bet the only ones were the, um, selfies taken in the home."

"Are you saying for certain neither you nor your brother looked at any of them?" Dale studied his son closely, waiting for his response.

Chase shook his head adamantly. "Not me, for sure. And Flynn never fools around on my computer, and besides, he would rather . . ." He paused, looking horrified at what he'd been about to say, but Dale waved him off.

"Yes, we all know what Flynn's more interested in," said Dale. "We've known for years," he added, and Tracey nodded.

"So many years," she murmured, and just like that, Flynn Patrick Ryan was out.

Turns out Tracey had planned ahead and made sandwiches: tuna salad on whole wheat and egg salad on rye with chips and lemonade.

"I almost cut off the crusts," she admitted. "Force of habit." She shook her head, no doubt missing the kids she served lunch to every day.

"I'm sorry, Mom," Chase said. "I screwed up," he added, looking at the crumbs on his nearly empty plate. Tracey sat up straight, smiling at her son.

"You did, sweetheart. You really did. But you'll get past this. We won't let a stupid mistake ruin your life. Just tell the truth and do what Attorney Diaz and Aunt Randi ask you to do. Got it?" Chase nodded, seeming grateful for his mother's understanding and support.

Feeling optimistic federal charges would not be filed, we discussed the state's case against Chase. I agreed with Justin that Chase stood a better chance in front of a jury than having his case decided by a judge. Justin left after ensuring his client would only access the family desktop computer to complete his make-up homework assignments, and if further questioning were to occur, Chase was forbidden to say a single word without prior approval. He promised and went to take a shower before heading to work at Alden's, the local hardware store, on his bicycle. Eric was one of their best customers, and he had approached Bill Alden. Chase had been put on the schedule the next day. Dale went back to work and Tracey and I poured more iced tea and went to sit on the back deck.

"That went well," I assured her. "Seriously. Justin was an excellent choice."

Tracey nodded and closed her eyes, enjoying the early summer sun on her face.

"Yeah, he's great. And we could never afford him without your 'friends and family' discount." I had no response, but Tracey opened one eye and slipped her hand into mine. "Thank you." I squeezed her hand, and we sat for a while, just enjoying the sun and the slight breeze and being together.

I finally broke the silence, needing to confirm what I already suspected. "You two good? You and the big guy?"

Tracey blushed and nodded happily. "We are. Fantastic," she said. "Ever since you told him to come clean with me and admit how shaky things were with the business . . . Jesus, that's another thing I owe you for. You're gonna keep my kid out of jail and you single-handedly saved my marriage. Is there anything you are not good at?" she asked, a note of wonder in her voice. "Any other special skills I should know about?"

I squirmed uncomfortably. As often as I found myself in it, I didn't enjoy being the center of attention and had never learned to take a compliment.

"Anything I'm not good at?" I asked. "Let's see, I gave Eric a complete list the other night . . ."

"Between the sheets," quipped Tracey, and I shook my head.

"Mind out of the gutter," I said. "I'm thinking dancing, frosting a cake, games, and, um, planning a dinner party. Oh, that reminds me. Do you want to come to dinner next Saturday night? And the boys too. I'm gonna see if Skip and Sarah can join us."

Tracey studied me, a look of surprise and a tinge of doubt on her face.

"Do you mean like with food? Food you'll cook and serve?" she asked suspiciously. "If so, who are you, and what have you—"

"I'm good at cooking. Some things," I added. "With supervision and a recipe with pictures. You'll see. So, is that a yes?"

"Yes for me and Dale. I'll have to check with the boys now that they both have jobs."

"Great. I love that you guys are 'you guys' again. I hate it when Mom and Dad fight," I said with a pout. Tracey grinned, looking happy and significantly less stressed than when Justin and I had shown up a couple of hours earlier.

"Let me know what time and what we can bring. And if you need the name of a good caterer—"

"My work here is done, oh ye of little faith. Now if they located McMurphy, I could put my feet up and relax. But . . ."

"No rest for the wicked," said Tracey. Reacting to the pained look on my face, she added, "Too soon?"

Yeah, maybe just a bit.

CHAPTER 41

Despite an APB and police officers combing the southern part of the state, Daniel McMurphy, aka Mick, aka Dante, had yet to be found. He had been on supervised release since leaving prison six months earlier, and assigned to a parole officer named Joseph Swensen. The overburdened Swensen claimed he had met with Daniel earlier in the week at their appointed time and had seen nothing out of the ordinary in their time together, but he noted McMurphy had been pleased about his new job as a grunt on a construction crew.

McMurphy had no family left in the area. Shortly after his conviction, his elderly parents had sold their home and moved out of state. No one in the New London police department had heard from him since he had been fired from the force ten years earlier. His only recent acquaintances were his boss and co-workers at the convenience store and members of the construction crew.

His cellmates at the Danbury State Prison had changed countless times during his ten years of incarceration since apparently no self-respecting convict wanted to room with a cop. Those who were still locked up had been questioned at length on the off-chance McMurphy had talked about his plans post-release. Comments ranged from "He was a pretty good guy for a pig," to "The only thing he talked about was how we're all sinners and we're all gonna be punished," to "He let me have his pudding cup sometimes." None recalled any mention he might have made of his future life on the outside. Kevin, the lay leader for the men's Bible group, claimed to know Daniel well and was not surprised to learn he had gotten himself into trouble so soon after being paroled. According to him, "Daniel is a good man, but a troubled one. Without revealing any confidences, I can tell you he is racked with guilt over the crimes that put him in prison, and he feels the only way he can be redeemed is by saving another sinner."

When Rick told me this, all I could think was how my salvation was now tied with McMurphy's. Awesome.

I divided my time between puttering in the kitchen and working on ideas for the next few radio shows. I kept busy, but it was hard to concentrate, and despite regularly assuring Eric, Tracey, and Pop that I was "fine, just fine" several times a day, I jumped whenever the phone rang or someone knocked at the door. Ours wasn't what I would call a close-knit neighborhood, but Louise came by with a Frito-topped tuna casserole that was surprisingly tasty. I don't know if she knew exactly what sort of trouble had overtaken the Quinn-Hansen household, but I appreciated her generosity and her support.

I had worked out a menu for our upcoming dinner party featuring grilled salmon and a variety of cold salads and sides. Easy-peasy! Tracey would bring dessert, and Pop and Sally were planning a charcuterie board. I teased Pop about even knowing what a charcuterie board was, let alone how to assemble one.

"This old dog has plenty of new tricks," he assured me, which had made me smile.

"Is it too early to set the tables?" I asked Eric one morning.

He looked up from his newspaper. "For what? You've gotta give me something."

"Our dinner party, of course." Duh, why else would I set the tables on the patio?

"The one taking place in what, six more days? Do you mean *that* dinner party?"

"It sounds silly, yeah? It's just I have the time now, and by Saturday I could be busy again." Or Dante could blow up my studio or kidnap me—or worse. "I told you I suck at planning dinner parties," I added.

Eric shook his head at me, looking rather amused at my obvious frustration. "Babe, you're anxious. It's okay. But I'm betting it has more to do with Dante still being on the loose than deciding which napkin rings to use."

I slapped my head in mock frustration.

"Damn, I forgot about napkin rings. *Now* I'm stressed," I told him as I crossed the kitchen and went to sit on his lap. "Why do napkins even need rings? And why do you always know what to say to make me feel better?" I asked.

He leaned in, nuzzling my neck and whispered in my ear, "Action speaks louder than words, babe. I can show you how to feel better rather than just tell you . . ."

I pulled away from him, frowning. "Justin is coming over with Tracey and Chase," I reminded him. "We don't have time this morn—"

"I'll be quick," Eric promised. "Really quick. And you can watch the clock the whole time." He started to pull my T-shirt over my head.

"Sounds dreamy. And so romantic. You sure know how to woo a girl." We were interrupted by the sound of the doorbell. "Saved by the bell," I said, giving him a quick peck on the lips. I raced to the door, pulling my shirt down as I went. "Love you," I called over my shoulder. "Rain check!"

CHAPTER 42

At last, there was a break in the case! Not the "Dante is a crazed zealot who wants to help me turn my life around" case, but the "Chase Ryan is *not* a pedophile or a sex offender" one. Daniel McMurphy would eventually be brought to justice; I could say that with close to one hundred-percent certainty. But this morning was all about Chase. Also, I'd been told in no uncertain terms to stay away from any sort of investigation of McMurphy by Rick, Chief Cronin, Eric, Pop, and Tracey. Focusing my somewhat divided attention on Chase made perfect sense.

Eric left for work after a whispered, "Damn straight rain check!" message for my ears only, and we got settled on the patio with cold cans of seltzer and bottles of iced tea. Today was going to be a scorcher, and my offers of coffee had been refused. According to Tracey, Dale had wanted to join us but got held up with personnel issues and would need to sit this one out. It was an important strategy session, possibly the last one before court next week. Justin started the meeting on a positive, almost jubilant note.

"It's good," he began, failing miserably at hiding the huge grin lighting up his face. "Parker has found the proof we needed. It proves Chase's situation is only the tip of the iceberg," he announced dramatically. I sat back, feeling relief wash over me. Tracey and Chase looked at each other, then at me.

"Are you saying you have evidence proving the whole thing didn't start with Chase? For sure?" Tracey squeaked, and Justin beamed at her.

"Yes, that's it exactly. You weren't the only one, Chase. Not by a long shot. I think we have the makings for a class-action lawsuit as long as we can prove damages."

Tracey pointed at her son. "There's your damage right there. Suspended for the last week of school. Reputation destroyed. And what about my daycare center?" She looked at her son, who was looking miserable. "I'm sorry, sweetheart. I didn't mean . . ."

"But what about the pics of me and Chloe? Does everyone have those too?" Chase asked. He flushed a deep red, mortified at the idea, but Justin was quick to reassure him.

"No, my friend, that's your specially curated semi-private collection inadvertently shared with most of the students and faculty at Old Lyme High School. We're still trying to track how that happened. You're not off the hook, not entirely, but the federal charges against you will be dropped. And I plan to talk with the DA, and I expect we will plead you out on a lesser charge. One that will keep you out of jail and off the sex offender's registry." Tracey burst into tears and threw her arms around Justin, wrapping him in as big of a hug as her tiny frame would allow.

"Thank you," she sobbed into his elbow. "I can't thank you enough." While Justin patted her on the back and tried to extricate himself from her grip, I turned to Chase, who was sitting stock-still, staring into space, looking dazed.

"C'mon, bring it in here, bud," I said, and he fell against me, tears streaming down his face.

"Thank you, Aunt Randi," he said, and I turned to face him. I tried to keep my tone friendly, but it was important he understood the severity of the current situation.

"Listen to me carefully. Justin is correct. If it all goes according to plan, you won't do jail time and you won't get your name added to the registry. But, and this is important, you'll need to keep your nose clean until you're at least eighteen. For that matter, plan for the rest of your life. No parties where there is alcohol or drugs. No girls in your bedroom, and stay out of theirs as well. No sex, at least not for a while, yeah? And you make damn sure the next girl you kiss is at least sixteen or older. Hell, eighteen. And when you decide to have sex, make sure your partner is ready, willing, and able. No means no, consent is *not* implied, and if you get lucky, wear a damn condom, okay? She says she's on the pill? Good for her. Don't care. Suit up if you want to play. Do I make myself clear? Crystal clear?" When I stopped talking, Chase was gawking at me, dumbfounded. Tracey and Justin were staring at me in amazement. Tracey spoke up first.

"Will you give Flynn the exact same speech, Ran? Well, you can skip the part about the pill. No, on second thought, leave it in. You never know," she added with a grin. I got another hug from Chase.

"You're so cool, Aunt Randi. You should record yourself and post it on social media. Just leave my name out of it," he added. "It would go viral, for sure. They're always preaching abstinence, but who are we kidding? We're normal, healthy—"

"At what point did you hear me say run right out and hook up? What I said was to be careful, use protection, and take your time."

Chase grinned at me and hopped up to leave. "Just having a go with you, Auntie. Gonna bike over to Alden's to see if he'll put me on today's schedule. Thanks, Justin. See you in court, ha ha. Later, Mom. I love you." And just like that, Chase was gone. We watched him hop on his bike and head toward the center of town.

"Do you think he understands he still has a lot of hurdles to jump through and there's still a lot that can go wrong?" I asked.

Tracey was already texting an update to Dale, but she looked up from her phone. "I think," she said with a smile that didn't quite reach her brown eyes, "I'm gonna give him today to feel normal and let him enjoy it. Tomorrow, Dale and I will sit him down to discuss what this all means." She paused for a second before adding, "And I hope one or both of you will be there to help me cuz I'm not sure I understand it myself."

"You'll do fine. I have an early court date and need to prepare. I'll be in touch," said Justin as he headed for his car. I assured Tracey I would come over in the morning before Dale and Chase went to work and we would have "the talk."

"Maybe you could pick up a paintbrush and join me after," Tracey suggested. "I'm repainting the play area." Ugh. She must have picked up on my reaction as she quickly retracted. "Just kidding. You have helped the Ryan clan enough this week. But will you stick around for waffles?"

I grinned in response. "I will always make time for waffles."

CHAPTER 43

After two weeks off, I couldn't wait to get back on the air. At 7:55 on Monday night, I sat in my chair, primed and ready to go. Skip gave me a thumbs-up through the glass separating us, and I winked in return. I was excited but anxious too. Dante was still out there, and I fully expected him to call in tonight. The affiliates had been advertising the return of *Miranda Nights* all weekend, and I was certain he would have heard the news by now.

The topic I wanted to talk about tonight was child custody and all the ways it could go wrong. I had done plenty of advance research and had a handful of anecdotes to share from my own experiences. I had located an expert willing to speak on the topic, a Dr. Ernest P. Whitmore from Columbia Law School, who was expecting a call from me at exactly 9:00 p.m. We had spoken twice this past week, and I felt he would add a sense of authenticity to tonight's show. I shuffled through my notes and took a quick sip of water. Skip gave me the five second hand signal: 5 . . . 4 . . . 3 . . . 2 . . . 1 The prerecorded welcome played. "Live from New York, it's *Miranda Nights*, featuring your host, Attorney Miranda Quinn." New York? Yeah, I know, but it sounded better than Old Lyme, right?

"Good evening and welcome to *Miranda Nights*. I'm Miranda Quinn, and I am thrilled to be back on the air after an unscheduled hiatus. I am looking forward to talking to you this evening on the topic of child custody and at 9:00, I'll be talking live to the pre-eminent expert in the field and author of the best-selling book, *Put the Children First*, Dr. Ernest P. Whitmore. You'll want to hear what he has to say, and hopefully you'll have the chance to call in and ask him a question of your own. As is always the case on *Miranda Nights*, there is a topic or theme for the evening, but all callers are welcome. I am here to answer your questions, listen to your concerns, and provide whatever resources I can to address your legal concerns. My producer, Skip, um, Stephen, is on hand to field your calls and welcome you to the show." Damn, I had almost forgotten Skip was going for a more sophisticated persona and had asked me to please call him by his real name on the air.

"Who is our first caller, Stephen?" I saw on my screen it was Linda from Queens, but I liked to give him some air time whenever possible.

"It's Linda from Queens, New York, and she has a question about custody issues tonight. Linda, you're on the air."

"Hi, Miranda. I'm a first-time caller, longtime listener. I love your show so much. I missed you the last couple weeks."

"Thank you for calling in tonight, Linda. What is your question?"

"I have this situation with my ex. He is trying to get sole custody of our little boy, and I feel like he is going to win." Her voice broke into quiet sobs.

"I'm sorry to hear that. Tell me, do you currently share custody? And how old is your son?"

She sniffed a few times before responding. "He's, um, three, and yeah, we have shared custody since we got divorced last year. He has barely spent any time with Owen since he left us. But now he has a girlfriend. My ex, I mean. Not my son. He may have already married her. His sister says he doesn't want to pay child support, plus his girlfriend wants a kid, so we think he wants to take Owen away from me and give him to her. No support checks and no pressure to have another kid right away, you know?"

I shook my head. Wow, that was messed up.

"I want you to listen to me, and I want you to stay on the line. My producer will give you some contacts to help you, okay? Can I assume you don't currently have a lawyer?"

"No, not yet. My ex says we don't need one." *I'll just bet he does. What a bastard.*

"We're going to help you with that." I watched Skip already going through my battered old-school Rolodex for numbers for legal aid in Queens. "The first thing I would tell anyone in a custody battle is to do your research. Find evidence. Voicemails, emails, text messages. Save everything. Receipts too—did you have to pay a sitter when your ex was a no-show? This kind of evidence will support any claims or accusations you might make and can strengthen your case and weaken your ex's. If you can collect evidence and prepare it properly, you'll save on attorney fees, increase your negotiating power, and help your attorney build a more effective case. All things being equal, and by that I mean no criminal record, no substance abuse or mental health issues, prepared parents prevail. Got it? Prepared parents prevail. Best of luck to you and Owen, and let us know how it's going. Thanks for the call. Here's Stephen." I ended the call after I watched Skip talking to her, and we went to a commercial break. In all my years in the courtroom, I still could not fathom the ways two people who once loved each other got locked in a battle guaranteed to destroy everything in its path.

Lost in thought, I almost missed Skip's signal we were going live. I quickly welcomed listeners back and asked who our next caller was. Not sure if it was my imagination, but the volume of incoming calls seemed light tonight. Maybe the word hadn't gotten around I was back on the air. Or maybe it had.

"Miranda, our next caller is Walter from Greenwich. He has a question about child support. Walter, you're live on the air with Miranda."

"Hello, Walter. This is Miranda. What is your question for me this evening?"

"Hey Miranda. Thanks for talking my call. First-time caller, new listener. My question is, do I have to keep paying child support if my wife is remarried and her new husband makes a lot more money than me?" Good question! I asked Walter if he wanted to be a part of his children's lives, and he said he did. Next I asked him if anything had changed, besides his wife remarrying, since the divorce papers were signed.

"Like what?" he asked. I suggested changes in health or employment or his own relationship status, and he said he was seeing someone and she wanted kids and was already pregnant. I assured Walter adding to his own family did not diminish his responsibilities to his existing family, but suggested he could ask if a portion of his support payment could be put into a trust for college expenses, as it did not appear to be needed for living expenses.

"Good luck, Walter. Take care of your children," I advised and thanked him for his call. During the next commercial break, I asked Skip about the call-ins. He confirmed the overall volume of calls was lower than usual but reminded me it was a Monday night, which always started out a bit slowly, and it was still early.

"I'm trying to feel out the callers. I've rejected a few who just want to know when your stalker is gonna call in and if we know his real name yet." I stared at Skip. *What the hell?*

"They said that?" He nodded.

"Yeah, it was almost like it was a game or something. But that's what listeners are waiting for. They don't want to tie up the lines in case, um, Dante is trying to get through. Crap, thirty seconds, Randi," he called as he hurried back to his sound booth.

As I watched him go, I tried to focus. This dangerous fanatic's ravings were being considered entertainment. I wondered if even more listeners would tune in if they knew the truth?

I welcomed my listening audience back. "We have a little time until we hear from our expert in family law, Dr. Ernest P. Whitmore, so let's continue with tonight's topic of custody and why the children don't *always* come first." The next few callers had stories to share and comments about custody and moving out of state, and I listened more than I spoke, which was ideal because my head was spinning with questions about Dante and what he would do next. We took a short commercial break just before 9:00, and I placed the call to Dr. Whitmore. His phone rang several times as I waited. I tried again, and this time I got his voicemail, asking me to leave a message. I couldn't understand what was happening. Had he taken ill, had some sort of emergency? I left my name and number and asked him to please call in to the show as soon as he could. I gave him a private number, allowing him to bypass other callers, and asked Skip to watch for incoming calls. He was giving me the five-second warning, so I cleared my throat and went live.

"Welcome back to *Miranda Nights*. I am your host, Miranda Quinn. We are having a bit of an issue reaching our scheduled caller tonight, Dr. Whitmore, author of the best-selling book, *Put the Children First*. I am sure he'll call in soon, but in the meantime I want to share a story about how a parent who created a detailed journal won sole custody of his two children." I blathered on, all the while waiting for a signal Dr. Whitmore was on the line. I watched as Skip pointed to the phone, made a zero with his fingers, and shook his head in bewilderment. Not only had my guest expert ghosted me, but there were no callers waiting in the queue either. If you hosted a live talk show to a nonexistent audience, did you really make a sound? Finally, Skip signaled there was a caller, but he seemed to hesitate putting it through. I read on my screen: It's Jason from Milford, another one of the

DansFans. I motioned for him to put the call through. The only thing worse than talking to a fanatical devotee of a psychopath was not talking to anyone at all.

"Good evening, Jason," I began, perhaps a bit too cheerfully, but what can you do? "Thank you for calling in this evening. Do you have a legal question or concern? Perhaps an experience related to child custody or family law to share?"

"Yeah, hi, I'm Jason. First-time caller, fairly new listener. When's that guy gonna call in? The crazy one who is always warning you about evil and all the things you're doing to send you straight to hell?"

I forced a chuckle before responding. "Jason, are you referring to the occasional caller who likes to tease me about all of my bad habits, or at least what he perceives to be my bad habits? Why he's just—"

"He's crazy, man. He's all 'fire and brimstone' and 'you're a sinner.' The guy's freaking hilarious. My friends and I have a drinking game, like every time he calls you a sinner or says you're going to hell, we have to take a drink, but you never let him stay on the line long enough." Skip signaled more calls were coming in, so as much as I hated to do it, it was time to say goodbye to Jason.

"Speaking of staying on the line too long, thank you for your interest, Jason. Have a lovely evening. And now I have," I checked my screen, "Courtney from Rocky Hill, Connecticut. Hi, Courtney. What question or concern do you have for us tonight?"

"Yeah, like the last kid, Jason? When is that nutty guy gonna call in? He's so—"

I was not about to give Dante or his followers any additional free airtime, so I jumped in quickly. "I have no way of knowing if or when he'll call in, so I'll say good night for now. Thank you for calling, Courtney." I looked at Skip, who signaled the remaining calls on hold were more of the same, so I made a slashing motion across my neck, and he disconnected them and we went to a commercial break. I looked at the huge digital clock on the wall, something I rarely did. It was 9:45. I still had two more hours to fill, but with what? It was a goddamn call-in show, for Christ's sake. The notes I had made and the anecdotes I had planned to share would not fill the rest of the show. And without Dr. Whitmore, there was no context for any of it. But I had never not shown up ready for work. Not as an assistant DA, not on my podcast, and not on *Miranda Nights*. Skip was waiting for me to decide what I wanted him to do, and I shrugged helplessly. Then he signaled I had a caller. Hmmm. *Eric* from New Rochelle, wanting to ask about the importance of witnesses in a custody battle. My Prince Charming! If ever I needed saving . . .

"Welcome back and welcome to our next caller. Hello, Eric, how can I help you this evening?"

"Hi, Miranda. Big fan, first-time caller."

Leave it to my husband. Only one floor away, and yet I felt like he was sitting right beside me, with his arm around me, trying to cop a feel. I shared the pros and cons of using witnesses and filled nearly seven minutes of airtime. When I was done, he thanked me profusely and told me to have a great week. God, I loved that man. I looked at Skip, who was grinning ear to ear, signaling we had another caller. Okay! *Tracey* from Stonington with a question about the most valuable types of evidence that could be presented in a custody hearing. And we were off. A couple of legit callers followed, then *Dale* from Niantic, followed by *Flynn* from Waterbury. And more callers. The next time I looked at the wall clock, 11:10 glowed in red. We were nearing the finish, and I felt relief wash over me. During the next commercial break, Skip came in looking confused rather than jubilant.

"Hey, bud, it's all good," I said. "We've had some great callers, and the topic of custody has been discussed *ad nauseam*. And we're almost off the air. Why so glum?"

"I just got a call from Dr. Whitmore," he said. "He heard your message, so he called in on the private line. Said there was some sort of mistake. He claims I, or someone who called himself Skip, called him right before we went on the air to cancel his call. Said there had been a programming change, sorry for the last minute, blah, blah. But of course, I didn't call him, so what the fuck? Sorry, Aunt Randi, what the hell is going on? Crap, we're on in fifteen seconds." He hurried back to his studio. Freaking Dante, that's what was going on. He must have heard about Dr. Whitmore from the promos over the weekend, somehow got his number, and called just as we went live so neither Skip nor I could confirm the change. Son of a bitch.

We got through the last half hour. There were only a few callers, half of them requesting "the crazy man." The sponsors would be happy since their commercial messages ran more frequently than scheduled, and I watched the clock as it slowly ticked its way toward the end of the show. Right before midnight, I was about to wrap up when we had another caller. I read the screen.

It's him

Dante was back!

CHAPTER 44

I had been prepped for this call by both Rick and Chief Cronin. The strategy had changed. Rather than shut Dante down, the current goal was to draw him out, let him say his piece, and hopefully bring this to an end. To be honest, I wasn't entirely sure this was the best approach. I had voiced the opinion that to give him anything—a name, airtime, credibility as a genuine threat—would stroke this guy's overinflated ego and lead to more grandiose acts resulting in even more attention-seeking behavior. But I had been outvoted, and I needed to respect that. I cleared my throat. *Here goes nothing!*

"Good evening, Daniel. Oh wait, I see you gave your name as Dante, but what's in a name anyway, am I right?" I got a low chuckle in response. Oh great, I was amusing this psycho! "What is your question for me this evening? Or perhaps you have a comment or a question about child custody issues?" Silence. "No? So what is the purpose of your call? We only have a couple of minutes left, I'm afraid."

"You're afraid? You should be, Ms. Quinn. Afraid of eternal damnation unless you repent for your sins and change your behavior. I think I have been quite clear on this from the start. I don't understand your refusal to heed my messages."

I forced a chuckle of my own. "As much as I would like to tell you where to shove your messages, Daniel, I must admit your calls are the highlights of the show according to some of my listeners. Which goes to show you there's no accounting for taste, am I right? Now, if there was only some way to use this energy of yours, which appears to be dedicated solely to my salvation, and rechannel it elsewhere. Somewhere for the greater good, perhaps? Thoughts?"

"Listen to me. I am your only hope. Your sins, your shameful behavior, your fucking arrogance have cost me—"

"Hold on there, Danny Boy. This is a family show, and we don't allow profanity on the air. Thanks to our handy-dandy five-second delay feature, our good listeners did not have to hear you just spew the F-word." I looked at Skip for confirmation. He shrugged his shoulders before giving me the one-minute signal to wrap it up. I made the "cut him off" signal we had agreed upon before continuing.

"I am afraid that is all we have time for this evening. Thank you, Daniel McMurphy, for, whoops, I'm not supposed to say last names on air. My bad. The only last name I can say is mine. So thank you for listening to this evening's edition of *Miranda Nights*. I'm your host, Miranda Qui—" That's when I heard his voice. He was still live, still on the air.

"Have a good laugh for yourself, Ms. Quinn. I'm glad your arrogance amuses you. After tomorrow, you'll have nothing left to laugh about ever again."

And with that, the episode was over. I looked over at Skip, who was shaking his head, looking more upset than I'd ever seen him. He left his sound booth and came out to join me.

"Randi, Christ, I'm so sorry. I thought I had ended the call with that nutjob. I was looking for the topic for Thursday's show. I was gonna post it on your screen for your close. I don't know how . . ."

I studied him closely. I loved this kid like he was my own. He was more than my nephew and much more than my sound engineer. I had always counted on his support, his skills, and his judgment, but tonight he had let me down. A mistake? Yes, but a careless one that could have been avoided.

"Mistakes happen. Do better, Stephen," I said with a frown. The door opened, and Eric came in. He gave Skip a quick one-armed hug before turning to me.

"Babe," he said, and I fell into his arms, holding back tears. We stayed like that long enough for Skip to gather his things and leave with a subdued "Good night," before we locked up and went upstairs to bed.

Long after Eric had fallen asleep and began snoring softly at my side, I lay awake. Thoughts were whirling around in my head, and I couldn't seem to put any of it aside. Not after tonight's shit-show featuring four long hours of an on-air disaster. Dante had effectively energized a young and vocal group of listeners who apparently tuned in only to hear the rants and raves of a psychopath. By canceling the call from a well-known expert who might have restored a sense of professionalism to the show, Dante had ruined my chances of a successful comeback following an unplanned hiatus he had orchestrated. I needed to call Skip first thing to apologize. The poor kid did not deserve my curt dismissal of an honest mistake. I had certainly made enough of my own!

I fully expected to get calls from the folks from Infinity in the morning. I had breached a serious rule of etiquette in radio broadcasting by revealing Daniel's last name and had been negligent, allowing him to stay on the line after dropping the F-bomb. Granted, that had technically been Skip's error, but it was my name on the show, and the buck stopped with me. Would they cancel the show? Put me on unpaid leave or slap my wrist and demand an on-air apology? Did I care about the repercussions, or would I just prefer to see the whole thing disappear? I could focus on my bread and butter, my blog and weekly podcast, and think about writing another book? Or get Eric to buy a Hobie Cat and just sail away? I couldn't quite imagine an extended life at sea and doubted Hobie would enjoy it either. And what about Pop and Tracey? My extended family? Dale and the twins? I flipped my pillow over, and the fresh side felt cool against my sweaty neck and shoulders. Focus on the positive, I told myself. Think of something good.

The only bright spots from the evening were the calls from Eric, Tracey, Dale, and Flynn. I had always felt their love and unwavering support, but never more than I had tonight. And we had a fabulous dinner party coming up. My breathing slowed enough to make me feel like sleep was a distinct possibility. Then the smoke alarm went off, and Hobie started howling. The sounds woke Eric, and we stumbled down the hall in search of whatever fresh hell was heading our way.

CHAPTER 45

The scene in our backyard was something out of a horror movie, but this was real life—*our* lives—and it was nothing short of terrifying. Our firepit had become the backdrop for an image I will never unsee. We listened as the sounds of fire trucks grew closer and closer. I had no words as I stared in shock at the dreadful tableau no one other than Dante could have created.

All I could say was this: Picture watching yourself burning in the eternal fires of hell. Try it, but you'll never match the horror of what we were seeing with our own eyes. A full-size cardboard likeness of me holding up a sign. The flames hadn't gotten up past my double's waist, so it was easy to read the message in crude lettering:

I deserve to burn in hell for my sins

Thankfully, Eric had the sense to snap some photos before he turned the hose on the flames, which was helpful, as it was hard to visualize the display within the sodden, smoking pile of embers. When the firefighters arrived, there was little for them to do other than take a quick look around and spray the firepit themselves, just to be sure. Apparently, enough smoke had come in through the screen window to set off the smoke alarm, but the whole-house alarm system we'd recently installed had not made a peep. I went inside to change my clothes after realizing I was shivering, wearing a threadbare nightshirt barely covering my lady parts and a pair of panties. The early morning air was chilly and damp, so I found a pair of sweats and a long-sleeved T-shirt from Nirvana's *Nevermind* tour. I found Hobie hiding under our bed, and I tried to soothe him with some snuggle time and a handful of treats.

I went back into the kitchen, figuring I would make myself useful and produce a pot of coffee and some snacks for the men in my backyard. It was becoming a habit, I realized. I was like Martha Stewart for break-ins and fires. If Infinity dumped my ass, maybe there was a new career for me catering for tragedies and disasters. I watched Eric in conversation with Chief Cronin. Although I couldn't make out his exact words, it was clear my husband was royally pissed off. I watched him as he came into the kitchen. He studied me for a moment before shaking his head.

"No more wet T-shirt?" he asked. "What happened? The other contestants are already on their way."

"You okay?" I asked, already certain of the answer he would give.

He studied me closely. "Yeah, I'm great," he said. "Really great. We've gone from a crank caller to a homicidal maniac trying to burn down our house. What's next? Locusts? An outbreak of pestilence? I can't wait to find out."

I went over and hugged him close to me. He remained stiff in my arms before finally yielding to my touch. We held each other until we were interrupted by a flow of traffic, beginning with the chief, followed by two firefighters who had heard there was coffee. Next up, Pop and Sally came hurrying in, just minutes ahead of Tracey and Dale. The Ryans had stopped on the way over and produced two large boxes of hot coffee, three dozen donuts, and a bag filled with cups, spoons, sugars and creamers, and a stack of napkins.

As I tried my best to calm Pop, who was almost as upset as Eric had been, I set out the spread on the breakfast bar, aided by Sally and Tracey.

"No one was hurt," I assured my dad. "It was a stupid prank gone awry, that's all."

He clearly wasn't buying it. "You two can't stay here. You're going to come home with us until this dies down and they catch the son of a bitch. The bastard already brought shame to his department when he broke the law, and now this? What kinds of jack-offs are they letting on the force these days?"

He had a full head of steam, and I debated the merits of just letting him get it out of his system versus trying to make him see reason. But who was I kidding? There was no reason as far as Daniel "Dante" McMurphy was concerned. I looked over at Sally, but she shrugged in a "What can you do? You know your father" kind of way and continued setting up our impromptu feast.

Minutes later, there was a line of folks grabbing donuts and getting their early morning caffeine fix. I noticed Pop, Dale, and Eric had retired to a corner of the room and were deep in conversation. I couldn't tell if they were planning to carry out an act of retaliation against Dante or tossing out ideas on how to remove the smoke and soot damage from the patio. I decided I did not want to know, so I snagged a couple of glazed donuts and poured myself a coffee. I saw Tracey sitting on a bench in the foyer, and it looked like she was finishing up a call, probably with one or both of the twins, and I went to join her.

"Thanks for the donuts and coffee," I said, and she squeezed my arm. I noticed her eyes were shaded with dark circles, and she didn't even try to cover up a wide yawn. For the first time, I realized it was not even six a.m., and I had gotten no sleep, not even a catnap. I yawned back at her and, after a sip of coffee, put the still-full mug on the floor, "Donut?" I said, holding up a slightly smushed pair. Her eyes brightened briefly, and she reached for one. She bit into it hungrily. She chewed just long enough to swallow it and leaned toward me, a tiny wrinkle appearing between her dark brows. Her skin would age well, I realized, not for the first time. I had laid beside her at Soundview Beach for hundreds of hours during our teen years. My fair Irish skin freckled, burned, and peeled, and the resultant wrinkles and age spots had already appeared on my face. Despite logging the same number of hours, Tracey D'Amici Ryan had more melanin, and her olive-toned skin was unlined and freckle free. It wasn't fair.

"What are they doing to find this jerk?" she demanded, tearing off another piece of her donut and chewing it angrily. "And why are you so freaking calm?"

I shook my head, stifling another yawn. "I'm not calm, I'm numb," I said. "After last night's broadcasting debacle, I couldn't sleep. Plus I was kind of mean to Skip. I was laying there wide awake when the fire alarm went off at about four, and I've been up ever since." I rested my aching head in my hands and let out a long sigh that grew into a noisy yawn. "But don't worry. Once I get a little sleep and take a shower, I'll be damn furious. You'll see. Danny Boy McMurphy will feel my wrath!"

"Um. Deadly sin alert," said Tracey. "Wrath is one of the seven."

"Oh terrific, do you suppose that's what he had in mind all along?"

Tracey rolled her eyes. "Who knows what that freak has in mind," she muttered. "He can't get away with all of this."

Damn straight. Threats, vandalism, my home, my job, my kitty . . .

"He won't," I said. "We'll find him and make him pay."

CHAPTER 46

After a two-hour nap, which left me even more exhausted, Eric and I drove over to the Old Lyme police station for a meeting at eleven. I got the usual greeting from Mike behind the desk, and Monty escorted us back to Chief Cronin's office. Bob looked fairly fresh for someone who had been awakened before dawn. He greeted us warmly, as did Dennis Reynaldo, the detective assigned to the case. I had suggested to Eric it would be a good idea to keep his temper in check, advice he appeared to be taking under advisement. He responded with a touch less than his usual upbeat greeting, but I was probably the only one who noticed. Coffee was offered, but as I recalled the quality and usual age of the brew served by the OLPD, I turned it down, and Eric did as well. The chief spoke first.

"The district attorney will join us, Randi. We figured it would save time to get everyone in the same room." I was surprised Rick was coming out this way, but when a former ADA is threatened, it made sense to get up close and personal in the case. I smiled in response.

"That's great," I said. "Eric and I are up for anything that will lead to the end of all of this." My voice broke near the end, and I realized once more just how anxious I was. Combined with exhaustion, it was the perfect storm for someone like me: semi-paranoid, occasionally delusional, and, let's not forget, stressed out and starving.

"Hopefully, he can shed some light on how the state police are handling this," added Eric with just a touch of "hopefully better than you chumps." I squeezed his hand and turned my attention back to Bob.

"Is there anything you can tell us before Rick arrives?" I began just as Rick breezed in the door. He looked around the table, ensuring he was familiar with everyone. He started speaking with no preamble. Classic Rick.

"I wanted to bring you up to speed with what we have on former police officer McMurphy," he said. "When one of our own is threatened, the entire unit is at risk. We are here to offer you anything within our power to help you through this." His eyes illuminated his narrow face. This was politician Rick, ready to serve and protect the good people of New London County. And get re-elected.

"Thank you, Rick," I said as Eric chimed in.

"We appreciate your concern. Can you fill us in on what's being done to capture McMurphy and to protect Miranda?" I smiled gratefully at him.

"Yes, yes, of course. Here's what we know." Rick spoke briskly, consulting a small leather-bound notebook as he did. "Based upon McMurphy's appearance at your house at approximately 3:45 this morning, we obtained traffic footage of the entry points into Old Lyme. The suspect was seen on camera driving a 2016 Chevy Malibu. He must have gotten rid of the Camry. He was driving southbound on I-95, and his image was picked up once more when he took the beaches exit heading to the scene of the crime. Your home, I'm afraid," he added sadly. This was new-to-me Rick. He seemed genuinely sympathetic to our situation, and I felt tears well up in my eyes, which I rubbed away quickly. No crying, I told myself.

"All we know is he snuck into your backyard. He must have parked a few houses from yours. He staged the cardboard cutout in your likeness with the sign saying, well, you've all seen the sign, before he set it on fire. It looks like he carried his own accelerant and matches. I'm sure there was kindling or something like it in the firepit already, and—"

Eric cut him off. "Rick, I'm sorry, but you need to cut to the chase. McMurphy drove to our home, and he set the fire. Where did he go from there? He can't go back to his rooming house, and he can't show his face on one of my fucking job sites, so where is he?" Eric turned to me. "Miranda has said all along she suspected McMurphy had remained in the area all this time. Everyone else thought he had fled, but this proves they were wrong. And she was right," he added, gesturing at me. "So, and excuse my French, where the fuck is he?"

Oh man, I had never seen Eric so pissed off. Normally, I was the one with the potty mouth, but this guy was a contender, for sure. Swelling with pride, I squeezed his hand again before I spoke up.

"Eric is right, Rick. Where did he go when he left our house, and where is he now? Is there any CCTV footage to help us?" Rick was not accustomed to be spoken to so, um, directly. But as I watched, he leaned forward and told us what he didn't know.

"I hate to say this after the night you've both had, but honestly? It's like he disappeared into thin air."

There was a knock on the door, and Mike stuck his head in.

"Chief, there's something you have to see." He went to the computer, hit a few keys, and turned the screen to face his boss. "At 5:17 this morning, a woman on Kenilworth Drive reported her car had been stolen during the night. She works the early shift at Electric Boat, and when she went out to her car, it was missing."

I saw Bob trying hard to keep his temper in check. "Thank you, Officer Williams. Issue a BOLO for her stolen car—"

Mike stopped him, apparently pleased with what he had to share. "It was a Dodge Neon, Chief. A lime green 2014 Dodge Neon. But that's not the best part." The chief cut his eyes at him, and he hurried on. "In her car's parking space was a replacement car, keys in the ignition, doors unlocked. It's a dark blue Chevy Malibu. Isn't that the car you're all looking for?"

The chief nodded at his desk sergeant.

"Yes, it is. Put out an APB for the Neon. Do it now. He's already had a six-hour head start."

Half an hour later, Eric dropped me off at the house, promising to return after checking in at a few of his job sites.

"Get some rest," he called out as he watched me walk up the steps and unlock the door. I waved and shut the door behind me. The alarm had not been reactivated, so I punched in the code and headed for our bedroom. I caught a whiff of my hair and the clothing I had been wearing for hours and wrinkled my nose at the unpleasant odor of smoke. Shower first, I decided and minutes later I was surrounded by steam as I lathered my hair for a second time. It felt amazing.

I came out of the bathroom, tying the belt of my terry-cloth robe, feeling refreshed. Instead of trying to nap, I decided to pull something together for lunch. We had eggs, so maybe a—I stopped suddenly, shocked at what I was seeing. There on my unmade bed sat Daniel McMurphy, holding a sleeping Hobie in his lap.

"I missed this little guy," he said, and I saw my cat was unconscious, lying limp. What had he done?

"What did you do to him? How did you—" I began, my heart racing as I tried to make sense of it all. Was Dante armed or just dangerous?

He gave a low-throated chuckle in response. "Just a little something to calm him down. Don't worry. He'll be up and at 'em in no time."

I tried to slow my breathing as I glanced around the room. The door to the hallway had been closed, and all the windows were shut tight. My phone? I remembered leaving it on the kitchen counter when I had arrived home a short while ago. I could make a run for it, if I—

Daniel was shaking his head at me, clearly sensing my thoughts of escape. "You need to listen to me. We need to talk, Miranda. Just imagine how quickly I could snap our little friend's neck," he said, his hands stroking my baby's fur. "I don't want to, but I could. I think you know that."

"What do you want?" I asked, my voice sounding strangled and sharp. "How did you get in here?"

"You all left in such a hurry this morning. The alarm wasn't activated, and the lock itself was easy to pick. Too easy. You need to be more careful." I glanced once more at the door leading out to the hallway. If I tried to escape, would he really hurt Hobie? Was I willing to find out?

"My husband will be home any minute," I lied. "You won't get away with this."

"I will not hurt you, Miranda. That has never been my intention. I'm sorry—"

"Sorry? For threatening me, harassing me? For breaking into my house and setting fire to my yard? For taking my cat? You're sorry?"

Daniel shook his head. "I have been trying to get your attention. I've tried to warn you, to get you to see the error of your foolish ways."

"Why me? What did I do to you? If you blame me for your conviction, I was just doing my job. The evidence against you was staggering. Surely, you can see that."

"Please, just give me five minutes. That's all I'm asking. I am sorry for . . . all of it. Will you let me explain?"

"You've got five minutes," I said in my best no-nonsense tone, leaning against the wall.

"You never responded to my note," he said.

"Which note? The one on my windshield or the one stuck in my doorway?"

"The one I gave to my lawyer after I got arrested ten years ago."

I tried to recall any form of communication between us, but came up empty. "What are you talking about? I never saw a note."

He sighed and shook his head. "My lawyer said you were the prosecutor on my case. I never forgot you from when I testified in court. Do you remember?" He looked so hopeful, and I nodded briefly. Satisfied, he continued. "I wrote you a note saying I wanted to talk to you. To explain a few things. My lawyer swore to me he passed it to you."

I shook my head. "I don't recall ever getting a note, Daniel. And it might have been considered *ex parte* communication anyway. How about you just tell me what it said?"

He drew in a breath and let it out slowly. "You had seemed nice, caring, when I was on the stand testifying for you. I wanted to let you know why I did what got me arrested." I made my "get on with it face," and he continued. "I was trying to scare them. The girls I was arresting? I needed them to realize the path they were on and how bad it could get for them. They needed to turn their lives around. I thought you would understand."

I tried to take it in, to follow this twisted path of . . . What? Rationalization? Justification? Bullshit?

"So let me get this right, you're saying you had sex with young women before you arrested them as a warning to scare them straight?"

Daniel became animated, nodding his head and smiling. "Yes, that's it. You understand. See, if I had talked to you before court back then, none of this would have happened."

"And because you thought I ignored your request to meet, you've threatened me, set fire to my home, all that?"

He grew still, deflated by my failure to understand him. "Yes, of course. You, you ignored me. Refused to listen to me."

"Even if I had, that's no reason to get back at me the way you did."

At this, he grew agitated, his eyes hard as he glared at me. "What is wrong with you? Are you that blinded by arrogance? You took an oath to protect and serve. First, do no harm. I've tried to warn you again and again. You will burn in hell for your sins, Ms. Quinn. I am powerless to help you." He threw up his hands, continuing to rant, and Hobie slipped out of his lap, landing on all fours on the rug. He staggered toward me, and I raced over to grab him before Daniel could react. Clutching Hobie close, I raced to the door and down the hall. I heard Eric and screamed to him.

"He's in the house. He had Hobie," I shouted just as Eric came into view. "He's in there," I said, gesturing to our bedroom, and Eric ran past me, already dialing 911.

"He's gone," he said after taking a quick look around. "He must have gone through there." He pointed to the open window. "I'm going after him." Before I could stop him, my husband-turned-action figure vaulted through the window facing our backyard. Seconds later, I heard Louise screaming, and I left Hobie sleeping on the couch and exited through the back door. I was running across the patio toward the Donnelans' when I saw them: Eric, Daniel, and Louise wrestling in a pile of orangey-red mulch.

Minutes later, a couple of local cops showed up, followed by several state police troopers. Daniel was practically foaming at the mouth as he was restrained and read his rights. He was shouting my name as they dragged him through the yard. The state guys must have won the coin toss because the last I saw of Daniel, he was slumped over in the back of a white sedan with state plates, heading to who knew where. I could only imagine a psych ward was in his immediate future. I turned back to Eric and Louise, the latter wearing a very skimpy bikini. She had been sunbathing when she saw a "strange man" running through our yard. She had gone to the edge of her property to investigate when she'd seen Eric heading toward her at a dead run.

"I've taken some self-defense classes," she had informed me when I asked her what in the hell had made her think that tackling Daniel had been a good idea. Eric later told me he'd watched Daniel trip as he made his way through a wide swatch of mulch and that Louise had jumped on him and held him down until Eric arrived. When Eric had tried to help her up, she had slipped and pulled him down with her. I suggested that a Jell-O pit might be a better venue to practice their wrestling moves but kept mum on suggesting my neighbor find a robe to cover up with.

"Thank you for everything," I told her. "Bet you never thought you'd be rolling around with a psycho stalker today." And my husband.

"I need a drink after all this excitement," she called out as she headed home. We watched her wave as she zigzagged across the yard to avoid the mulch.

"Eyes back in your head," I told Eric as we went inside. "Go shower, and I'll make coffee."

He shook his head. "How about going out for lunch? Let's celebrate," he said. "He's locked up. We never have to deal with him again."

I looked at Hobie, who was still lying on the couch, trying to shake off the effects of whatever he had been given. "I'll order grinders from Fortuna's while you shower. I want to stay here and keep an eye on this guy. He's been through a lot." Eric kissed my cheek, and then headed down the hall. "And I'm bringing him in for a check-up tomorrow if he's not back to a hundred percent."

"Sounds like a plan."

After placing our lunch order, I paced around the kitchen feeling restless and full of nervous energy. I called the desk at the police station.

"You've had an exciting morning," Mike said.

"Is he talking?" I asked. "Has he asked for representation? And no, I am not volunteering for the job. Just curious as to his state of mind." I hoped Daniel would ask for a lawyer, showing he was lucid and able to assist in his own defense.

"He's been ranting and raving, not making a lick of sense. We have him in lockup," Mike said. Damn, that did not bode well. Any decent defense attorney could get him declared *non compos mentis* or "of unsound mind." But at the very least, it appeared he would be locked up for a while.

"Okay, keep me posted, yeah?" I said, nodding to Eric as he came into the kitchen.

"Sure thing, Randi. Gotta go. A bunch of bad guys to lock up," Mike said and ended the call.

I turned to face Eric. "McMurphy is behind bars. Thanks to you and Louise."

"Yeah, about that. We're planning on taking our wrestling act on the road," he said. "I wanted you to be the first to know."

The doorbell rang. Lunch!

"Sounds good. But can we eat first? I'm starving."

CHAPTER 47

After lunch, Eric studied the desk calendar with my work commitments and the one hanging on the kitchen wall marked with get-togethers and birthdays. "If only there was some way to merge them," he said. "How are you supposed to keep track of a calendar with important social engagements and a second calendar detailing work responsibilities?" He mimed pulling out his hair over the conundrum before trying to physically combine the two calendars with the goal of creating a single one. I shook my head.

"I know. It shouldn't be that hard," I said. "The online meetings with Infinity are set fairly far in advance. All I have to do is look and make certain I have nothing else going on when they want me for something."

"And yet our family get-together is still on for Saturday, as is the compulsory-attendance drinks meetup with affiliates in Manhattan at, hmmm, the Plaza. Will they comp your room? Do you need a plus-one?"

"Aarrgghh. I don't know what to do," I told him, staring at the square white boxes filled with writing on both calendars.

"You know what this means, right?" At my blank look, Eric went on. "We charter a bus and move our dinner party to midtown. Kill two birds, am I right?"

It sounded dreadful. I was looking forward to having everyone here for dinner for a lovely, quiet evening. It would never work, and even if we could pull it off . . . Of course he was kidding. My phone buzzed, and I read the quick text from Brian.

Sat drinks off. Ed on wagon. Sunday lunch at his in Rye @ 1. Deets to follow.

"Well, we have to cancel the family, right?" Eric asked before he saw me smiling. "What's up?"

"The good news? We are no longer double-booked. The slightly less good news? We have to go to Ed's estate out in Rye on Sunday for a dry lunch instead." I was relatively new to the organization but had heard our VP gave up alcohol and going to places serving it every few months. "Still want to be my plus-one?"

"Sure, as long as we can stop at the package store on the way and stock up on shooters."

I rolled my eyes. "Everyone knows you go to the *packy* for *nips*," I corrected him.

"Either way, we need to get you set up with a calendar on your phone. One calendar where you can keep track of all your appointments. I can help."

"Hell no," I said. "The last time you tried to 'help' me install software on my laptop, we didn't speak for days."

"Hmmm. Fairly certain it was maybe forty-five minutes, but anyway. You just have to pay attention and follow the directions I give you. It's simple."

"When I tell you I don't understand, all you do is repeat the same instructions over again in a louder voice. Doesn't help!"

"Yeah, you're right. We don't communicate for shit. Except in bed. Then when I tell you what I want you to do, it works—"

"Flynn," I blurted out. Eric looked crushed.

"Here I am talking about being in bed with you, and you bring a sixteen-year-old boy in. Into the conversation, that is. Not our bed. That would be—"

"Perv," I said, already texting. Seconds later, yes! "He's in. He'll be here before work in the morning to set me up. Said it would only take a few minutes, that it's not hard." I watched as Eric turned to me, a grin on his face. "Don't say it," I yelled just as he responded in the way I knew he would.

"That's what she said."

###

Later that day, I got the call from Rick I had been waiting for. He sounded pleased as he recounted the charges Daniel Murphy would be arraigned on.

"Criminal mischief, criminal trespass, arson, two counts of criminal harassment, and attempted murder. The whole ball of wax!"

This was seriously good news. But . . .

"What about his mental state? Will he be deemed competent to stand trial?"

"I believe so. But we will have to call in some experts to assess his capacity," Rick said, sounding fairly confident. He ended the call after promising to keep me in the loop. Trying to channel my inner-Eric, I started slicing and dicing everything in the fridge, and when Eric came home, we had a veggie stir-fry and a night on the couch. Hobie was now recovered fully, and after gobbling up all of his food, he followed us to bed just after nine.

CHAPTER 48

The day of our dinner party started out beautifully. Coffee in bed, walk on the beach, breakfast sandwiches from Brennan's Café. Just perfect. The weather looked good, cool for late June, but that was fine as it kept the humidity low as well. By late morning, however, the sun had all but disappeared, and the clouds grew dark and ominous. Because I was me, I had already started setting the tables out on the patio. I hoped the colorful tablecloths would detract attention from the scorched pavers surrounding the firepit in the corner. A lovely reminder of Dante. When it started to sprinkle just before noon, I raced out and gathered everything up. I tossed the damp tablecloths in the dryer, found new napkins, and dried the plates. And I waited, but not for long. The skies opened up, and Hobie and I watched from the kitchen as the rain grew so intense I could barely see across the lawn to our newly laid mulch.

"Plan B," I told him, and he watched as I installed the extensions to our farmhouse table and pulled extra chairs from the storage room. I unearthed the only tablecloth I owned that would accommodate a ten-foot table. There would be thirteen of us, as the twins and our niece Sarah weren't joining us. Eric arrived home from the fish market, where he had gone to purchase six pounds of salmon fillets. He was soaked and looking glum. Now what?

"We're in for it, babe," he said as he pulled off his wet shirt and gratefully accepted the towel I handed him. "I just heard the latest weather report, and it's not good."

I groaned and started looking through the sodden bag he had carried in.

"Well, that just sucks," I began before studying the contents. "What's this? Pollock?"

Eric shrugged. "No salmon at the market," he confirmed. "The guy said pollock was an excellent substitute."

I stared at him, unwilling to accept this news. "When have you ever seen me order pollock or buy pollock? The glaze I was just going to whip up is for salmon, not pollock."

Eric threw up his hands. "No matter how many times you say 'pollock,' it doesn't change the fact they were out of salmon. It's fish, and it's fresh, and we'll figure out how to cook it, and everyone will love it." He saw me start to relent and added, "You always say Coyne's is the only place to buy fresh fish, so I didn't bother going to the grocery store."

Yeah, I did always say that. Crap. What with the rain and the change in the menu, this dinner party was in trouble. "So I guess we'll eat in here," I said, pointing to the mostly set table. Eric nodded his agreement.

"Table looks great. I'll dash back out after a bit and buy some flowers for the centerpiece. How does that sound?"

It sounded good to me, so while Eric busied himself googling "How do you cook pollock?" I heated some soup and melted cheese on a plate of whole wheat crackers. We ate by the window, watching in awe as the rain continued to fall.

By late afternoon, I was ready to throw in the towel, wave the flag of defeat, and order a pizza to binge Netflix with. The rain had continued unabated, and the calls had begun. First, it was Jake. Clem had the sniffles and had been running a fever, and they didn't want to bring her out in the rain, and Meg had already canceled the sitter. Next up was Pop. Sally had been under the weather and complained of feeling light-headed. She had been napping all afternoon, and Pop didn't want to disturb her. When my caller ID showed my stepsister, Julie, was calling, I considered tossing my phone out the window.

"Hey, Jules. What's up?"

"I was planning on a pasta salad, but I couldn't remember who didn't eat onions. Is it Eric, or am I thinking of someone else?" I assured her onions were fine with Eric, and she said she would chop some up and see us before too long.

"You know your mom's not coming, right?" I asked.

"Yeah, your dad called. I have to tell you, Ran, I am not happy with that doctor of hers. She's been to see him a bunch of times, and she never seems to feel good."

I hated to admit Sally's health, while of concern to me, was not something I felt all that up-to-date with. I would talk to Pop in the morning and find out what I could.

"We should plan to go with her to her next appointment. One of us or both?" I suggested, and Julie agreed.

"See you at six," she said, and I stared at the phone, wondering if there was more about his wife's condition Pop was keeping from me. I needed to get my eyes on her and soon. I saw I had a text from Tracey. Now what?

Flynn's shift got canceled tonight. They're sending everyone home cuz of the storm. He wants to join us.

Terrific, I texted back. *The more the merrier.*

He wants to bring a friend. David.

No worries. Plenty of room and tons of pollock.

Okay. See you soon. T (smiley face emoji, heart emoji)

I studied my table again. We were down four guests, but up two with Flynn and David, so I removed two chairs and two place settings. Eric had already chilled three bottles of white wine and opened a bottle of merlot to let it breathe. Besides the pollock, which sat wrapped in white paper in the fridge, there was Julie's pasta salad and Tracey's dessert. My sister-in-law,

Tricia, had said she would bring a side dish, but if she had told me exactly what it would be, I sure couldn't remember. And that was it. No charcuterie board and no tossed green salad from Jake and Meg. I would need to improvise. I started digging through the pantry and found two different types of packaged rice mix, several cans of corn, and a can of diced tomatoes. Sally would know what to do with this motley assortment, but she wasn't here, so I put everything in the Crock-Pot on high and would check it in an hour. How bad could it be? Instead of a salad, I sliced cucumbers and tomatoes into a bowl and drizzled olive oil on top. Done! Next, I opened a bag of tortilla chips and located a jar of salsa, and suddenly this was looking like a party. Kind of a lame-ass one, but still.

Eric came up from the basement, where he had been installing an additional layer of soundproofing in my studio. He sniffed suspiciously.

"What's cooking?" he asked. I showed him the rice stew simmering in the Crock-Pot, and he nodded gravely. "I can run to the store," he offered. "I was going to buy flowers anyway." He looked around, noting the bowl of chips and the jar of salsa. "I can get some hummus and veggies. Or cheese and crackers. What do you think?" I assured him we would be fine.

"I think my rice will turn out great. We'll have plenty."

Julie and Brad arrived first, and it gave us a chance to catch up. They had driven the fifty or so miles from West Hartford and claimed the roads were not as bad as they'd expected because of the lack of traffic in the middle of a monsoon. I stowed the enormous bowl of pasta salad in the fridge. It looked delicious. Eric poured drinks, and I emptied the salsa into a bowl and set out cocktail napkins. Why had I been dreading throwing a simple dinner party? This was going well. I was planning on following them to the living room, where Eric had the gas fireplace roaring to take the dampness out of the air. I heard some lively jazz emanating from the speakers and figured it was guests' choice since Brad was a huge fan. I went over to inspect my rice stew. What was left of it. The bottom had burned and all the liquid had evaporated, leaving behind a dried-out slab of, um, not sure what exactly. But clearly nothing edible. I unplugged the pot and filled it with warm water and dish detergent, figuring I would scrape it clean in the morning.

Tracey and Dale came next, carrying bags of food and a platter loaded with brownies, blondies, and hermits. All homemade. I studied the assortment carefully.

"No Rice Krispie treats?"

"What burned?" Tracey asked, sniffing the air with a frown on her face.

"Nothing good," I assured her. "What's in the bags?"

She shrugged apologetically. "Eric asked us to stop and pick up some basics." She pulled out tubs of hummus and dips and bags of pre-cut veggies.

I started to tell her she didn't have to do all that, but she obviously had, so I decided to just roll with it. I arranged everything on plates as she opened the last bag. *What the hell?* "Is that steak?"

Tracey was trying to be all kinds of nonchalant, but when you were laying out packages of what looked like a dozen or more filet mignons on someone's kitchen counter, trust me, they'll notice.

"Don't blame me," Tracey said. "When you texted there was plenty of pollock, I was like, pollock? And Eric asked us to stop at the store, and I said, 'What goes with pollock?' and Dale said, 'Why not steak?' So here we are. If you don't want to serve them, throw them in the freezer. There goes my kids' college fund, but whatever." She managed a smile, and I smiled back as Eric came in beaming.

"This looks great. We can do surf and turf, babe," he said. I told him it was a terrific idea as John and Tricia arrived soaked to the skin from the quick sprint from the car. They were carrying two bottles of wine, flowers, and an enormous bowl of pasta salad. Eric took their jackets and offered towels before they followed him into the toasty-warm living room, carrying glasses of wine.

"Oh boy," I said as I shuffled the contents of the fridge around to make room for the salad, which also looked quite appetizing. Shortly after Skip, Flynn, and his friend David, a tall, thin boy about Flynn's age with a mop of unruly brown curls and a shy smile, arrived, and after they got settled, Eric and I met in the kitchen to discuss the cooking of the steaks and fish. We set the broiler in one oven and turned the other on to bake just as the lights flickered and died. *Are you freaking kidding me?* Power to the home had been lost, and the backup generator ordered months ago was still on back order. After calling around, we learned all the area restaurants had closed, so there was no way of getting pizza or anything else delivered.

So we lit candles and sat around the fireplace, eating two kinds of pasta salad, hummus and veggies, and talking. It was so relaxed and fun I almost forgot I was co-hosting the worst dinner party in the history of dinner parties. Flynn and David were sitting next to each other, cross-legged on the floor. I watched as Flynn tilted his head briefly to rest on David's shoulder and the look that passed between them was positively joyful. Tracey saw it too, and we grinned at each other.

"I like Julie's salad more than Tricia's," Eric whispered in my ear. "Too many black olives," and I agreed.

By the time I got out paper plates and napkins and passed around Tracey's dessert tray, I was feeling rather festive. Because of the copious amounts of wine consumed compared to the relatively small amount of food, most of the adults were no doubt over the legal limit. Skip drove his parents and said he would come by in the morning to get his car, and Flynn took his folks home with David following behind them. Brad had been the designated driver, so he and Julie left after turning down a night in our guest room. After everyone left, we gathered up empty plates and cups and blew out the candles.

"Worst dinner party ever," I said. "Let's do it again soon."

"Definitely," Eric said with a smile.

The next morning, the sun was shining and the only evidence of last night's storm were the branches and leaves scattered around the yard. The power had come back on just before midnight. When I located my phone, I saw a text had come in from Brian an hour earlier.

Lunch canceled. Rye estate w/o power. Ur off the hook. B

Happily, Pop and Sally joined us for a hastily organized brunch with Skip, Tracey, Dale, Flynn, and Chase. Sally looked good, tired but in good spirits. Eric and Dale cooked the steaks on the grill, and Tracey and I made a mountain of scrambled eggs with cheese and peppers. The pollock was relegated to the freezer in the garage.

It was the best morning-after party I could have imagined.

CHAPTER 49

On Monday, Daniel McMurphy was arraigned and pleaded not guilty on all charges by reason of mental disorder. Bail was set at five hundred thousand, but with no financial resources available to him, he sat in jail awaiting his trial date set for next month. I had not gone to the courthouse but had been told the former cop was quiet and well-behaved, with no signs of manic behavior. I celebrated with a mocha shake and a walk on the beach, followed by an early dinner with the hubs. It was a great day.

An hour later, Skip and I met to discuss logistics. It was a half hour before we were live.

"The most important thing is to weed out the callers who just want to get Daniel to call in," I said. "I don't want to announce on air he's been arrested. Okay?"

Skip nodded vigorously. "No DansFans," he agreed. "I'll ask them what topics they want to talk about, the same as I always do. But do you think I should bring him up just to see how they react?"

I shook my head. "No way, he's had enough free airtime. I guess you'll have to play it by ear and see if you hear any hooting and hollering in the background."

"Sounds good," Skip agreed. "They like to listen in group settings, from what I hear."

I shook my head at the idea of social gatherings planned around some fanatic spewing warnings and threats with religious overtones. I rubbed my damp palms against the legs of my jeans. It was like my first night on the air. I was feeling anxious and less than confident I could carry the show for four whole hours. What if no one called in? I texted Skip to be ready with backup "best of" tapes, and he gave me a quick thumbs-up. I smiled and shrugged, and he nodded back at me. If only all communication was this straightforward and effective! No mixed signals, no misunderstandings. Everyday topics worked well with us, but I still wanted to know more about his visit with Becky. Regarding matters of the heart, my nephew and I were worlds apart. I looked up and saw him gesturing to me and giving the two-minute warning. I pulled on my headphones, slicked on some lip gloss, and began watching the clock. At the thirty-second mark, I cleared my throat and took a tiny sip of water. It was showtime! I waited for the prerecorded welcome to finish before I spoke.

"Good evening and welcome to *Miranda Nights*. I am your host, Attorney Miranda Quinn, and I'm here to answer your questions or provide some insight into any of your legal issues or concerns. Although I am a practicing attorney, my remarks are general information for entertainment. Legal *advice* can only be provided by your own attorney. The phone lines are open. Wide open," I added as I saw Skip gesturing to a mostly dark phone bank. I motioned for him to pass along any calls. Anything was better than dead air. Make that almost anything. I checked my screen and greeted the caller.

"Hello, Brenda from Rocky Hill, Connecticut. Welcome to the show."

"Hi, Miranda. Thanks for taking my call. Loyal listener, first-time caller."

"Do you have a question for me?"

"Yes, I do. I'm having a problem with tenants in the duplex I own. I live on one side, and they're driving me crazy. Cars parked everywhere and I'm pretty sure there is another couple living there as well. They keep saying they're just visiting, but they are always there. Is there anything I do?" she asked. I smiled. Great question. Fairly straightforward and definitely in my comfort zone. No heavy lifting with this caller.

"Brenda, I'm going to give you a checklist of actions you can take. When I'm done, my producer, Stephen, will take your address, and we'll send you some forms to get you started. How does that sound?" Brenda thought it sounded great, so I shared with her what she needed to know about being a landlord. Predictably, the next call was from a disgruntled tenant, Mark from Stamford, and we discussed tenants' rights, another of my favorite legal topics. The evening progressed from there, and before I knew it, Skip was giving me the sign to wrap it up. I motioned for him to let me take one more call, and he did.

"Hello, this is Miranda. You are our last caller tonight, um, Tony from Bridgeport. What question do you have for me?"

"Yeah, oh hey, Miranda. First-time listener, and first-time caller, Yeah, duh, right?"

Damn, I never seemed to quit while I was ahead. "Hi, Tony. What's your question?"

"Okay, I'm just passing this message along from a friend. Well, more of an acquaintance, I guess." I saw Skip telling me to wrap it up again when Tony added. "Um, Daniel says he will see you in hell. And, um, sooner than you might think. He says even though he's been reborn, he did some bad things and so did you. I guess that's it. Um, sorry." Skip ended the call, and I stared at my screen. The closing announcement was airing and my *Night* was over. He could get to me from jail. Good to know.

I had planned to go right to bed, but according to Daniel, I was going straight to hell.

CHAPTER 50

I felt groggy and out of sorts the next morning, like I'd had way too much wine the night before. But I hadn't had a drop when I crawled into bed next to Eric. I had been shivering and huddled next to him, trying to absorb some of his warmth. He was essentially a portable heater wrapped up in a sweet and very sexy man, and I'd needed his heat. I'd lain there for hours, trying to imagine how Dante had found a disciple willing to call in to threaten me. Even from jail, he was sending a message he could contact me whenever he wanted. I must have fallen asleep at some point because it was now 7:17.

Eric came out of the bathroom wearing a towel, a billow of steam in his wake.

"Good morning, babe. I didn't mean to wake you," he said. I studied his face as he walked over to my side of the bed and my eyes started to focus. The left side of his face was covered with a thick layer of what? Shaving cream? Wishing it was whipped cream, I shifted in bed, allowing him to perch on the side.

"Eric?"

"That's me."

"Why do you have shaving cream on half your face?"

"I'm only going to shave half. I might grow a mustache, and this way I can compare with and without," he announced. "Thoughts?"

I buried my face in my pillow. "I have never seen you with facial hair," I mumbled.

He chuckled. "That's because you haven't been paying attention. Look through my photos in the attic. There are loads of them throughout college and well into my thirties too. I mean, I wasn't any competition for Sam Elliott or Tom Selleck, but still. I think I wore it pretty well."

I groaned. "They're like twice your age, so *not* the most convincing argument. But I guess as long as it's not some porn 'stache like the guy from the show."

"The show?"

"The prison show. The orange one."

Eric nodded in recognition. "No way. Trust me, babe. I probably won't look like that guy at all."

"But if you grow it and I hate it, you'll shave it, right?"

Eric considered this for a moment before shaking his head. "My face. My choice," he said. "Sorry, but it's my constitutional right to decide if I want to be clean-shaven or not."

I scoffed at that.

"Oh yeah, what do you know about the Constitution, huh?" I sat up in bed and leaned closer to him. "Seriously, tell me one thing about the constitution."

"It was signed in 1776," Eric said triumphantly.

"Wrong-o," I said. "It was 1787. The Declaration of Independence was 1776, and there's nothing in either document about facial hair. Trust me."

"That's because all of our founding fathers had facial hair. It was assumed."

I shook my head. "Babe, I aced Constitutional Law. You should quit while you're only slightly behind."

"I am nothing if not a graceful loser," he conceded. "But the least you can do is help me get over the shame of my defeat with consolation sex."

"Replace the shaving cream with whipped cream, and I'm all yours," I said.

"I'll do it, but you have *got* to brush your teeth first. Deal?"

Sure, why not? I was going to brush them anyway.

CHAPTER 51

Later that morning, I picked Sally up, and we drove to her doctor's appointment. Julie was waiting for us in the parking lot, and the three of us went inside and checked in at the desk. Sally had been strangely quiet the whole time, with none of her usual chatter. Pop had balked at our offer to accompany Sally to her appointment, but Julie wore him down, and here we were.

"Mom, we're worried about you. We just want to talk to the doctor and see what we can do to get you feeling like your old self again," Julie reminded her as we sat in the examining room. Sally nodded, and I squeezed her hand.

"Maybe you'll get a sticker or a lollipop," I told her, and we all smiled. But when we left the office less than an hour later, we were no longer amused. Heart disease was no laughing matter.

We walked across the parking lot to a coffee shop, found an empty booth, and ordered coffee for Julie and me and tea for Sally. No one spoke for a couple of anxious moments. Finally, Sally cleared her throat and tried to explain.

"I'm sure you have a lot of questions, and I'll try to answer them. I love you girls, and I didn't want you to worry about me. At first, I told myself my doctor was being overly cautious and if I just kept up my exercise and took a nap in the afternoons, I'd be fine."

"Mom, that's not how this works," Julie insisted. "Heart disease doesn't just go away on its own. You need treatment and you need to take your meds. You had a stroke, for God's sake. And please don't tell me it was *just* a mini-stroke."

Sally nodded, resigned. "I thought I had more time," she said.

"What does Pop say?" I asked. "Does he know what's going on?"

Sally couldn't meet my gaze. "Not much at all," she admitted. "He was concerned about my dizzy spells, but I told him it was my blood sugar. He didn't question me or press me for details. You know your father," she added. Yeah, I did. Back when my mother, who had never smoked in her life, had been diagnosed with lung cancer and died only a few months later, Pop had lost all faith in the medical establishment. He didn't trust doctors much, and since he and I had always been healthy, it hadn't affected him. Until now.

"We all need to talk, Sal," I said. "Jake too. You can't go through this alone."

She agreed, and on the drive back to the condo, I called Pop to tell him we were on our way and Julie called her brother. Half an hour later, we were all sitting around their kitchen table. Pop had insisted on bringing it from the house I had grown up in, and although it was rather shabby and a 70s "antique," it warmed up the rather sterile space. Julie got the conversation started.

"Mom, your doctor has concerns you have not been following the protocol he set up for you, and he's worried. You are putting yourself in danger of another stroke. And this one could be much worse."

Pop looked at Sally, clearly shocked at the news. "What's she talking about?" he asked. "Why didn't you tell me?"

"I'm sorry Dez. I was planning to. But between the move and the cruise, there hasn't been enough time to—"

Julie cut her off. "You were told your blood pressure was too high last winter. Your cholesterol too. You've had months to get on board with the meds and the plan you agreed to." Julie was doing her best to hold on to her temper, but she was pissed and scared. We all were.

"I promise you. I will go over everything the doctor said. I'll fill all the scripts and watch my diet. I will."

Pop turned to his wife, studying her closely. "Sally, you are the most capable woman I know. But I won't sit by and watch you do all this on your own. Damn it, I'll count out your pills and buy groceries and get you out for a walk every day of the damn week. I won't lose someone I love again. I won't." His voice broke, and I watched him trying to hold it together. Sally had tears in her eyes and she let him pull her into a hug.

"We're here to help, Mom. Dez, you can count on us for anything you need. Twenty-four-seven, okay?" Jake said. "We're fifteen minutes away, and with the new baby—whoops. Meg is gonna kill me." He flushed bright red, shaking his head at his slipup.

"I'm going to be a grandmother again?" cried Sally. "When? How?" Jake and Meg had tried for years to start a family and had finally utilized *in vitro* fertilization to conceive their daughter. Jake was looking quite pleased with himself.

"This one will be another Christmas baby, due right around Clem's second birthday. And the old-fashioned way this time, I'm pleased to say."

Amid congratulations from everyone, Julie leaned in and whispered in my ear, "Way to steal the thunder, yeah? Typical Jake move."

"Trust me, Jules, now that Pop knows what's going on, Mom won't be able to skip a single pill or postpone an appointment," I said.

"You just called her Mom," Julie said with a grin. "You always call her Sally."

"Well, I love her like a mom, so why not?" And I really did.

CHAPTER 52

I arrived home to find a massive flower arrangement on the counter. Eric? I preferred chocolates to flowers, but . . . He came in through the back door while I was checking for a card.

"Secret admirer?" he asked.

"Not from you?" I read the card and burst out laughing.

Heading to the Hamptons, thanks to you. Wedding Bells ~ Save the Date! Taylor & Brian 8/15/22

I handed it to Eric, who looked confused.

"Who's Taylor? Why 'thanks to you'?"

"I gave Brian some advice, I guess. And as to Taylor? Your guess is as good as mine."

"That must have been some advice," Eric said. "I always thought Brian was—"

"Single," I said. "But apparently not for long."

Eric shrugged. "I wish it was one of those fruit-and-chocolate baskets. Hey, aren't you supposed to be in court?"

I checked the time on my phone. "I'm going to leave now. They pushed it back to three." Chase's case was going to be decided in juvenile court in less than an hour.

"I'll keep you posted," I told Eric, blowing him a kiss and heading back to my car. I arrived in plenty of time to hear the verdict. Tracey and I held our breath as the judge announced her decision.

"Chase William Ryan, you have been found guilty of a class C misdemeanor and are hereby sentenced to six months of probation and 120 hours of community service. You will meet biweekly with your probation officer, and I, for one, do not want to see you in this courtroom again. Is that understood?"

Chase nodded. "Yes, Your Honor. I understand."

No jail time and no detention center. This was excellent news. After it had been discovered it was Chloe's younger brother, Todd, who had found the pictures and shared them with the entire school, the charges against Chase had been reduced substantially. Now it was Todd who was in trouble, but at only thirteen, it was unlikely there would be any significant punishment. Tracey pulled me along with her to hug first her son, then Justin. I thanked Justin and gave Chase a quick squeeze.

"Do better," I told him, and he said he would. Leaving them to set up the logistics for Chase's probation appointments, I walked outside to a warm and muggy day. Just as I got to my car, a call came in. Becky!

"Hey, Bex. How are you? I've been thinking about you so much," I said.

"Do you hate me?" she asked, and I chuckled.

"Why would I hate you?"

"The thing . . . with Stephen?" It took me a second. Oh, Skip!

"I was surprised. I can tell you that. But honestly? He has barely said a word. What's going on with you two?" I asked.

"We're in love," she said simply. "He and Jesse and me, we want to be a family. After he graduates, that is. Until then, he'll be spending time here whenever he can, and I plan to head up north this fall for a few weeks too. We can make it work," she added a bit defensively. I pictured my young friend, her blond hair falling across her face, her wide blue eyes, and her sweet disposition. She had overcome childhood abuse, homelessness, drug addiction, a couple of years as a sex worker, an unplanned pregnancy, and threats to her life from a powerful group of lawyers. And here she was on the other side. Happy, healthy, set for life financially, working as a paralegal, a great mom, and in love with our nephew. What a comeback story!

"Congratulations, sweetheart. There's no one who deserves happiness more than you. And welcome to the family!" I said, and we spent the next several minutes catching up before she had to get back to work.

"See you in September," she told me. "And please get your butts down here to visit. You're not a fan of winter, and I've got plenty of room."

I told her it sounded great. "Kiss Jesse for me," I said, and we ended the call. I drove home grinning from ear to ear. No jail for Chase, and Becky and Skip were officially a couple. I couldn't wait to tell Eric! When I arrived home a few minutes later, he had news for me as well. Great news! I had missed a call from Rick, but he had reached Eric.

The psychiatrist who had interviewed Daniel McMurphy had submitted his report, stating he had found no evidence to support the claim my stalker was incompetent to stand trial. The state agreed to drop the attempted murder charge in exchange for a guilty plea, and it was expected McMurphy would be sentenced to fifteen-twenty years in jail with no possibility of parole. It was finally over.

Six months later . . .

It was New Year's Eve, and we had just finished a dinner of grilled shrimp and asparagus over rice.

"No more rice for a while," I reminded him. "We're going low-carb, remember?" Eric rolled his eyes at me, and I wondered why I had ever felt the need to teach him this important skill if he was going to use it against me.

"I honestly don't recall agreeing to that," he said. "I vote for *lower*-carb, and that means ice cream is out also, or have you figured a way around that one?"

Hmmm. "How about we cut back on weekdays and have cheat weekends?" I suggested.

"Weekends start at five on Fridays?" Eric asked.

"Duh, of course. Until midnight on Sundays?"

He laughed at that. "When is the last time we willingly stayed up until midnight?"

"But now we'd have a good reason." We raised our glasses and toasted each other.

"Happy New Year, babe. It sure has been an interesting one, yeah?" he said, and I had to agree.

"We have a new nephew, so that's exciting." Theodore Quinn Colby had born early in the morning on Christmas Day. He weighed in at a respectable eight pounds, eight ounces and measured twenty-two inches long. Clementine was thrilled she now had a baby "brudda," especially one born in time to attend her second birthday party.

Eric shook his head in amazement. "I don't know how Jake and Meg pulled off a party just two days after Teddy was born, but it was fun."

It *had* been fun. Exhausting, loud, and chaotic, but fun.

"I'm glad Sally is doing well. She's happy to be looking after Clem two mornings a week to give them a break. And I think Pop is even more excited," I said. Sally's last few checkups had gone extremely well. Her blood pressure and cholesterol were in the normal range, and she hadn't felt dizzy in months.

"Do you think they'll still be up for going to Florida with us in March?" Eric asked, and I thought about it before answering.

"I hope so. But only if we can pull her away from that adorable chubby-cheeked baby," I said with a smile. "I'm really looking forward to seeing Becky and Jesse."

"The timing is perfect, with your show ending and all. But I hope we won't interrupt Skip's visit. It's his week of spring break."

"But that's why we're staying nearby," I reminded him. "He was all for it when I talked to him on Christmas Eve. Right before he hopped on a flight to be there in time to open presents with Jesse," I added. And Becky, of course. Young love!

"You still good with your decision?" Eric asked.

"I'm thrilled," I said. "I can't wait."

I had chosen to not renew my contract with Infinity Holdings. After the show had expanded to three nights a week, I realized just how much I disliked working until midnight. *Nights* just weren't for me. I still had two months left on my current contract before moving on. Starting in April, I planned to volunteer three mornings a week at the free legal clinic in New London and resurrect my weekly podcast *Miranda Writes* as well.

Eric was thriving as a senior partner at his old firm. With help from Tim and Dale, he had opened up a branch office in nearby Niantic, and they were on track to beat budgeted first quarter revenues by fifty percent. He had received a healthy year-end bonus and, fulfilling a longtime dream, had purchased a sailboat currently docked in Florida. After visiting with Becky, our plan was to put Pop and Sally on a plane home and sail our Hobie Cat around the Gulf of Mexico. Just day trips to start, but Eric was already talking about getting a bigger boat in the future.

"Yeah, quite a year, babe. I wouldn't have wanted to spend it with anyone but you," I told him.

"Right back atcha, sweetheart."

We talked for a while longer before loading up the dishwasher. A short while later, we were both yawning. It was a few minutes past nine.

"It's still technically a cheat day," I said, thinking longingly of the pint of coffee-fudge ice cream in the freezer. "This lower-carb deal doesn't start until 12:01."

"But tomorrow is Saturday, so you can eat ice cream all day long if you want to," he reminded me.

"Sounds good. Let's go to bed, yeah?"

"Early to bed, early—"

"No proverbs," I reminded him. "No platitudes, no axioms, no adages, no cliches. . ." No deadly sins, nothing. I yawned again.

"You sure you don't want to wait up? Watch the ball drop?"

I shook my head. "You've seen one ball, you've seen them all," I said. No argument from Eric. Minutes later, we were lying in bed, our large gray tiger stretched out between us.

"Eric?"

"Mmm?" came his muffled reply.

"What are we going to name the boat? We can't call it Hobie cuz this is Hobie," I said, stroking our cat's shiny fur.

"You'll think of something, babe," he told me. "You're the clever one."

"I thought I was the funny one."

"Mmm, yeah. Clever *and* funny, that's you. Happy New Year, Quinn," he mumbled as he drifted off.

There was more I wanted to say as I studied my sleeping husband, but I would tell him in the morning. He might think I was the clever one and the funny one, but I knew the truth.

I was the *lucky* one.

THE END

P.S. Want more Miranda?? Here's the first chapter of *Miranda Writes*. I hope you enjoy it!!

Miranda Writes

CHAPTER 1

Despite a brain still foggy from endless champagne toasts, I was feeling good. Yesterday had been a wonderful day. I finally had something to celebrate, following the demise of what had once promised to be a stellar legal career. My blog-turned-podcast, *Miranda Writes*, had recently garnered enough attention that the Sterling Broadcast Group had brought my closest supporters and me to New York in a limousine to sign a lucrative contract to host a daytime TV show. Things were looking up after a few tough years.

We had arrived back to Old Lyme, CT in the early evening and dropped off my dad and his girlfriend Sally, followed by my best friend Tracey and her husband Dale. Then, with help from the limo driver, I had carted all the floral arrangements and fruit baskets from future sponsors into my house. I was awestruck by the outpouring of support I had received. When I first started blogging, I had never imagined that it would lead to this. Honestly, back then I had been writing to maintain my sanity, nothing more.

The local network affiliate had already started airing promos of my upcoming show and I had stayed busy all night, fielding phone calls, texts and emails from friends, neighbors and former classmates. The calls stopped around 11:00 p.m., but I had lain awake for hours, my mind buzzing with topics for shows and names of legal experts I wanted to invite as guests. I had finally fallen asleep and was still in bed, debating the merits of a pot of home-brewed coffee and a slice of multigrain toast versus a drive-through latte and a cinnamon roll roughly the size of my head. My phone buzzed beside me. Probably a long-lost law school classmate or a childhood friend calling to congratulate me or to wish me well, I guessed. I checked the time as I found my phone. 5:45 a.m. Too early for a friendly call, I thought with a flicker of concern. *Hmmm*, unknown number.

"Hello."

"Um, hello. Is this Miss Quinn?" The voice was soft but familiar.

"Yes, this is Miranda. Can I help you?"

"Yes, ma'am. I need to talk to you, Miss Quinn. I don't know if you remember me—"

"Who is this?" I asked, barely masking my annoyance. I was rarely up for a game of twenty questions, and never before I had my coffee.

"It's, um. Becky. Becky Lewis." I sat bolt upright in bed, the chill I felt having nothing to do with the sudden loss of my down comforter. Becky Lewis? Yes, I certainly remembered her.

"Becky? Of course, I remember you. What's um, up?"

"I'm sorry, Miss Quinn. Really, I am. I saw you on TV last night and I thought I should get in touch with you about what happened." I was struggling to follow her. What had happened?

"What do you mean?"

"He did it again, Miss Quinn. He hurt that girl. Just like me and the other one." My heart sank. I knew who she meant. Of course, I did. Three years ago, I'd had the chance to put him away, and I had blown it. Now he had attacked another woman, and it was all my fault. This one was most definitely on me. But I still needed to ask. To be sure.

"Who, Becky? Who is *he*? What did he do?"

"Terry. Terry Kane. He raped another girl."

To keep reading, order your copy of *Miranda Writes* today!!

ABOUT THE AUTHOR

Gail Ward Olmsted was a marketing executive and a college professor before she began writing fiction on a full-time basis. A trip to Sedona, AZ inspired her first novel *Jeep Tour*. Three more novels followed before *Landscape of a Marriage*, a biographical work of fiction featuring landscape architect Frederick Law Olmsted, a distant cousin of her husband's, and his wife Mary.

Miranda Nights is a sequel of sorts to *Miranda Writes*. Both are contemporary novels with a legal twist, featuring attorney Miranda Quinn. Olmsted enjoys writing about quirky, wonderful women in search of a second chance at a happy ever after.

NOTE FROM THE AUTHOR

I hope you enjoyed *Miranda Nights*. I love to hear from readers and you can find me on Facebook at GailOlmstedAuthor or email me at gwolmsted@gmail.com.

Please consider leaving a review for any of my books or even a quick rating on a website of your choice, including Goodreads. Reviews help to increase a book's visibility and mean the world to authors. Your comments are very much appreciated.

Best for now,

Gail O

We hope you enjoyed reading this title from:

www.blackrosewriting.com

Subscribe to our mailing list – *The Rosevine* – and receive **FREE** books, daily deals, and stay current with news about upcoming releases and our hottest authors.
Scan the QR code below to sign up.

Already a subscriber? Please accept a sincere thank you for being a fan of Black Rose Writing authors.

View other Black Rose Writing titles at www.blackrosewriting.com/books and use promo code **PRINT** to receive a **20% discount** when purchasing.

www.ingramcontent.com/pod-product-compliance
Lightning Source LLC
Chambersburg PA
CBHW050156120726

47903CB00002B/643